Rescue
of
Undaunted
Spirit

Pam Kumpe

Pam Kumpe

Copyright © 2015 Pam Kumpe

Photo on Cover: Pam Kumpe

ISBN- 978-0-692-46716-9

DEDICATION

To my twin sister, Melody
You are connected to my heart!

To a friend's son, Jacob Daniel
Your mother loves you!

To my 'Ladies in Purple' in recovery
Some of my best friends!

Pam Kumpe

DISCLAIMER

Pam Kumpe

Staircase of Pain

The pebbles flew from my clenched fist, clunking against the wood door of Taddy's second floor apartment. Screaming at him with each toss, I pulled more rocks from my overall pockets. "You are not my friend."

Standing at the bottom of the staircase in the entry, my angry words mixed with the musty air and my mood became like mildew. I assaulted the silence between each breath, hurling ugly words from my throat at my best friend, who hid behind the closed door. "Go ahead. Kiss your mama on the cheek. Be sure and hug her, too. I have no one to hug or kiss. Don't worry about me." I put my hands on my bony hips, blubbering another round of muck at Taddy. "I don't need you. You are a two-faced, bore of a boy who plays with acorns."

I spun around and plopped to my bottom, sitting on the first step, gritting my teeth to keep my shouts inside. I shook my head, and thought about how we rode the train home from Wheelock Academy after the horrible-terrible there. The terrible included death and sorrow, all packed inside the suitcase of my heart. Taddy lost his Aunt Margo, and I lost my grandma and a new friend, Eleanor. Sure, Taddy's mama is alive, but since we got off the train, Taddy's moved from being with me to moving away from me.

So far, I hate being eleven.

I rose from hugging my knees, twirled, and faced the top of the stairs again. "Taddy, you aren't nice to me. You don't play with me. Or talk to me at school. You make faces at me, and you keep ignoring me. It's Friday again, and I'll have the whole weekend to be by myself."

A man stuck his head from behind the apartment door to my right, his baldhead shiny. His presence caused me to swallow the last bit of hate words clogging my throat. The man squealed at me. "Quiet. Whoever you are, we don't allow shouting here. Knock it off. Go away, and be quiet. No children are allowed to run wild in here."

"I'm not running." I stuck my tongue at the man, and he slammed his door shut. I resumed my barrage of angry accusations at Taddy, leaping up a step on the stairs. I shook my fist at Taddy's apartment door, grabbing the dark cherry rail. The hallway above me felt like thunderstorms of clouds ready to collapse, and below I imagined a pit ready to swallow me up, one filled with quicksand. I was sinking and my anger festered, as I became a volcano of hate. I sank into the pit of screams like Mahlee uses when she's mad at me.

Living across the street from Taddy at Grandma's manor on Beech Street for this last year sent me and Taddy to the same school, to the same creek church services on Saturday, to playing in trees. Now, it's like I'm invisible. But I'm not. "Taddy, can you hear me?"

I kicked the gold molding at the edge of the next step, and thought about how life rolled hard with sorrow, thought about how the past few weeks count as the loneliest ever without my grandma. Her funeral by the tracks at Rose Hill Cemetery near Union Station placed her body next to my daddy's marker. His spot doesn't even have a body in the dirt, since he was never found in the river near Memphis—after falling from the boxcar.

Pastor Cody invites me to Church by the Creek every Saturday morning, saying Slow Tom and Fast Tim miss me, telling me he needs help passing out the hymnals. I'm not in the mood to talk to God, because I'm busy trying to get Taddy to talk to me since he's axed me from his list of friends. He's mad at me for snatching the letter from inside Margo's envelope, the one from her coffin, the one talking about her being his real mama. The one saying she's Priscilla, and how Priscilla is Margo, whom we call Taddy's mama. Goodness, it's all so confusing. In short, it seems the twins changed places when Taddy was small to keep him protected from the crazy twin, who is now buried at Wheelock.

I wiped the drip on my nose, and ran my fingers through the end of my ponytail, whispering, "Taddy's family is crazier than mine. Or maybe I just know more than I need to about them."

Taddy's current mama, Priscilla, the twin recovering from broken legs and a head injury, she is inside the apartment upstairs, to the left on the second floor, next to the rail. She's the real mama for now, no matter what the letter says. I mumbled, "Taddy might be right. I might be right. It doesn't even matter anymore. Taddy has a mama. Or maybe he was lucky enough to have two for a while."

I jumped up another step. I don't have a mama, or a daddy, or even a grandma. I'm alone, except for Mahlee, but she's busy sprucing up the manor for new boarders. She's hoping her fiancé, Ernie, the reporter with the fancy car, comes home from Florida. She hovers next to the wall-phone, hoping for his call every night. So far, nothing. Nothing.

Nothing is what I feel. I can't cry. Or laugh. Or play. But I can shout. I need Taddy to help me get back to writing poetry. He's my best friend. We're perfect for each other. He has everything and I have nothing. I pulled another rock from my pocket and chunked it toward Taddy's door.

Thunk. Thud.

I can't sleep in my bed at night because no one misses me, or tucks me in. No one looks for me, or calls me, or plays with me. No one makes me do chores. No one bakes me a chocolate cake, except Mahlee did for my birthday last month, but it was dry. Dry like sand in the desert, like sand over tombstones. Not moist like Grandma's cakes.

I rocked in my shoes, leaping up another two steps. "Taddy, can you hear me?" I slammed my fist on the rail. "Come out and talk to me like a fifth grader who's not afraid of my punches."

Creak. A shuffle swish-swish of the door revealed a face over the railing, a wavy-haired boy, and a familiar gaze with mad eyes. Taddy shook both hands in a wave of swoops. "What are you yelling at me for? You scream at me on the playground. You throw rocks at my window from your tree at night. You come over here every afternoon and bellow, whining your little girl words at me. What is wrong with you? Can't you see I need to be with my mama?" He bent down, gathering up two of my boulders. "Is this how you get me to play with you?"

I charged up the stairs, two at a time, deepening my voice to eliminate any girlish or whiny sounds. I shook my fist at him. "Your mama's better. She can sit in her wheelchair, and Mahlee said she's getting stronger. Priscilla will walk soon, and the nurse stays with her day and night. She even knows who you are now. You could come outside and sit in the tree with me, or talk to me, or run with me, or let me sock you. I need my Taddy, but he's missing. He's gone. He has left me—like everyone else. You're my best friend and now you act like I'm a ghost. Like you can't see me." I touched my arm. "I'm right here. Waiting for you."

Taddy squawked. "I can more than see you. You are a pest." He flew around the railing, leaping at me in the middle of the staircase, wobbling side-to-side, huffing and puffing, tossing the rocks at my feet. "Stop bothering me, Annie Grace Kree. You need to stop the yelling, too. You're selfish, and you don't know when to leave things alone. Everything isn't about you." Taddy folded his arms, turning his back to me, taking a step up, like he was retreating to his apartment where mamas get to live.

I reached for his arm, digging my nails into his soft skinny elbow. "You can't talk to me like that. Don't call me Annie Grace Kree. Call me Shoelace. Use my hobo name. It's who I am. Besides, I saved your life, and helped with your rescue. I was there when you were tied up by the tree, and Chula gave me a knife to free your wrists from the rope. Me! I was the person who set you free from Scar and Red!" I shook Taddy like a rag doll. "You act like I'm your enemy, like I have the measles, like I'm contagious."

Taddy yanked free, spinning around, and pointed his finger. "You are trouble. You get in the way more than you help. You are worse than contagious. You are a disease. You hid the letter from me, the one from Margo. You don't tell the truth, and you keep too many secrets. I'm finished with you. I don't want a friend like you. If I'd never met you, my mama wouldn't have gone with your grandma to Oklahoma. She'd never gotten run over by a wagon. We would have been right here in Texarkana, safe and sound."

"You're wrong. The letter would have come from Boswell even if I'd never showed up. That didn't have anything to do with me. You're lucky I did come to town so I could go on the trip with you. Remember, I saved you. You should be glad you had me along." My tears leaked from the corners of my eyes like a water fountain ready to explode. I was about to cry for the first time since my grandma died.

Taddy wrung his hands together. "Go home. Find a new friend."

I pushed Taddy. "Fine. I'll find a new friend. I'm finished with you, too. Who needs a Taddy in their life? Not me. I don't need anyone." I leaned in closer to whisper more pain into Taddy's heart. "Don't think I will forget this. I will never speak to you again." I spun in a circle, fast enough to sling tears to the steps, fast enough for Taddy to miss my combustion of sadness showing up on my face, leaking from my nose.

A tug on my overalls made me turn around, and my spin put me nose-to-nose with Taddy. He yelled a firm growl of a sound, one I hadn't heard before. "You are a hobo girl without a family. Leave me alone. I am not your friend. Get off my stairs." Taddy's finger gave me a single tap on the shoulder. "Go. Get out of here."

I pretended to stumble, to lose my footing, to make Taddy think he shoved me too hard, only for my untied shoelace on my PF Flyer to get caught under my other tied shoe. I danced a twirl of chaos, with arms swinging, and my hand slapped Taddy in the jaw like a branch whipping back in a tornado.

Taddy's hand flew to his cheek. "Ouch! You've gone and hit me. It never ends. Get out of here, and never come back." He grabbed the rail, steadying himself. "I never want to see you again."

I reached for the rail too, unable to balance myself, and Taddy's words engulfed my anger. *Achooo!* I sneezed like Taddy, and fumbled for a steady hold of the rail.

Taddy scolded me. "Stop playing. I know you're not falling."

"Help me … I am … falling." I tumbled sideways, leg over leg, and my shoe flew off. I bounced from step to step like a wagon wheel wobbling down a rocky road. I bounced off the wall at the bottom of the stairs, hitting my head on a metal chair by the door. My shoe slapped me in the face before hitting the floor.

I stood to attention and shouted at the empty staircase, to the backside of Taddy who rushed inside his apartment. I screamed at the steps, the rail, the walls, and at the whole world. The silence of the next seconds crashed into my chest like a heavy boot stepping on my heart, and I whined, "We can still be friends. Please … come back."

I slipped on my shoe, stepped to the porch, and slammed the entry door behind me. Smashing my nose against the glass next to the doorway, I peeked inside—for one last glance, in case Taddy returned to check on me. I whispered, "Taddy, you can rescue me right now, if you want." I slumped to the ground and sat on the concrete, rocking. I leaned on the windowpane with my back, sobbing like a toddler who had lost her way. I wept for a grandma, for a daddy, for a mama— wailing for someone to hug me, to climb a tree of hope with me. I only had sobs.

I thought about the last three weeks, and how Priscilla had lingered between sleeping, moaning, and remembering. How she first talked out of her head like a mule without any sense, but then she recognized Taddy, which changed everything. He stopped talking to me when she improved, and he acted as if the whole world was about to snatch him up and take him off to the whistling ghosts in Oklahoma again. He's safe. He has a family.

But I'm alone. Flat out alone. No one wants me. No one. I jumped to my feet, looking at the bare branches on the trees near the side street. "White Beard? Where are you? Here kitty-

kitty." I jogged to the side of the apartments, climbing up Taddy's tree, sitting on the branch beside the window next to his apartment.

I wished for Taddy to open the window. Wished he would at least peek from behind the curtain. Wished he would sit in this tree with me.

Meow. Meow.

My kitty jumped from a branch to one above me. "White Beard. Come here. You're my only friend."

Meow. Meow.

He sauntered from the branch above my head and curled into a ball in my lap. But no matter how white or soft he is, White Beard can't replace a best friend. Or give me a family. One I don't seem to have. One I can't find in this town.

When Staircases Crumble

The scratchy quilt rubbed my face like claws from a cat, and I rolled over in my feather bed, the dingy yellow sheets in need of washing. But Mahlee and the laundry mix like collard greens and syrup. She's behind on her housekeeping and not once has she ordered me to pick up my dirty clothes, or put my shoes in my closet. The dust on my dresser is thick enough to shovel into mini volcano mounds.

Rolling over, I squinted my eyes at the sun peeking through the balcony glass door. The streaks of brown revealed stained and dirty windows, too. Dingy with soot. Gritty floors like a sandbox. My shirts scattered like pebbles of sadness, along with my overalls in heaps on the hardwood floor. The littered mess a reminder of the sloppy way I live without supervision, but if Mahlee ignored me for much longer—I will run out of clean clothes.

"Shoelace, get up. Saturdays aren't for slouching. Taddy and Priscilla will be knocking on the back door. Time for church with your hobo friends. Time to carry biscuits to the creek. Time to help pass out the songbooks. Time for …"

I flew from beneath the covers, jumping to my feet. I stood on the mattress, and my gown flapped around my knees. The call of hope bounced off the wall in my bedroom from somewhere—somewhere in my mind. I looked for someone, but found no one. From across the room, my wrinkled overalls were draped on a hook on the wall beside my dresser causing me to take a double glance, because the outline appeared like a shadow of a person. "Grandma? Why did you have to die?" I slumped to the mattress, knowing she's gone, but saying

15

goodbye to her hurts worse than any broken bone. I sniffled, "Grandma. Grandma."

I buried my face in the quilt, pouring my sorrow and loneliness into the fabric. I sobbed, "I'm hearing voices now. I'm losing it. I need my old friends, the ones on the rail. I need to see them. I need to go. I might leave. I might. I'm a messenger of doom. I break things. I am a lone spirit without a family. I touch things and they die. I might fly away like a cardinal. I might join the circus with Sally. I might go away and never return."

Meow. Meow.

Picking up my cat, I nestled my nose in his fur as he arched his back, licking me on the cheek. "I love you, White Beard. You are mine. Wherever I go, you go. I'll take care of you. I won't let you die. I can be your mama."

Meow. Meow.

I petted his head, rubbing his spine, and his skin rippled with each stroke. "I didn't know my grandma's heart was bad. I should have been a better granddaughter. I was trouble. I was too much for her. Taddy was right. I am a bad person."

Meow. Meow.

White Beard lunged from my arms, landing on a patch of socks on the floor, tearing into them with all four claws. He darted. He scooted. He dove at a sock floating away, and then shook one paw when one of them got hung on his claw. He flip-flopped in a wild roll, leaping like the sock was a new tail, a sock tail attached to his paw.

I giggled. "Let me save you. I can save you. I can …" I fell to the floor like my crumpled laundry, wishing for Grandma to come home, wishing for a life like other children, the kind where mamas and daddies live, and tuck you in bed at night. Who ask you to pick up your clothes, and make your bed. My giggles turned to sobs, and I crawled to each piece of clothing, gathering up smelly socks and stained overalls. "Grandma, I'll clean my room. Just for you, even if Mahlee doesn't ask me."

I dressed, and wobbled to the closed door with my laundry in my arms, ready to take the load to the carriage house, to wash my clothes, to make them fresh like sunshine. I cracked my door and stepped into the hallway at the top of the stairs. I lost a few socks with each step, which caused White Beard to begin his attack again.

**

Ack! Ack! No! No!

The screaming stopped me at the top of the stairs, and I dropped more clothes. At the bottom, Mahlee wiggled on the floor, her screams were a fit of madness worse than my tantrums. She shouted into the phone. "No, Ernie. Come home. You can't break up with me. I'm yours. And you're mine." She crumpled like a stack of dirty socks, clasping the phone, only to wave the receiver in her hand like she wanted to pull Ernie through the phone line. She caught me staring at her, and shook the receiver at me. "Girl, get out of here. Can't you see I'm … I'm …"

I charged down the stairs like a deer set loose from a trap. "Mahlee, what did Ernie do?" I tossed the rest of my clothes to the floor.

"Nothing. Get. Go. I don't need a girl in my way. I need Ernie."

I snatched the phone from her hand, listened, but the beep-beep dial tone was the only rhythm keeping time with Mahlee's shouts. I motioned her to the front room, and let the phone dangle from the wall. "Come sit on the sofa. Talk to me like a grown-up."

"No. I like the floor. Leave me be."

"Really? Get up. Stop acting like me."

"Leave. Get away from me before you're sorry."

I grabbed a pair of dirty overalls from the floor, tossing them at her head. "Come on." Mahlee acted like the old Tin Can Mahlee who rode the rail with me in the past. Her arms shook, and her eyes blinked way too fast—she made me afraid, afraid for her, and afraid for me.

She pushed me. "Stop. Leave me alone."

I yanked on her hand. "Come sit over here. The O'Malleys are supposed to be here this morning. They'll be pulling up anytime. Do you want them to see you like this?" I squeezed her arm, and Mahlee unfolded herself from the floor. "Tell me what happened."

At the sofa, Mahlee slugged the cushion with her fist—pounding the fluffy pillow until the fluff became flat. "Ernie's staying in Florida. He's taken a job at the Miami News, and he thinks we need to wait to marry. Can you believe it? He's leaving me before we even get to the church." She threw the cushion at my cat.

Meow. Scat.

I patted her knee. "You could go with him. You could move to Florida. We could both go."

"I told him I'd come. He said no. He said no twice. He's sorry he rushed things with us. He wants out."

I scooted closer to her, but she jumped to her feet, leaving me on the sofa. Mahlee rushed to the stairs. "I'm going to my room. I'll be up there for a bit. If the O'Malleys get here, show them what needs to be done. They can start cleaning in the kitchen. Everything's a mess. I haven't been up to the task since losing your grandma. I got this front room clean, but the rest of the manor is cluttered. They will know what to do."

She stormed up the stairs, trembling as if her heart might stop, and White Beard darted in and around her feet. She scolded me. "Get your blasted cat away from me."

I jumped to my feet. "Here kitty-kitty."

**

Bam.

I raced up the stairs, hovering outside her bedroom door, and cuddled my cat.

Mahlee screamed through the doorknob. "Girl, go downstairs. I know you're out there. My business is not your business. Get to your own business. You are on your own."

I left before she changed her mind and opened the door to slug me. I let White Beard scamper down the rail of the staircase, and I hopped down each step, picked up my clothes, and ran through the kitchen.

Jogging, I headed to the carriage house, across the backyard, and tossed the whites in with the dark. I could almost hear my grandma's voice in my head telling me to sort them while I poured soap powder into the wringer washer. Hurrying to my tree beside the manor, I shimmied up the branches, sitting on a fat limb next to the spot where I keep my can of poems.

I grabbed the rusty coffee can, popped the lid, and unfolded the poem Taddy wrote to me last year. His poem is all lies. He didn't mean what he wrote. I crumpled it up, ripping the paper into a million pieces, letting them float to the ground like snow. "I don't want any poem from Taddy. Not one. Mahlee is right. I am on my own."

A female voice called, "Who started this laundry? We have suds rolling into the alley like lava. Shoelace? Where are you? Are you responsible for this?" The familiar voice of Ms.

O'Malley sent birds from their perches, and their flapping wings clapped a singsong of taps in between her calls for me.

"She's over here. In her tree." Sally O'Malley ratted me out, and smiled her great-big-cousin smile at me as I gazed down at her from my branch. I held onto the limb, and swung to the ground. "Sally! Hi! Leave the paper on the ground. It's broken snow that won't melt. I'm on my own now. Mahlee said so."

Sally giggled. "Were you going to live in a tree now?"

"Yes, until I get hungry. Who knows, I might just r...un a...way." The whistle from a nearby train rolling into town or maybe out, drowned out my last words.

"You best be helping my ma with those suds. I'm sure you're the reason for this laundry disaster. We're here to help clean up the manor. My mama's on a mission to get you and Mahlee on track so you can reopen the boarding house."

I skipped in a circle around Sally. "Your mama's not going to get much help from Mahlee. She's locked herself in her room, and Ernie broke up with her. She's ranting and screaming, and acting like me. She'll be there for hours."

Sally hugged the tree. "Come on. I'll help you with the chores. Mama says the faster we get finished, the faster we can play."

"Play? You want to play with me?" I gave a quick look across the street at the second floor window of Taddy's apartment, and whispered to no one, just to the air. "Goodbye, Thaddeus William Day Jr. I can play with Sally." I carried my can, deciding to keep the snow paper. "Let's put the snow in here for now. I might need some paper to write a poem on someday. Let's hurry, we have to catch up on our playing."

Sally laughed. "We have to catch up on chores first, and my mama will probably give you a lesson on doing your own laundry."

Leftover Clothes, Leftover Life

"One towel. Two. Three rags. Four." I counted the clean towels on the narrow table at the top of the stairs. I sighed, wishing for Mahlee to get up, to come from her room, to want me. Maybe she could at least pretend to be a mama. "Mahlee, you have clean towels for your bathroom and wash rags. Ms. O'Malley left them by your door. Everything's polished, waxed and shined. You might want to thank her. I helped, too."

No response, only a creaking high-pitched sound tingled my ears, and the squeak came from downstairs where Ms. O'Malley and Sally were finishing up supper in the kitchen.

The afternoon of washing clothes, of rinsing suds from the bricks in the alley, to dusting windowsills and the piano had left me achy and hungry. Laughing and doing chores with Sally made the day zoom by like a chicken hawk swooping by for lunch, swooping by for fun. We played like wild animals set loose from a cage, like elephants stomping in mud puddles, and like lions roaring in the wind.

Sally called to me from the first floor. "Shoelace, we're leaving. Thanks for helping me balance on your front porch rail. I can join the circus now. I'm ready. The Dailey Bros. Big Railroad Circus comes to Texarkana, April 22. Remember, you have to go with me."

I giggled, yelling at her from upstairs. "You can't join the circus. You're not a high wire walker; to become one takes more than an afternoon on my porch. You need more practice. And yes, I'll go with you to the circus. I like the lions and those elephants. They balance on little stands and don't fall off. I have trouble standing on my own feet."

"You're right. I may need another lesson tomorrow, and thanks for chasing off those monsters from the roof on the carriage house. I love singing with you because it's the only time I feel like I'm with someone who squeals as much as I do."

"You're welcome. You do sing like a cat with a furball in his throat."

Ha! Ha! Ha! Sally waved her arm from below, and disappeared from my sight.

"Bye, Sally. See you tomorrow."

I started to return to Mahlee's door, but Ms. O'Malley called to me. "Shoelace, be sure and keep watch on the meal."

I leaned over the rail. "Yes, ma'am."

Ms. O'Malley's green scarf tied on her head shined almost more than the sweat on her face. The headband reminded me of my grandma's scarf. Which reminded me of the times I'll never get back.

She held her neck, wiping off the dampness with a handkerchief. "Don't forget the vegetable soup is warming on the stove. And do turn off the burner. The cornbread is in the oven. Tell Mahlee we missed her, but we hope to see her tomorrow after church unless you'd like to ride with us to the chapel in the morning. Mr. O'Malley can swing by if so."

I smiled at the woman who loves Sally, the best mama around, but she makes being alone—feel lonelier. "Yes, ma'am. I'll watch the stew. Mahlee's not answering my knocks. I can't even hear her breathing. She must be sound asleep." I jumped down a few steps. "I don't think we'll go to church. Mahlee might need to stay home, and I'll stay with her to keep her company."

"Great idea. We'll swing by after service and check on you both tomorrow."

"Yes, ma'am."

"Be sure and lock up the manor, close the blinds, latch the windows, and double check everything. Since the Phantom Killer swept through Texarkana last year, we can't be too careful."

"I will lock up tight. Bye."

I crumpled to my knees beside Mahlee's door, trying to peek through the keyhole. The bit of light was darker than smoke, but lighter than walking on train tracks at night. "Mahlee," I turned the knob. "Mahlee, are you going to sleep all day? It's nearly six."

**

I draped my clean sheets over the long wall-table to make me a tent in the upstairs hallway, using Mahlee's towels and rags for a soft bedding. The stew is in the fridge now, and the pan of cornbread is all gone—since I shared most of it with White Beard. His belly is pooched out from under the towels next to my feet. "Poor kitty. You ate too much. We should have saved some cornbread for Mahlee."

Meow. Meow.

"Oh no, I forgot to lock the house." I tossed the tent flap to one side, flew down the stairs, and charged to the front door.

Click.

"Good, the door's locked. I better check the kitchen latch." I paused at the sink, taking a peek out the window facing Taddy's apartment. The light shone through the curtains, and a small shadow peeked from between them. I scooted to the side, not wanting Taddy to see me snooping on him, because he would use my nosiness against me sometime when he got mad. He couldn't get much madder than yesterday after school though. I took one last glance. No shadow now. I sat down at the table in one of the chairs and watched the curtain, hoping for one more glimpse of Taddy—but it never came.

I folded my arms, put my head down and dozed for a few minutes. Well, it seemed like just a few. My eyes popped open and the light at Taddy's apartment was now off.

I remembered I hadn't latched the hook on the back door, did so, switched the light off, and shuffled upstairs. The tick-tock on the wall clock by the phone counted off a chiming sound.

Ding. Ding. Ding.

I twirled around to glance at the time, the light from upstairs shadowing me, making me look like a giant in the half-lit staircase. "It's almost midnight. I slept forever, and Mahlee has slept too long. I'm waking her up. No one sleeps for twelve hours. Not even her. No wonder I'm yawning."

I pounded on her door, scaring White Beard, and he wobbled in slow motion downstairs and into the darkness. "Mahlee, get up. I'm scared. You need to take care of me. No one is here. I'm on my own, but I don't want to be. Being alone is no fun. Come out." I hugged the doorknob with both hands, twisting and jerking, and screaming. "Mahlee, I'm going to call the police. I am. I can. I will. I'll call Pastor Cody. He'll make you wish he didn't bring his Bible. He'll fix you. He has a verse for every sin."

I slumped to the floor, catching my foot on my table-tent, yanking the fabric, and it swooped over my head. I sat there like a ghost without anyone to scare, like a ghost who is afraid of her own shadow.

I unfolded myself from beneath the sheet, wiping tears from my face, and hurried to my room. I poured my treasures from my satchel onto my mattress, picking up a handkerchief, the one I'd found in the train after sitting with the stranger, the day Grandma died. I held it to my nose. Sweet honey. It reminded me of sweet honey on pancakes. I found my arrowhead, the one I brought back with me from Wheelock Academy. I held six soda pop caps. Two nickels. An old pencil. My harmonica. And a long slender nail from one of my walks with Taddy after school. I clasped the rusty nail in my hand, wishing for one more stroll with my best friend.

I rushed across the hall, stuck the nail inside the keyhole and jiggled it up and down, twisting and turning and poking. Then, on my last jiggle, I turned the knob and the *creak* told me the entrance to the tomb holding Mahlee captive was open. It was so dark, even a ghost might get lost. I stepped into the room, a draft of cold wind rushed past me. I found the light switch, and lifted the shadows from the room.

The lamp next to the window lay on its side. The curtain dangled in the breeze coming through the half-closed window, and one side of the fabric was torn off the rod. I placed the lamp upright, and my socked foot kicked something, sheets of paper. I knelt, and picked up my Grandma's will. It was her last statements where she left certain things to certain people, but not me.

I stepped backwards, clutching the will with both hands and sat on the white bedspread, the one with beaded balls of fuzzies all over it.

Where is Mahlee?

From somewhere, White Beard pounced to the nightstand on the other side of the bed, and the sparkle on the stand grabbed my attention. Not one sparkle. But two. Mahlee's engagement ring, and the blue ring Priscilla gave Mahlee last Christmas sat on the table. What? She never takes them off.

I rushed to Mahlee's clothes wardrobe, opening the double doors. Her old skirts were gone. Her old boots, too. I rushed to the window, calling into the night. "Mahlee, are you out there? You wouldn't leave me here all alone? Would you?" The rustle of freezing air shot through me and told me February had turned a ghostly cold. Was I alone for real? Mahlee wouldn't leave me after everything I've gone through, would she? Even if Ernie had just ripped her heart apart and crumpled it like dirty laundry, Mahlee wouldn't disappear without telling me, would she? My questions landed like ghost words in the wind, like a blank page of sadness written on my heart. A goodbye without a goodbye, a farewell like a haunting of my past.

I shut the window, put Mahlee's rings inside my overalls pocket, and crawled to the hallway, unable to stand for fear I'd crumble from the sadness. I remade my tent over the table in the upstairs hallway and sat underneath the wooden cave, holding a broom for protection after Pastor Cody didn't answer his phone. The O'Malleys didn't answer either. But I was not calling Taddy, no matter how many howls the night ghosts made and no matter how long until sunrise. I pulled White Beard close to my chest with my free hand, and inhaled a gasp of fear, exhaling breaths of despair.

After saying goodbye to my daddy and Grandma, and watching Scar and Red hurt people, and after seeing Eleanor die at Wheelock Academy, and after losing Margo a few weeks ago—I should be braver. But so far, I'm like soapy suds rushing down the alley of life. I had to stay awake, to keep the ghosts away when I sleep. My nightmares never ask me when they can come, but when they do, they swallow me up and take me to the grave where Grandmas never return—where everyone leaves, where shadows lurk, where life is darker than a rusty nail in a keyhole.

My eyes got heavy, and I fell sideways on the clean towels, hoping for dreams of cuddling with Mahlee in her bed, but instead I've got a cat. White Beard purred at my feet. "God, why is it so hard to give me a family? What have I ever done to you?"

Silence fell into my heart, a sign God was leaving me alone, too. I have no one. I am alone. Or maybe, I'm not.

Tour to Goodbye

I wiped my eyes, peeking from beneath the table. "Mahlee? Mahlee?" I crawled on my knees into her room, sat back on my legs, sighing as if last night was a lost and leftover nightmare—until I saw the tear in the window curtain.

I hopped to my feet, ran my hand along the bedspread, touching the softness and wondering how Tin Can Mahlee could decide to leave me. I don't call her with a 'Tin Can' anymore. These days, I simply call her Mahlee. She appeared settled in at the manor, content to get married, and seemed happy learning to cook and bake. She acted like a regular person, not like a hobo afraid of town folks.

Last year, when I sneaked off to do my 'vestigating at the Stamps farm, she scared the living and the dead out of me. I remember how she wore all of her skirts, too, and how she plopped behind me in her old brown boots. She lied to me about hitting the rail. She was planning to run off then, but when the chicken hawk dove at my cat, and me—Mahlee stayed in Texarkana because I'd gotten hurt. She never stays in one place too long, neither did Daddy and me. Somehow, I figured I'd be in the picture with her, no matter where she lived—since she's all I have. Since I'm all she has.

I wiped snot from my nose, in between sobs, and collapsed to the mattress, hitting the pillows. First the flat one where she must have slept, and then the fluffy pillow, fatter, like brand-new. I screamed at Mahlee even though she couldn't hear me. "You are so selfish, Mahlee. Worse than selfish. So a man leaves you, and now you leave me? I need you! Don't you see?" I shook my head. "Never mind. I don't need you. I don't. If you don't want me, I don't want you either. Daddy has lots of friends on the rail. I might go find me some new friends, and a new family. I'm eleven. I'm strong. I can fend for myself. I know my way to the missions, to the alley trashcans. I can leave, too. I'll go find my way, since this world loves having its way with me. I'll have my way with the world."

The fat pillow smelled like mothballs, and Mahlee's pillow like dirty-oily hair, like burnt vanilla. Mahlee baked cakes and muffins, using more flour and sugar than Grandma did in a month. No wonder her pillow reeked of dried cake. I almost smiled. Her cake isn't too hard to swallow if you make sure you have a glass of milk.

I shouted. "What if she never comes back?"

I touched my pocket, stuck my fingers inside and pulled Mahlee's rings out. The engagement ring is now the break-up ring, and it reminds me of how Mahlee grinned at Ernie, how she lit up when he walked into the room, especially when he kissed her. I'm not sure why she liked him. For a reporter, Ernie's lanky and mousy for a man, and not much to look at. His fingers tend to have ink on them, and he's happier typing or driving his new car than being a friend. He snapped at me more than once. I won't miss him, but I will miss Mahlee.

Clasping the blue ring, I couldn't believe she left this one behind, let alone take the ring off. She loved opening the box with the ring inside at Christmas, a gift from Priscilla. Oh, how happy it made her. Well, I hope she's happy now. She's deserted me without even asking me. Who does such a horrible act? Who up and leaves? I swallowed hard. "I'm leaving, too. I don't want to be here if no one is here for me." I smothered my face into her pillow trying to sniff in as much burnt vanilla as I could, in case I never saw Mahlee again.

Knock. Knock. Knock.

30

I jumped from the bed, leaping to the window, while stuffing the rings into my pocket. "Mahlee? Did you forget your key? Did you come back? I'll let you in." I raced down the steps as if my feet were on a sled flying across a snow-covered hill. I unlocked the front door, turned the knob, and came face to face with Taddy, who was dressed in his Sunday brown slacks and loafers.

I frowned. "What do you want?" I shoved the door part way closed.

Taddy stepped forward. "My mama's making me apologize to you. She heard us fighting on the stairs when we argued Friday, and I told her you fell down the steps. She knows what it's like to fall, to get hurt, and doesn't want you suffering. She thinks I'm being too hard on you." Taddy worded his phrases with precise, clean, clear, and concise enunciation. "I'm here because she's making me. I'm not finished being mad at you."

"You told her I tumbled down the stairs? So you did know? And you let me fall, and you didn't come to check on me? You had no idea if I'd broken my arm or a leg. I could have died." I shoved the door to close it, but Taddy's arm swung between the facing, stopping the door.

He moved the wavy piece of hair from his forehead. "Wait. At first you were faking your fall, and we both know it. You will do anything to get attention. It's not my fault you tumbled down those stairs, and if you broke anything you would have called for help. Your falling wasn't my fault."

I opened the door wide, pointing my finger at Taddy. "What? A best friend would have come back to see if I was alive."

He chuckled. "I saw you outside my window in the tree with your cat. You were fine, and you were sitting on my branches, not yours."

"I only used your tree to climb across to my oak tree." I paused. "So you were snooping on me? You do care."

"I might care. And I'm not a snooper. At least, not until I met you. I saw you watching me from your grandma's kitchen window last night. Yea, I might care, a little."

I laughed. "So we're both snoopers?"

Taddy rubbed his finger across his chin. "I'm not sure I am, but if you say so, I'll agree. I'm tired of arguing with you. It hurts. Besides, I have to tell you something before I leave."

"Before you go to church?"

"No, before I leave town."

"What? Where are you going?"

Taddy handed me a basket. "Mama made these this morning. She believes a good warm biscuit can help start your day off right."

"Thank you. Your mama does know how to make my tummy happy. But, where are you going?"

Taddy charged at me, swinging his arms around my neck like a monkey, hugging me so hard I gagged. "Taddy, what's wrong?"

He let go. "I'm sorry. You are my best friend. You always will be. I don't want to stay mad."

My monkey arms grabbed his neck. "Taddy, I'm sorry, too. I think after I act, and forget to act after I think. So much has happened in Oklahoma, and here. I was never so happy than when I found you alive."

Taddy sighed. "I know. Being kidnapped mixed me up, and I didn't know whom to trust. I'm your friend. I am." He stepped back a couple of feet. "I'm glad Mama sent me over here because I was going to tell you Friday, but your temper flared up faster than my words found a way to get out."

"What? Tell me." I wrinkled my nose.

32

"Don't get mad again. I have something I need to say. I'm going away. Mama's sending me to Uncle Carl's for a visit. He came to town last week, and they made the plans. I don't even know him. He's my grandma's brother, or a brother to another cousin. I don't know. I just know I call him Uncle Carl. And now I'm staying with him while Mama gets all well. No one asked me, but she wants me to finish my schoolwork at his farm, and to focus on my studies. She will stay here with her nurse, and I'll come back by summer when she's walking and stronger. I'll write you, so don't be mad at me. You're the only friend I've ever had. So promise me. You will write me back, won't you?"

I sucked in snot running down the back of my throat. "What? You're leaving? Now?"

Taddy nodded. "I'm leaving on the bus tomorrow morning after I get my assignments from Ms. Reece at school."

I shook my head, and a million faces ran through my thoughts. Grandma. Priscilla. Taddy. Mahlee. Pastor Cody. Ernie, the heel. Sally. Ms. O'Malley, the mama I wish I had.

Taddy shook me. "Are you there? Hello, anyone inside your head?"

I blinked. "I'm here. I'm so … so sad. Taddy, I need you. I will miss you. And I will miss your birthday." I sighed, saying words in my head, but not aloud. *I hope to see you again someday.*

Taddy squeezed me with a giant hug as if he liked me. "Write me. Promise. I'll be back before you know it." He skipped from the porch, out the front gate, and ran to his apartment building.

I stood there frozen like a snowman caught without any snow. Shocked, I shouted to the howling wind, placing the basket down, and sat down on the porch steps. "My Taddy is leaving me, too. Now what? I'm alone. No one wants me.

Well, the O'Malley's would. Or Pastor Cody." I shook my head harder than I should have, shivering from the cold February gusts, and then one of my pierced earrings flung from my earlobe to the wooden slatted porch.

Clink. Clink.

"Oh my, I can't lose an earring. These were Eleanor's." I reached for the earring, slipping it back into place. I rubbed my eyes hoping to wipe away the soot of the weekend, and bounced to my feet. "I have to make up my mind. The O'Malley's will come by after church. Sally will ask me to move in with her. She's adventurous and nice, but she will have pity on me. I don't need pity. I need ... I need my grandma. Or Mahlee. But she doesn't want me."

I hurried inside with the biscuits, slammed the door, and put the latch in place. I leaned against the door and slipped to my knees watching the fire crackle in the fireplace, the embers of ash mixed with the damp smell of old wood. The new windowpane to my left behind the sofa let in the morning sunshine, and I inched to the middle of the front room, touching the sofa cushion where my grandma often sat. I ran my fingers across her books on the bookshelf, and held her favorite copy of *Life Magazine*, the one with the stain from her sweet tea.

"Grandma? I need you. Why did you have to die? Why couldn't God have given you a heart ready to live and beat longer?" I screamed at God, knowing I'd have to tell him sorry for being mad—later.

Ding. Ding. Ding.

I glanced at the clock, and was reminded how slow time goes when you have nowhere to go. I didn't want to stay here anymore, because others will treat me like an orphan. I'm no orphan. I'm … I'm free. I can come and go. I'm going. I'm leaving before the O'Malleys get here.

Upstairs, I packed some overalls and clean shirts in my satchel. I tossed in my treasures, my tin can with my poems, and tied my PF Flyers in double knots. I folded my white dress from Eleanor's funeral, tucking it into a side pouch for special things. I slipped my coat on, rushed downstairs to the kitchen, and grabbed White Beard.

Meow.

"Not to worry kitty. You're with me. You may be a scrawny cat, but we have each other. I'm not going to an orphanage. Not going to the O'Malleys, either. Don't want to mess up their love for Sally. I'd ruin their family. I'm an extra wheel with a broken axle."

I packed some of Priscilla's biscuits inside my satchel, using one of Grandma's dishtowels, and then I wrapped Grandma's cat apron around my waist, pretending to dance with her. I looked at my kitty whose eyes were bugging out of his head from my twirling, and realized kitty had no idea what dancing with a hobo girl meant.

I sniffed the blue and white apron and saw blackberry cobbler stains on the front. She helped Ms. Motes bake cobblers when we were at Wheelock Academy. The apron smelled like Grandma, like old soap, and Vicks Vapor Rub. I stuffed the apron into my satchel and snapped the bag closed.

The lone whistle of the train rolling down the tracks sent me out the back door, darting to the alley, clutching my cat. I headed toward Union Station on the side roads, ready to hop a train out of Texarkana, but first I needed to make one last stop.

A Gift at the Coffin

The sun hung from the sky like a yellow balloon ready to pop, ready to release the pain of my being a hobo kid. I rode into town with Mahlee's help, after losing my daddy to the river, and I reunited with my grandma. She gave me and Mahlee a home. But now—I'm back where I started. If only my real mama had lived after I was born.

Sucking in the dust whipping between the buildings in the alley, I took the familiar walk of misery. No one will miss me. No one will know I'm even gone, until I can't be found. No one will even come looking for me. I thought Mahlee loved me, but she doesn't, or she wouldn't have left without saying a word.

I squeezed my satchel hard, my fists tight, stepping in a leftover puddle from the night. "God, I can't do this. My heart is beating, but I'm like a circus balloon. I'm ready to bust. I could just float away in the sky, or down a river, and no one would care. I'll float away to a land where no one knows me. I can't stay here. I want you to know, God, I don't want anything. Nothing. Well, except ..." I wiped my nose, tumbling over the wooden crossties on the tracks leading across the bridge next to Swampoodle Creek. "Never mind, God. You're probably too busy to listen to me. Hey, keep up, kitty. It's a long walk, or a long ride to nowhere, but we're going anyway."

I straddled the ties on the tracks, glancing at Swampoodle Creek below. It reminded me of the night I fought with the masked man last year, the night I tumbled from the boxcar right from this spot, and how no one ever caught the killer. I'll never forget his eyes though, the way they looked right through me. Which is the same way Ernie's eyes have a way of slicing straight to my heart like a knife, too. I shivered, shaking off the memory of both sets of eyes, running the rest of the way over the bridge.

I gazed back. "Come on, White Beard. Hurry it up."

The paws of my white cat danced a perfect balance on the track, and he twitched his ears with each bird singing, with each rustle in the bushes ahead. He moved with a purposed step like a lion ready to roar at anything, or something. I was ready to roar, too, at everyone with a family, who has a daddy, who has a mama, at anyone who dared to get in my way.

Nobody knows what I'm facing, or knows how lost I feel. It's as if I'm in the valley of "No Way Out," surrounded by cemetery markers with no future, with memories I can't count on. "Come this way, White Beard."

I jogged to the right down a trail, stopping under the arch of the entrance to Rose Hill Cemetery where my family sleeps in dirt and darkness. I know they're not in the ground, but I'm finding comfort in being surrounded by corpses. I shuddered, feeling a flutter in my heart. Oh, no. I hope I don't have a bad heart. I held my chest. Maybe my heart is pumping the wrong way. It's a valve short of being whole. No one would want someone with a bad heart.

I kicked at a clod of dirt, and shuffled to the first set of crosses lining the middle of the dirt road, those next to the green moss on the edge of the bricks. I read names, army people buried in a rectangle with a memorial sign posted at the end. These people fought in the war. I'm fighting a war, too. A battle I'm losing.

I picked up my cat and inched toward the side part of the cemetery to our family plot, where the concrete bench with the name Kree etched on it, sits. The bench rests at the foot of my mama's marker, close to my daddy's marker. Grandma's tombstone rests next to my grandpa's marker.

Screech. Meow.

White Beard bounced from my arms, roaming to the bushes and trees behind the bench. "Come back here, and get out of the tree. We're leaving. You're on this crazy road with me. I can't do this alone." I fell to the bench, rubbing my hand across the engraved letters of the family name, four letters, which felt like a foreign language, a name without a living person to care for me.

Chug. Chug. Chug. Crackle. Chug.

I rose up, squinting my eyes. One car. Two. A pile of cars followed each other to the west side of the cemetery. I shook my head. "No one should bury someone on a Sunday, or at lunchtime. Sundays are the day for rest, or running away. Maybe they don't know what day it is.

Rubbing my nose, I gazed at the sun peeking from behind the trees. The O'Malleys will be at the manor wondering where Mahlee is, wondering why I'm not answering the door. Thank goodness, I left the front door unhinged, along with a note letting them think Mahlee and me went downtown to the Grim Hotel for chicken fried steak. This way, we won't be missed for hours. No one will care anyway.

I licked my lips, remembering the luscious food and the rolls at the Grim, wishing for one last meal with my grandma there.

Across the way, the first black car with the shadowed windows told me it was a coffin-car. I slipped from the bench and ducked behind it, and sat on the cold ground. Leaning my chin on the slate bench, I spied on the people, hoping they'd hurry up and say their goodbyes.

A woman with red hair, long and wavy like a grapevine, moped in slow motion toward the spot where some chairs sat. She stared at the hole in the ground, not moving, only shaking her head. Two men joined her, wearing suits, and they and a couple of other men placed a coffin on a stand by the hole. A round man with skinny legs placed flowers on a shiny metal holder.

From the third car, another woman emerged, chubby and flabby like a grandma but not old enough to be one. She opened the door in the back, "Girls, come on. Walk with your auntie. We need to go be with your mama. This day is hurting her heart, and we need to let her borrow ours."

The taller girl, with long red hair, ran ahead and stood next to the coffin like a human tombstone. The mama wrapped her arms over her daughter's shoulder, and together they shuddered in unison.

I touched my shoulder, wishing for an arm to drape around my neck, to love me, to pick me. I sniffled, "God, would you let me know you love me? I can't feel you right now. I don't see you. I feel so alone."

Meow. Meow.

White Beard pounced to the bench and nestled close to my face. I rubbed his ear. "Love you, White Beard. You are my family. The only family I have."

A gust of wintery wind chilled my legs, burning my face with a sting of pain, like bees attacking. I rubbed my cheeks. "It's getting colder. Must be a storm coming. Hope there's no snow with it." I shook, cuddling my cat.

A voice shouted from the opened door of one of the cars. "I want my daddy to wake up. He's asleep. Not dead. Don't put him in the grave. He's my daddy. He has to wake up." A girl, smaller, bony like me, with pigtails flopping, charged the coffin. She jumped and cried. "I want my daddy."

I moved closer, standing behind a tree, watching the funeral unfolding before my eyes. Their yelling pierced my ears, reminding me how Mahlee held me at Grandma's funeral, how she'd let me sit in her lap in my white dress. The one Eleanor stitched in her sewing class. The one the matron gave me at Eleanor's funeral last month.

I ran to Grandma's tombstone, crumpling over it, whimpering, "Grandma, come back. Don't leave me. You have to come back to me. Mahlee's not here. She's left me. She's gone. I need you."

I sobbed, dripping the leftover tears, those that had gotten stuck inside me. They rained from my eyes like a winter storm set loose in a cemetery. The words at the other funeral echoed with my aching heart.

Digging into my satchel, I pulled an envelope from inside. "I wrote you a letter, Grandma. It's more like a poem to lift your spirits when you miss me. You will miss me, right?" I sat the envelope next to her tombstone. "I love you, Grandma. Tell God to watch out for me."

I knelt next to Daddy's spot in the dirt, and touched the postcard-size marker with my finger. I couldn't cry anymore, all my tears were spent on my grandma. And on losing Mahlee. I toppled over, hugging the brown grass poking me like needles of death, not sure how long I stayed there, except all of a sudden, a rush of heavy breathing drifted toward me.

Wheeze. Whistle. Sniffle.

I jumped to my feet, sense that the wheezing and sniffles were whistling near the angel tombstones, next to a group of towering crosses. I stood there frozen, watching a pastor cradle his Bible, talking to the family and to others. They hovered like low flying planes ready to crash land.

Folding chairs held some of the family, and the mama lady. Her two girls. One older than me. One about the same age as me, with blonde hair. I moved my bangs to the side, slipping over to a wrought-iron fence surrounding a group of tombstones. I crept along the fence, listening to the pastor who spoke through crackling words. "Mr. Rivercoon loved his family. He doted on his girls—Tonya, so mature for fourteen, and Cindy, so kind at ten. He loved them like they were precious pearls. I considered him a friend, and the accident took his life too early. This world is cruel, but we have his memories."

Cindy charged the pastor, knocking his Bible from his hand. "I don't want a memory. I want my daddy."

The mama hurried to Cindy, picked her up and cuddled her, calming her with whispered words I couldn't hear. She sat down in her chair, motioning for Cindy to do the same.

Those standing behind the chairs used their handkerchiefs and caught what seemed like a gallon of snot. They wiped their noses, and their coughing made me clear my throat. Their pain leaked from their faces, and somehow knowing they hurt, made me hurt less. It made me thankful for knowing my daddy and my grandma, for having some good memories.

I tired of watching their goodbyes, and needed to be on my way. I wandered back to the Kree bench where I sat down for one last cry of my own. "Grandma, I'll never forget how you took me in, and wanted me. I'm sorry for sneaking out so much. I'm sure I made your heart tired. I'm sorry for being so bratty."

Cindy, the small girl, shorter than me, walked up to the flowers on her daddy's coffin. I couldn't help but watch, and then she gave me a glance, and I turned away. Then I looked back and she was coming towards me. I jumped to my feet on the bench, towering higher than the marching girl. "Go away.

This is my side of the cemetery. Don't bother me. I'm talking to my family. Leave me be."

Cindy clutched a flower, a white rose like the paper ones the Choctaw girls made for Eleanor's funeral. She held the flower out. "I want to give you this." She held up the stem with the most perfect rose, an offering of kindness. Unexpected. Like God sent her.

I reached for the flower, "Thank you," and jumped with a somersault dive to the grass. "Your family is getting in the car. You better catch up."

She twisted her head, "My mama will wait. She won't leave me."

For every step I took around the graves, Cindy shadowed me. She moved closer like an approaching boxcar, like a steam engine filled with hope. I wanted more than anything to have hope, but not from her. I wanted my grandma back. "Get away, or I'll …"

"Or you'll what?" The words of the determined girl flew at me.

"Or I'll hit you." I shook a fist at her.

"Are you going to hit me on the day I had to say goodbye to my daddy? Why would you hit me? My daddy died last week falling down a flight of stairs. He hit his head on a wall and never woke up. So if you would feel better, go ahead and hit me." She folded her arms, and pursed her lips.

"I don't want to hit you. I'm just flat out mad. I need to be alone." I coughed up more words, doing my best to run her away before I slugged her. "Thank you for the flower, but I'm not all together—together."

Cindy smiled, and then sobbed, "I … I loved my daddy. He's in heaven now. Maybe he's with …" She turned to the markers. "Who died?"

"My grandma. Her heart gave out before I wanted it to."

"I'm sorry she died. I didn't want my daddy to leave me, but God gave me my daddy for ten years. Wasn't God nice?" She flinched, her arms shaking. "I'm going to miss him. He played the piano for me at night. I'll miss hearing him sing."

I tried not to smart off, but it wasn't happening. "Good for you. You had ten years. I only lived with my grandma for a year."

"Where were you before you stayed with her?"

"I lived with my daddy and Tin Can Mahlee." I told her enough, without telling her too much.

Cindy pointed to a marker. "But who do those two markers belong to? Your parents' graves?"

"Yes. Mama died when I was born, and when Daddy died I came here to my grandma's house. I knew her from when I was small. I'd been gone a few years. My grandma was the kindest, most patient, and bestest person I've ever met. She made the bestest chocolate cake, and she gave squishy hugs, too."

Cindy hugged my neck. "Then make her proud. Go be the bestest granddaughter."

I jerked free, walked to Grandma's grave, and placed the rose across the top of her plot. "I don't know how." I squinted my eyes at Cindy. "You talk like my friend, Taddy. He talks all grown-up, too."

"Thaddeus William Day Jr.? I know him. He's smarter than six eighth graders all rolled into one giant Tootsie Roll." Cindy sauntered next to me. "So why can't you make your grandma proud?"

"Because I'm running away. No one wants me." I snatched my cat, darted into the woods, and headed toward the tracks. Taking us away from town, down one of the splits, I charged ahead, not caring where I went. I wasn't sure, but I was headed somewhere, even if I landed nowhere.

I heard Cindy yelling at me, "But you don't understand, my mama says you can't outrun your life."

I called back to Cindy; she heard none of my shouts, "I'm gonna try."

The whistle of a train rumbling on the nearby tracks, picked up speed and called to me like a coffin with wheels, and I hung low at the edge of the bushes, out of sight from funeral criers. I no longer could hear Cindy calling for me to come back, either.

I stuffed White Beard into my satchel, and his paw slipped from under the flap. "Kitty, you stay put and hold on." I called to the cemetery. "Goodbye, Grandma. I love you."

My PF Flyers charged alongside the open boxcar, and a hand reached out of the shadow from inside the door. "Take my hand. I'll lift you up."

In one swoosh, the man yanked me into the boxcar, tossing me across the floor of the car. He hovered too close. "What do we have here?" He ran his hand through my hair. "Such a pretty girl. What's in the bag?"

The wrinkled face hung over me like one from my nightmares!

Road Trip

If my life were a cartoon strip, I could erase the ugly face breathing sour whiskey odors and leftover cigarette breath up my nose. This man was sending a burn up my nostrils, making my tongue stick to the top of my mouth. I'm not a cartoon character and neither is this man pulling on me. "Stop. Leave me alone." I kicked my feet, alternating them like I was playing kickball. Zeroing in on one spot on his chin, my tennis shoe belted his jaw.

The bent man slobbered, rubbing his face. "Little brat, stop the kicking."

"No, let me go. I never did anything to you. Not yet, anyhow." I hollered like a black bear with no claws, clutching my satchel. I squeezed White Beard too hard, and he squalled. *Meooow!* "Sorry, kitty."

"What have you got in the bag?" The polka-dotted face with little craters spewed more words at me, but the thud-thud, clack-clack of the wheels drowned out my response.

I tossed my bellows into the air anyway, and the man picked me up, leaving my feet dangling. "Leave me be."

The slobbering man shoved me over a stack of crates. *Slam-skamp-slam.*

"Ouch, you helped me in and now you do this?"

"I want your food and your money. I'm hungry."

I pounced onto a crate, dropping my satchel behind me in the corner, holding my fists, ready to sock someone. "Seems like you drank your food in a bottle. You need to stop the booze. It's bad for you. I'm not giving you my biscuits, either. You best get away from me."

The hum of the train squealing sent the boxcar into a jerk-stop-jerk motion, causing me to wobble like a circus performer in training. The man with the glaring green eyes stumbled near the opened boxcar door, grabbing the side. "I get what I want. I take what I want. Hand me the satchel."

From the shadow behind the drunk, an arm extended like Superman without a uniform, without a cape. Superman yelled, "Mister. You will regret getting in this boxcar. Enough! This little girl is not yours to steal from."

The surprise-hands of the super hero yanked the ugly-man into the other end of the boxcar in one swoop.

Ahh. Ahh. Ahh.

Superman shouted in a kind sort of way. "Stay put, and don't bother the girl."

A wounded whisper rose up in the corner. "I'll leave her be."

Superman shot from the shadow toward me. "Are you alright?"

I leaped from the crate, bent down to get my satchel, and stepped into the beam of light coming through the boxcar door. "I know you. You're the man from … my grandma's train when we came home from Oklahoma. You let me sit in your lap, and you held me when she died from her heart attack. I didn't get to say goodbye." I rushed to him, and he gathered me up, offering me an embrace like a hundred hugs from God, tight, firm, warm, and with love.

He put me down, kneeling in front of me. "What brings you to a boxcar on this Sunday afternoon?"

Meow. Meow. Meeeooow.

I unclipped my satchel, ignoring his question. "White Beard, I'm sorry." My kitty slipped from the bag to the gritty floor, his white paws crisscrossing in a prance of freedom. I petted his ear. "Now don't fall. This train's picking up speed."

Meow.

White Beard's tail swirled in the wind, going straight up, and he balanced himself with a wiggle and a pad-pad prance.

Superman touched my coat sleeve. "Try and focus. Why are you on this train?"

I stepped back. "Tell me why you are. Are you following me?"

"Following you? I was on this train before you sprinted from the bushes at the cemetery. So, tell me, why is a little girl like you hopping a train? From what I remember you had folks at the train station when we arrived in Texarkana. They're going to miss you."

I put my hands on my hips, giving him the Popeye, one-eyed look. "What do you mean a girl, like me? You don't know me. I'm a hobo girl. Me. It's just me. I don't have any family. They're all gone. Gone! Did you hear me? They either died or left me! Gone!" Tears leaked from my eyes.

Superman lifted my chin, pulling out a handkerchief, dabbing my cheek. "There. There. Don't cry."

I grabbed the handkerchief. "I have your other one."

"My other one?"

"Yes, you left your handkerchief in the passenger train when we first met. I kept it." I reached inside my satchel, digging around. "Here it is. Do you want it back?"

"No, you keep it. They tend to come in handy for days when we cry."

"I don't cry." I dabbed my face to hide those last tears. "Hobo girls don't cry. They don't." I'm not sure he believed me, or if I believed me, but either way—my eyes were leaking.

Pam Kumpe

"You have a way of not answering me. So where are you headed?"

"I'm on a road trip. Me and my cat."

The slobbering man got up, and wobbled towards us. "Let me at her. I'm going to see what's in the bag."

The man with the handkerchief made a fist. "I told you to leave her alone." Superman dove at the ugly man who charged at me from the shadows. "Buddy, I don't think this boxcar is big enough for all of us."

"Then you'll need to deal with me."

They rolled on the floor, heads flopping, and arms socking, with White Beard hissing at them. I tasted fear in my mouth, and wondered if I should have hopped another car.

Superman grabbed the drunk by the collar, pulling him to his feet. "I've had enough. I see we're taking a bend. You best hold onto your shoes, you're out of here."

With those words, the ugly and grouchy drunk tumbled out of the boxcar door with one push from the man saving my life. I realized I had no idea what my savior's name was, nor did he know mine.

I rushed to the opened door, watching the loner fall, a slow-descent, like a picture show stuck on the screen. He landed in a padded spot of ground packed with what looked like leftover hay, like a pillow of straw. It's as if the hay was placed there just for him.

I yelled into the wind, my head bending backwards as we chugged on down the tracks. "He's not hurt. You timed your shove just right."

Superman stuck his head out, too. "I'd say so. It looks like God managed the landing. I simply did the shoving."

I moved from the door, sitting on a crate. "Phew. I'm glad he's gone."

"Me, too. So where are you headed?"

I cleared my throat. "I'm off to the circus. I'm headed …" I almost told him more than I should, almost told him I had the address of the house Grandma left for Mahlee.

"Circus? Life can seem like a circus. There's the clowns. The animals. And the people. Some people come at us like clowns who hide behind white faces."

"I'm not hiding. I'm in the open. I'm right here."

He patted my arm and sat down across from me on a crate. "Well, some people roar to keep others away, so no one will know they're hurting, or sad, or even mad."

"I'm not sad. I'm not mad, either. I'm tired of hurting, though. I'm making my own decisions, so I'm leaving. Everyone leaves me first; it's my turn to do the leaving."

"I've noticed how the animals perform for the ringmaster, but they long to be free. You remind me of a caged lion who is ready to roar."

I smiled, wiping my hair from my brow. "I am a lion."

He chuckled. "I see a cub. You might need someone to take care of you until you get stronger, bigger, and even wiser. You might have found your roar, but your body hasn't caught up yet. The drunk could have taken away your roar."

I pounced up, folding my arms. "I can take care of myself."

Superman squeezed my arm as if checking for a muscle. "Is that why he tossed you over those boxes? Is it because you let him?"

"No, he caught me off guard. He helped me get inside the boxcar, and I never figured he'd steal from me."

"Well, your figuring is off by about ten lion years."

"What? What do you mean by lion years?"

"You need to grow up. You're just a cub."

"Stop using playing words with me. I'm not in the playing mood. You never told me how you got stuck on a freight train. Last time I saw you it was in a passenger train when we rode to Texarkana from Millerton, Oklahoma, and now you're in a boxcar hitching a ride. And I don't even know your name."

"My name is Archie Gabs, and I hit the gambling tables at the Grim Hotel after we got to town last month. I'm not proud of losing my money, but it happens to the best of us. We make mistakes, get in trouble, and run away."

"I'm not running away. I'm moving away." I shook my head. "They don't have gambling at the Grim."

"There's a gambling table in every bar or hotel, if you look hard enough."

"Whatever." White Beard rubbed his back on my legs.

Archie reached down to pet my cat. "So is this a permanent road trip?"

"You're trying to trick me. Do you think by knowing my inside thoughts you can fix my outside world?"

"We can't fix things ourselves, but God helps us when fixing is hard."

"Stop talking in circles. You're acting like a know-it-all who carries handkerchiefs for noses, who thinks he has all the answers."

"I don't have the answers. But I know who wipes away tears."

"You, right?"

"No, Jesus. He wipes away our tears. And holds us."

"He doesn't hold me."

"You'd be surprised."

"He forgives people for things, but he's too busy to stop me from leaving."

"You'd be surprised."

50

"You said that already."

"I did. It was worth repeating."

Meow. Meow. Meow.

I stuffed the handkerchief into my satchel, and unwrapped two biscuits. "Want one?"

"Yes, thank you." He bit into the crusty roll. "So tell me your name."

"It's Shoelace. See my red PF Flyers." I held up a foot.

"Yes, nice running away shoes."

"I'm not running away."

"Right, you're leaving. And your name is?"

"Shoelace."

After convincing Archie of my name, he slipped to the shadowy corner and curled up for a nap. I did the same at the other end of the boxcar, my lips cracking from the cold, my body shivering. I remembered how I used to cuddle with my daddy on the rail when he was alive. I'll never get used to—sleeping by myself.

Rap. Rap. Rap.

Archie tapped my foot. "Shoelace, get up. We've got to jump. We're coming to a town. The railroad cops will be checking the boxcars at the train station, and taking us to jail if we get caught."

"How do you know so much about railroad cops? Isn't this your first time to hop a train?"

Archie Gabs took my hand. "No, I've lost money before. This is not my first time. Come on, the train is slowing down. Ready, set, let's roll."

I tumbled to a patch of dirt softer than hitting a place with rocks. I landed under a bush, remembering my cat. I ran to the tracks, jogging alongside the boxcar. "White Beard. Here kitty, kitty. Come on. Jump boy. Jump."

My cat sat on his haunches licking his paw, and a railroad cop showed up from the bushes up ahead. "Hey girl. What are you doing? You hobos get younger and younger. Stay put. We need to talk."

The train inched to a stop, and the railroad cop slapped his club in his hand. He stood next to the opened boxcar door where my kitty sat, and he called to me. "Stay right there. You're going to take a ride to town with me."

Meoooooowwww! Scatttttt!

White Beard leaped from the boxcar onto the railroad cop's head.

"Get this cat off me."

I slipped under the boxcar to the other side of the train, darting beneath the tracks. I stayed on my knees hoping my cat saw me, calling to him. "Here kitty. Come on. This way."

White Beard came into view, and I reached for my cat. "Good boy. Good kitty."

A firm hand sent me spinning to my feet. "Archie, is that you?"

The freckled teen stood taller than me wearing an engineer cap, one like I used to have, like the one I gave to Lizzy Beth.

The boy whispered, "Nope. My name's Crush. Hurry up. Come with me. I know where you can hide."

A Debt I Cannot Pay

"Stop pushing my head, you've tucked me next to these sacks in the back of this truck like trash inside of a can."

The boy scolded me, speaking over the bed of the truck. "Hush, someone's coming. Act like a sack of sugar and be sweet, but mostly be quiet."

Squashing White Beard under my chin, his furry ears tickled my face. I listened, sucked in dust through my mouth from the burlap tossed over my body, and hid from everyone, not knowing why I obeyed this boy. Maybe I had no other choice, and hiding in this pickup might keep me from going to jail.

A man's voice rang out. "Boy, have you seen any hobos running past here? They usually don't come this close to the depot, but I've caught them wandering in places right in the open before. I could have sworn a girl in overalls ducked out of my sight. Where could she have gone?"

"No, sir. I did see a man in a brown suit run like an unsteady stick. He cut through the alley over by the drugstore. No one came this way." Crush ratted on Archie, but somehow, knowing he didn't tell on me was better. Sitting in jail or getting sent to an orphanage sounded worse than sitting folded in half with my kitty in this truck.

The man's questions returned. "What's under this cover?" The railroad cop's growl grew louder and more intense.

"Oh, we have thirty sacks of sugar for Marion Kane. He's from Jefferson. His shipment was short, so we drove to Atlanta to buy wholesale. We're about to load up and head home."

"Marion Kane? Well, he does make the best syrup in East Texas."

"Yes, sir. He does."

With my back up against the cab, I shifted my foot, wedging myself between the corner of the sacks, and my toes tingled. They were falling asleep. Shoving White Beard between my knees along with my satchel, I rubbed my itching nose, then wiggled, and pinched my nostrils. The bomb of a sneeze backed up in my head, but slipped through my mouth.

Achooo. Achooo. Achooo.

"Who sneezed? Are you hiding someone in the back of your truck?"

"No sir. Just the sugar. And Timmons and Tak."

I wrinkled my nose, tucking my face into my jacket sleeve, trying to figure out who or what Timmons and Tak were, or could be.

Crush hollered, "Timmons. Tak. You can come out now."

Rustling on the other side the sacks came with screams of joy. "You found us. We were hiding from you."

Two high-pitched voices snickered from the other side of the bed, in the opposite corner from me. They called, "We're playing hide 'n go seek."

One yelled, "We've been hiding for a long time."

The other one squeaked, "We were hiding from Mr. Marion."

Crush corrected the squealers. "Get down from there. You'll fall off the sugar and break a leg. The both of you. Get down."

I peeked from under the corner of the burlap, and saw four shoes, same brown leather boots attached to scrawny boys, no older than kindergarteners.

I glanced over at the railroad tracks, and the cop slapped his stick and disappeared toward the bushes, shaking his head, sporting a gun on his hip.

I popped my head out the whole way, staying low in the corner. "Who are they?"

Before Crush could answer, the boys crawled over the pile of sugar sacks, falling nose to nose toward me. The strawberry-haired boy and the cotton-haired boy spoke together, "Who are you?" Their freckles matched like brothers from the same mother, but their hair opposite like strawberry jam on one, like cotton balls on the other.

I sat down on a stack of sugar sacks, folding my arms, letting White Beard prance across the burlap. "I'm Shoelace. I'm eleven. I'm on my own. I'm joining the circus."

The taller boy with red hair moved in, touching my hair, sniffing my shirt. "You hair is like Tak's. Light and yellow."

I wrinkled my nose. "What are you doing? Don't touch me."

He backed up. "You don't smell like you work in tents or in the dirt. You smell all dignified and clean."

The smaller boy leaned in. "Yep. Dignified."

I dusted my overalls with my hands, letting crumbles of dirt fall to my shoes. "There's nothing wrong with being clean. Taking a bath is not so bad unless you get soap in your ears." I tapped the smaller boy on the shoulder. "What's your name?"

"I'm Tak. I'm sick on days when the sun shines, and even sicker in the winter—except on a good day. Today's a good day, and Mr. Marion let me and Timmons ..."

"I'm Timmons." The other boy pointed at himself.

Tak pushed his brother. "I was talking, don't be interrupting me when I talk. You get on to me for interrupting, so I'm telling you."

"Fine, go ahead." Timmons jumped from the back of the truck over the side, and leaned on the door panel with his arms folded.

I glanced at him, and he ran to a fat, bouncy man with a smile as far as the east is to the west. The man carried stick candy in his hand.

Tak turned my chin back. "Excuse me, Shoelace. I'm telling you a story. I like stories. Toby Raike tells us stories when he preaches. I'm gonna be a preacher someday like him."

"A preacher? I'm not so happy with preachers right now. They tell me God loves me, but I'm not so sure He does." I realized I was rambling. "Sorry, I have to go. I don't need anyone interfering with my plans." I climbed over the sacks toward the tailgate of the truck.

Tak followed me over the burlap. "You can stay with us. You don't have to leave. We can be friends. I need a friend."

I leaped from the truck to the gravel. "I don't need anybody. Sorry little kid. I'll be on my way." I called White Beard and we moved on down the dirt road, the one leading behind a bunch of brick buildings.

Tak tracked me, pulling on my arm. "I was telling you my story. Mr. Marion let me and Timmons come to Atlanta so he could get his sugar. He promised us a treat. He always has more than enough. He'll give you one, too, if you stay."

"I'm not here to stay, I have to leave."

Crush mouthed at us. "She can't move in with us. We don't have a home." He turned to me. "We stay in an old run-down house in Jefferson. Sometimes we sleep in this other old house, to keep warm or when the river's up."

I spun around. "Tak, see, you have a home. It's me. I'm the one who needs a home." I pointed my finger at Crush.

"Did you say you live in Jefferson, Texas? How far is Jefferson from here?"

Tak giggled. "Why? I thought you were going to be in the circus."

I pushed him away. "Never mind. Just leave me be."

Crush ran up to me, yanking on my arm. "I've left you to yourself here, and now you're being rude to my brother. I helped you out, now you can help us out. Here comes Mr. Marion. I need you to tell him how I saved your hide from the cops. He enjoys it when he hears I've done something kind or good. I've got my image to keep with him."

I yanked free. "Kindness shouldn't come with a price. You're making me pay you back. It's like a debt. You're not being kind."

"You're right. I have a price on every good deed I do."

"Then it's not a good deed if you hold it over someone's head."

The jolly man with no hair on top, but with some strands wrapped sideways near his ears, bounced up to me with Timmons, who licked a piece of stick candy. The man asked, "Who do we have here? Are you lost, little lady?"

"No, not lost."

Cough. Cough.

Crush cleared his throat, giving me a slanted head tilt, and eye squint.

"Sir, your son, Crush, saved me from the railroad cops."

Mr. Marion laughed, and his belly jiggled. "These are not my sons. Just some special young men I've taken a liking to. Crush works for me, and Timmons and Tak tag along."

I picked up my cat. "Then your worker boy helped me out. I wanted to tell you *how kind he is.*" I turned, and my satchel flew over my shoulder hitting me in the back.

"Where are you off to?" Mr. Marion quizzed me, and hurried to block my path.

"Sir, I'm going to the circus. I've got a meeting with the ringmaster. I'll be on my way."

Timmons and Tak jogged up to me, and they stood on either side of Mr. Marion. Timmons tugged on my bag. "Tak thinks you're going to be in the circus. So are you good with the elephants? Do you work with the lions? What do you know how to do?'

Tak answered for me. "She's probably the ticket girl. She doesn't know how to work with wild animals."

"I do, too. You two are wild. I could whip you in a second."

Mr. Marion stepped in front of the boys. "No need to cause trouble for these two little ones. They talk big, but little they are."

"Yes, sir." I sighed, wishing I would pause before yelling at people, but I wanted them to know what I can do. "Hey, Timmons and Tak." I tiptoed on a row of pebbles in the road. "I'm a high wire walker and I can balance myself in the air. I know how to do more than most girls my age."

Timmons pointed to his chest. "I'm seven. Tak is five. We know more than you."

"Why do you think you know so much?"

"Because girls in overalls and red shoes don't walk on wire. And circus workers don't smell like Ivory soap. I bet you're running away from home."

Mr. Marion stepped between us again. "Now, now. This girl is headed somewhere, and we're in the way of her being on her way." He pulled a stick candy from his shirt pocket. "Here, take this. It's a treat. I love sugar, and I love making sugar cane syrup and selling sweets to folks." He patted my head. "Take care, little girl. May your walk be short, and your future be filled with more syrup than you can eat."

I smiled. "Thank you, mister."

"My name's Marion Kane." He tipped his head down. "Until we meet again."

Crush rushed to my side, clutching my cat in his arms. He whispered, "Thanks for making me look good to Mr. Marion. I need him to keep me on at work, and if he thinks I'm slacking, I might lose my job. I've got to feed my brothers."

I almost said "you're welcome" but White Beard clawed Crush on the arm.

Scat. Scat.

Crush dropped White Beard. "Darn cat. I ought to break his little neck." Crush rubbed his arm, spitting on the spot, wiping it clean with his hand.

"You're not hurt. Not bad anyhow. White Beard likes most people, except for those he doesn't."

Mr. Marion ushered the boys off. "We've got a long drive ahead of us. Let's go, boys."

Timmons yelled, "Bye. Hope to see you at the circus." He giggled and ran to the truck.

Tak turned to me. "I like you."

I waved to them, but Crush blocked my view, standing in front of me. He whispered some ugly words at me. "I try to be nice to you, and look what happens. Your cat will pay if I ever see him again." Crush turned to catch up with the others.

I called to him, holding my kitty close. "Your nice and my nice don't mean the same thing. I hope I never see you again."

Crush turned around, charged me, and shook a fist at me. "A silly girl with a big mouth can come up missing."

I stomped his boot with my shoe. "And tall boys with no brains will get left behind."

"What do you mean?"

"Marion Kane is driving away. He's leaving you."

Crush hurried, running behind the pickup. "Mr. Marion. Wait. I'm not in the back of the truck."

The jolly man looked back through the cab truck window, the wheels slowed, and Crush jumped onto the towering pile of sugar cane. He gave me a scowl, but I gave him my Shoelace grin. "Good kitty. I don't like the Crush boy, either."

Choo-choo. Choo-choo.

The whistle on the train cut through the chill of the afternoon temperatures, and I tucked White Beard into my satchel. I ran past the train depot, hurrying to find a spot to hop the train leaving Atlanta. "Maybe I'll find a circus or start one myself. I could train my kitty to do tricks, to fetch, to roll over like a dog. Dog. I wish I had a dog, sometimes. Dogs keep up with you. Cats stray off, but not a good watchdog."

I knelt near the ditch as the boxcars left the station, and I rose, charging alongside of a car with a partially open door. A train with yellow and red boxcars, colors I'm not used to seeing on trains.

I reached for the iron ladder, gave myself a leap in the air, and swung into the boxcar. I brushed myself off, making sure I didn't squish my cat. I put him on the floor, and made sure no drunks were with me, although I sort of hoped Archie Gabs was here. But only a giant crate-like cage sat at the end, and it filled up most of the boxcar.

ROAR. ROAR. ROAR.

I tumbled backwards, falling to my hind side. The giant cat screamed at me from the cage, and a nose like White Beard's stuck out through a hole on the end. A giant nose. This was no ordinary cat. It was a lion!

Soaring Down the Rail

White Beard's claws stuck like nails into the wooden floor of the boxcar. His furry white body went flat, his scats and high-pitched meows unheard. Between the lion shaking the cage at the other end of the boxcar and the *click-clank-tak* of the train's wheels, kitty's cries evaporated like a mist. Kitty's whine was no match for the roar of a lion. I was no match for a lion, either.

Roar. Roar.

I gathered my legs, wobbled to kitty, reaching for him. He bounced like a kickball at my touch, my hand spooking him. He tumbled into a cat-fit into the air, his claws extended, ready to scratch anything or anyone who came too close. He was like a kitty doing an acrobatic act in the circus.

I hollered at him. "White Beard. It's me. Be careful, or you'll fall out of the train."

My words dropped like fear to the floor, and my kitty lunged out the opened door to the sandy patches of dirt flying past me, like an escape from the roar shouting certain death to us. "White Beard, wait for me."

I held onto the wall of the boxcar, making sure my satchel hung over my shoulder. "Goodness, we're moving too fast."

ROAR. ROAR.

I sucked in a deep blast of air, hoping it came with courage, and my fingers unfolded from the boxcar. I jumped, sailing into the gusts forcing me to the ground. "Geronimooooooo..." I rolled into a woven basket of weeds and sticks, like a padded cradle except for the sharp branches slicing my arm. "Ouch! Sticks and stones may break my bones, but a roaring lion is never gonna get me."

I sat on my knees, pulling out a shirt from my satchel, ripping it into pieces, and wrapping the cloth around my forearm. Another scar to have, another wound to heal. At least nothing is broken.

Clack-clack-clack. Wisp. Wisp. Clack-clack-clack. Flap. Wisp.

The train rolled ahead to my left with more yellow and red boxcars. One coal car zipped past me, sending me back in my mind to the day my daddy lost his grip, to the day his foot slipped from the ladder on the train over the river. I stomped my feet. "No! No! No! No more scenes of daddy's death. I want to remember his life, not his death." I shook my head, and the tan bandage on my arm showed a red spot of blood seeping through.

Wisp. Wisp. Flap. Wisp.

A sign flapped in the wind on one of the boxcars. It read, *Dailey Bros. Big Railroad Circus.*

"No way. I could have joined the circus. No wonder there's a lion on the train, but the circus is going on without me. And rolling right past me." I jumped up and down like a toddler waiting to see the big show. "Sally would have done anything to be in the circus. I can still be in the circus, and hiding with circus performers sounds fun to me, and not so alone. I can follow them."

I hurried to the edge of the bushes. "Wait for me. I want to be a part of your circus. I can do lots of things. I can. I can..."

Clack-clack. Tak. Tak. Tak.

The last boxcar rushed past me, and a wave from the man sitting with his legs dangling from atop the boxcar sent me running. "Archie? Archie Gabs? How did you get up there?" I screamed into the cold winter fog and into the gray evening. The clouds in my heart lined up with the clouds in the sky.

Archie waved a goodbye like a hello of yesterday, his body becoming a dot on the tracks until I couldn't see him any longer. Screaming, I cupped my mouth, "Tell them to stop and let me be in the circus."

Click-clack. Click-click. Click.

The train left a greasy oil smell in my nose, and my eyes burned from the grit and soot of sand landing on my face.

Crueowk. Crueowk.

I spit like a boy, and sneered at the tracks, squinting as the train disappeared around the bend. I yelled through the dust, running. "Don't leave. Stop the train. Stop…" I crumbled to my knees, sobbing, knowing I was alone. It was too late to go home. Too late to stay put. Too late to move on. "Nothing works out for me. Not one blasted thing. Not one. Nothing."

I turned to find my cat scampering up, purring. "White Beard, why couldn't you have stayed in the boxcar? We could have joined the circus. Do you hear me? The circus."

I rose to my feet and shuffled from crosstie to crosstie, dragging my shoes, while White Beard balanced his paw-steps on the rail just behind me. Repeating my words, I tried to convince myself I could do circus work. I needed to find something to do, something that matters, and something worth trying. The wad of birthday money in my satchel won't last long.

I pointed my finger at him. "This is your fault. When we finally find them, you're going to be fed to the lion."

Meow.

I bent down. "No, no, you can live. But don't be causing me any more problems. You don't want to get left behind. Do you?"

Meow. Meow.

I petted his head, remembering how it felt to sit outside Mahlee's room, to find it empty the next morning. I couldn't figure it all out. Why would a grown woman, even one who used to be a hobo—why would she desert me after my grandma died? What kind of person up and leaves a little girl? Mahlee! She does! She's a mean, horrible cook who has no one. Not even me.

Sitting on the track, I crossed my legs. To my right would lead me back to Texarkana. To my left I might find the circus. Where do I go when no one wants me?

Meow. Puuurrrrr.

White Beard curled up on my PF Flyers, rolling on his back, and licking his tail.

I sighed. "I'm sorry, Kitty. I'm not like Mahlee. I'm not ever going to leave you. Never. No matter if you scratch me. No matter what happens. You're my cat. Forever."

I jumped to my feet, skipping. "Come on, kitty. We have to catch up. They'll stop in a town somewhere to set up. This circus has Con Mercino in it, and he's the best aerial walker in the country. Sally told me so. I have to meet him. He has to teach me his trade."

I charged down the tracks with one arm straight out as if I were a small glider, holding my kitty tight with my other hand.

**

Catching up with the train may take longer than chasing a cat from a boxcar. The last hour of running, and of huffing and puffing hasn't stopped my cat's motor box from rattling; he's comfy in my arms, even if it comes with jiggles and bumps. I pulled the satchel around to my front, stopped running for a second and unlatched the flap, folding him inside. He curled into a ball, like he was getting used to riding in the bag.

I stuck my arms out like a glider, and swooped to the right, and dove to the left. I ducked down and twirled around, my tummy full from eating four biscuits. Bringing water along would have been smart, but maybe we'll reach a creek soon.

Splat. Splat. Splat.

Wonderful, it's raining. I pulled my coat closed, and hugged the satchel. Shelter. I need to find somewhere to sleep. Maybe under a bridge. Or an old barn. I spun around in a circle. Bushes. Trees. The wind whipped the branches together like spoons and forks. "God, I'm wondering if this is a good time. I know you know, I know, how mad I am at you for taking my grandma up to heaven to run your kitchen, but I need a favor. My grandma wouldn't mind if you answered me, I'm sure. Would you send me somewhere warm, somewhere safe, and somewhere out of this rain?"

I sighed, waiting for his answer.

Skrattle-splat-ka-bang.

"God. You are not funny."

The storm flashed lightning bolts across the tops of the trees, and I crawled to a bushy spot beside the tracks. The rumble under my feet, and the hum in the wet sand told me a train was approaching. I readied to jump a boxcar, but the howling wind, the soaking of the ground, and the zooming boxcars barreled down the tracks like a race to the end of the day. "I need to find a town and get on a train leaving out, one going slower. But right now, I need to get out of this rain."

The train sailed on down the tracks, and I hurried ahead on my journey, as a cloud parted and the rain slowed. The temperatures met with hot and cold pockets of air, and I found myself in a sunset, thick with fog. "God, first you sent lightning, and now you blind me with this fog."

I rushed ahead, staying between the tracks, holding White Beard over my shoulder in the satchel as it flapped on my back. "I see lights! To my left. Glaring lights shooting a beam into the haze."

For a split second, I saw Timmons and Tak—no, it's not them, my eyes were playing tricks on me. I charged forward, and my face smashed, *kaplowee.* My head slammed into something hard like a concrete wall, one straight up in the middle of the tracks, right in the railroad crossing of the muddy road.

Cold! Wet! Hard! Pain shot into my skull like a riddle of bullets shooting through my head. I slid down the upright pancake, and crumbled to the ground like a worm, and my knees buckled.

The sting in my head rushed through my body like a lightning storm. I touched the gash above my eye, where my skin peeled away from the veins, and my arms dropped to my side. My ears exploded from the pressure between my eyes. Fading into the past of my past, into nowhere, to a place where … where the circus of life cuts little girls in half—where darkness comes and death awaits. I lost myself and darkness fell. I cried, "God, rescue me from this daunting hole of nowhere!"

Room 19

I moved my eyes behind my eyelids, and light snuck under them. I blinked, rubbing my eyes, and my right arm stung. I touched my head, feeling gauze taped to my forehead. Sitting up, I focused my gaze, and wiggled in the scratchy sheets, rubbing my feet. These feel rough like my grandma's sheets. I darted under the quilt, pulling it over my head, and ran my hands over the fabric, rolling in the bed like a kitty squirming awake.

"Wait? Where am I?" I popped out from under the sheets and quilt, looking at the room. "This is not my room." Dizzy, I leaned on the pillow, closing my eyes, trying to think back on the how and why. "How did I get off the tracks? And who brought me here?"

I opened my eyes, and figures danced around the edge of the bed. A figure spoke to my left. "Remember to tie your shoes, Annie Grace Kree."

"Daddy? Daddy?" I mouthed again and again.

Next to him, my mama added her words. "Precious girl. You are a gift. You are a messenger of hope. Shine. Sail. Walk the tightrope with God."

I rubbed my eyes, and my grandma touched the quilt, squeezing my toes through the patches of fabric. "Get yourself up. Be brave. You are my joy. Always."

Next to her stood … stood … a bony, leaning-forward man who wiped a tear from his wrinkles. "Annie Grace Kree. It's your Grandpa Kree. I caused heartache in my family. I would have loved to have known you."

I crossed my legs, and yanked on the quilt, pulling it to my neck. "What is this? A dream? No, it's a nightmare. My mama's dead. My daddy, too. Grandma and Grandpa are gone." I ran my fingers through my tangled blonde hair. "What is this? Will someone just wake me up?"

A voice like sweet syrup spoke. "Little girl, Shoelace. It's me, your friend Marion Kane. It's great to see you awake."

I threw my pillow at him. "You? Why you? Why not my family?"

Holding the pillow, Marion Kane spoke, and sat on the edge of the bed. "Family? Who is your family? I'll find them for you. They are probably worried sick about you."

The next figure came into focus, the one standing behind Mr. Marion, and Crush asked, "Hey, you. Never thought you'd run into us again, did you? Are you feeling better?"

"My cat. Where's White Beard?"

Marion Kane pointed. "He's asleep on the chair cushion by the window."

The shorter two figures jumped on the bottom of the bed. One was Timmons, and he laughed. "I'm ready to play. Are you?"

Tak crawled up next to me, and touched my head. "You bled on my shirt when they put you in the truck."

"Truck? Who put me in the truck?"

Mr. Marion touched my hand. "Me, I held you while Crush drove us to the hospital. You ran smack dab into the side of the passenger door of my pickup. You showed up like a small train on the tracks. Crush was practicing his driving and we took the back roads, the ones crossing back and forth across the tracks near Lodi."

I squinted. "I'm in Lodi? Where's Lodi?"

"No, we're not in Lodi, we're down the highway. We're in Jefferson, and you're at the Jefferson Hotel. I own the syrup company here, and I own this hotel."

Tak cracked a grin. "He owns most of the town."

Mr. Marion shushed him. "Tak, my personal business is not everyone's business." Laughing, he turned to me. "The doctor patched your head with a few stitches, and you've slept for a whole night and day. It's Monday evening. I expect you're hungry."

My tummy growled. "I am. I'm actually starving."

Marion Kane picked up the receiver on the phone next to the bed on the nightstand. "Yes, this is Mr. Marion. Will you please send someone to the café and bring us …" He put the phone to his shoulder. "What do you like, my dear?"

I rolled my eyes, thinking. "I like chocolate cake."

"What about some real food first?"

"Mashed taters and … anything else you have."

"Let's get the Monday night special. Chicken fried steak with potatoes, green beans, and chocolate cake for dessert."

Timmons licked his lips, and so did I.

Tak cuddled close to me, whispering, "We thought you were a deer when you crashed into the truck. They dart in and out of the woods at dark, but when Mr. Marion saw you on the tracks, he brought you here. You left a dent in his truck though."

"I ran into you? You've got it backwards." I pointed at Crush. "I bet you can't drive, and you ran over me, and now you all feel sorry for me."

Crush charged to the other side of the bed, making a fist with his hand. "You are a mouthy, bratty girl. You have no manners. You don't know when to be grateful. Mr. Marion put you up in his hotel, and bought you those pajamas."

I looked down at the pink PJs. "Hey, who changed my clothes?"

A woman stepped from the bathroom off to the side. "I cleaned you up. Just you and me. I've got your clothes washed and all ready for you, too." The female voice clad in white smiled at me. "I'm your private nurse. I've been here since you got in the room. I waited all day in hopes you'd wake up. Now you have. Looks like my job is done here."

She strolled to me, kissed the top of my head, and turned to leave. "I'll check on you tomorrow morning. The doctor will be glad to know you're up, and wide awake."

I watched her nod at Marion Kane and slip from my room.

"Hey, where is my satchel?"

Marion Kane's belly jiggled each time he spoke. "Your satchel is on the back of the chair. Crush, enough firm talk with the fragile one. She was lost, and she was injured. When she collided with our pickup, it was simply an accident—or maybe, it was God bringing her in from the storm last night."

I held my noggin. "God has an odd way of answering my prayer. And I'm not fragile."

Crush cackled. "You're right. You should see the dent in Mr. Marion's truck." He wiped his nose. "So you prayed to crash into something?"

"No, I prayed to find a dry spot for the night."

Mr. Marion nodded. "And a dry place you found, my little friend."

Timmons rocked on the bed near my feet. "I'm glad you ran into us. I like you."

"I like you, too. Is it Timmons?"

"Yes, and remember my brother …"

"My name's Tak. Not like a tack on the wall, but like a T-A-K without the letter C."

I smiled. "I like you too, but I'm not so sure about Crush."

Crush sucked the air from the room. "You need a preacher. You need to talk with someone who can fix your attitude while you're getting dry and getting well."

I jumped to my feet, standing on the mattress "You're the one who needs a preacher. You're like the boys I used to beat up at school."

Mr. Marion asked, "And where was this school?"

I pursed my lips. "Somewhere down the tracks."

Mr. Marion ruffled my hair. "I see. I see."

Tak mocked me, jumping to his feet, holding my hand. "Crush, you need a preacher. You are worse than all of us."

Mr. Marion laughed, "Crush may be a couple years older than you, Shoelace, but I expect the two of you have more in common than you know. You could be siblings."

Together we screamed, "We are not!"

Timmons smiled, "I could use a sister. I like her."

I grinned, laughing at the red-haired boy who reminded me of Taddy.

Knock. Knock. Knock.

Tak leaped from the mattress. "I'll get the door." He skipped to the gold knob, twisted the handle, swinging the heavy white door open. A sign on the door with 'Room 19' showed me exactly where I was, but where I was, was still a mystery. I'm in Jefferson with people who are not family, but they were acting a whole lot like they were, with the arguing, the fussing, and the doting.

Mr. Marion moved to the door, and I couldn't see who was in the hall from my angle. Mr. Marion asked, "Who is it, Tak?"

"It's the housekeeper. She wants to clean the room. I told her to come back after we leave, after supper."

Mr. Marion motioned to the boys. "Let's go. We'll give Shoelace time to get dressed. Her food will be here in a minute."

Timmons and Tak ran to Mr. Marion, one on each side, holding his hands. Crush gave me a smirk, probably his last one since I'll not see him after today. He even made a face at my sleeping kitty.

Tak gave me one last glance, smiling, "See you tomorrow. We could go fishing if it gets warm outside. The Cypress Bayou is right behind the hotel."

I nodded, but my mind made other plans as they shut the door. I'll eat, get my clothes, and sneak out tonight. This Mr. Marion is asking too many questions, and he'll send a cop my way soon, with more questions. I'll be gone before sunrise, before the roosters in this town even know I'm up, before Marion Kane stops by with breakfast. Before Crush yells at me again. Before the nurse stops by to check on me.

Meow. Meow.

White Beard unfolded and stretched his neck higher than his body, arching his back. I ran to him, cuddling my kitty in this warm room, in this dry spot, where I was safe, and where God apparently thought I needed to be last night. I lifted my eyes to the ceiling hoping God can see through roofs. "Hey, God. Thank you for the warm bed, but I can't stay. I'm on a search for … for …" I didn't finish my talk with God, afraid He wasn't interested.

I curled into a ball with my kitty on the mattress, snuggling with him, and staring at the light fixture on the ceiling. I decided to talk to God one more time. "Sorry, God, I'm back. I wanted to let you know I'm headed to the circus. No time for people. No time for soft pajamas." I ran my hand down the pink fabric. "Well, maybe one more night won't hurt."

Pam Kumpe

From Fight to Flight

Smacking on the last bite of potatoes, I sighed with contentment. This meal almost tasted better than my grandma's cooking. I picked up the plate, licking the China glass clean, handing the plate to White Beard who found some stray crumbs. I patted my pooching belly, and stretched out like a fat cow in the sun, only I was in a fancy hotel.

The room reminded me of those I've seen in magazines. The quilt blue and white with flowers, the walls royal blue to match. The frame on the bed was brass, and so shiny. I placed the food tray on the nightstand, looking out the window at the gray colors falling from the sky. I touched the windowpane. "Cold. Too cold."

I hurried back to the bed, leaping into the middle of it. "I could get used to this, but even here, I'm alone. No one wants me. I couldn't tell Mr. Marion Kane where to take me because no one is looking for me."

I jumped from the bed, refusing to let something as small as not having a family ruin my last night in this hotel. "White Beard, I'm taking a bath. A nice hot bath sounds like a great idea." I slapped my leg. "My grandma would say she liked hot baths. Now, I'm sounding like her."

In the tub, I dove under the soapsuds and pretended to swim, although in real life, swimming isn't my idea of fun. I can't swim, and would sink if I fell into the bayou behind the hotel.

Wrapping my hair inside the white towel, I slipped on my clean shirt and my overalls, although I should have put the pajamas back on, bedtime is not too far off. I tiptoed,

74

practicing my wire walk on the hardwood floor without the height or wire. "White Beard, look at me. I'm a high-wire walker."

The not-paying-attention kitty pounced into his chair, circled the same spot from his nap, and twisted his ears into his belly, hiding his whiskers.

"Kitty, you're missing the show!" I danced to him, kissing his head.

Clump. Clump. Schalump.

I moved to the door. "Someone's in the hall, kitty."

Knock. Knock. Knock.

I leaned closer, with my ear on the door, my hand ready to open it. "Who's there? Mr. Marion?"

Tap. Tap. Tap.

"Housekeeping, ma'am. I'm here to change your sheets, and freshen up the room. The front desk sent me up."

I squinted at the door. Should I let this lady in? Should I say no? Should I see why the voice on the other side reminds me of someone I know?

Tap. Tap. Tap.

"May I come in?"

I twisted the knob, cracking the door open, and the brown boots the size of a man's shoes came into view near my toes. "You're not a cleaning woman."

An arm stuck between the door blocking any attempt I might try to shut the door. "Little girl, Marion Kane sent me up. I'm only following orders."

"You're not dressed like a housekeeper."

The force on the other side of the door sent me tumbling backwards, and the towel unraveled from my head, draping over my eyes. "You don't have to push me."

"Sorry ma'am. I've got work to do."

I recognized the voice and yanked the towel from my face, pushing my bangs out of my eyes. I jumped to my feet. "No! You? Tin Can Mahlee? How did you get here? Do you have a job here? And why here? Why Jefferson?'

Almost at the same time, Mahlee screamed, "You? You are supposed to be in Texarkana. What?" Mahlee dropped a pile of clean towels on my feet.

I pointed my finger at her. "Why did you leave without a word?"

"You wouldn't understand. You have a few questions to answer yourself."

"Me? You're the one who ran away and left me all alone. You left me, remember?"

"I left town. Leaving you just happened to be a part of what I couldn't control. I have people who ... who ... well, you wouldn't understand."

"Understand? Whatever. You're a grown up. I'm just a kid."

"A pretty smart kid, I'd say. So you followed me here?"

"Followed you? I had no idea where you went. You disappeared like a hobo from my past. Gone." I charged her, whipping my towel at her.

"Stop hitting me. I'm not letting you back in my life. It's complicated." Mahlee yanked the towel from my hand, and shut the door behind her, putting her back against it.

I yelled, "Let me out. I'm getting my satchel and my cat. I never want to see you again."

"Too late. We need to deal with this. Stop your fit. You're gonna get me fired."

"I don't care. You can get lost for all I care."

Mahlee sat her cleaning basket on the floor, inching forward, waving both arms. "Like I said, you don't understand. I've never been married, let alone engaged. Then Ernie dumps me. Dumps me like everyone else in my past. Pain follows me. I can't catch a break. The other phone call came after Ernie broke up with me, and I had no choice."

"Other phone call?"

"Yes, it's complicated."

"So you run out on me just like that?"

"Yes, to keep you alive. Staying with me is dangerous. You know that from our past. I even gave up my Lizzy Beth to keep her safe when I should have told your daddy ... should have told him ... that he was the daddy."

"What? You and my daddy? No way. Not ever. He ... he wasn't Lizzy Beth's daddy. He couldn't be." I pounded my arms in her side. "Why tell me this now? Why? You're mean and evil, and simply think of yourself."

Mahlee gripped my wrists, her hands stronger than mine, stronger than most. "Stop hitting me. You think you're the only one who is sad, who is hurting, and who wants life to be better. I needed a fresh start without the past."

I wiggled, standing on my toes. "So you run out when it gets tough."

"It seems you're doing the same. I heard Mr. Marion found a little girl, but I had no idea it was Annie Grace Kree."

"How could you hear this so soon? Did you already have this job lined up? It's only been two days ago that Ernie called you. I don't get it."

"I told you, it's complicated. I had a ride here. I had ..." Mahlee shook her head. "I've said too much. Never mind."

I kicked her. "You were planning to leave, weren't you? And don't call me Annie Grace, my name's Shoelace. Better yet, don't call me anything. Don't ever talk to me again." I jerked free, and jumped into the middle of the mattress, standing like a soldier. "Get out of my room before I call the people at the front desk. I'll tell them you hurt me. I'll … I'll fix you."

She picked up her basket, and stepped over the towels. "Your threats don't scare me." She wiped her face, and turned to the door. "I'm leaving. We've got nothing more to say to each other." Mahlee pointed to my head. "You're bleeding. You need to get someone to look at your wound."

"I don't have anyone!" I swiped my fingers over the damp spot on my eyebrow. "What do you care? I can't believe you waited until now to tell me about my daddy and Lizzy Beth. How do I know you're telling the truth?"

"I know. I just know. Why would I lie?"

"Why would you tell the truth? Why tell me now?" I scratched my ear, wondering about Lizzy Beth from Wheelock, wondering where she went, and knowing in my heart—she was the lost girl from Memphis whose mama is crazy, whose mama is Tin Can Mahlee. The adopted family who took Lizzy Beth lives somewhere. But where?

Mahlee spouted at me. "I wanted you to know. Always have. Hey, stop staring into space. You need a doctor for your head."

"No one can fix my wounds." I cupped my hands like I was holding something in them, and jumped to the hardwood floor.

"What are you doing?"

"I've been looking at our memories in my head since you left, and thought they were real. Thought you might love me. You were here for all my scars until now." I turned my hands over, acting like I dropped the invisible items from my palms, and I stomped on them. "No more. No more. No more wishing for you to be my mama. To be my family. You have killed my heart. I'm done with you."

Mahlee stepped forward like she started to hug me, her free arm outstretched, but she stopped. "How did you hurt your head?"

"What do you care?"

"I don't want you to hurt."

"Really? Well, you're too late. My heart will never get over losing you. There's nothing more in this world I wanted, than for you to tell me it was going to be okay. Instead, you leave me at the manor by myself!"

Mahlee sighed and the gray falling from the sky slipped into the hotel room through the window. She opened the door, and stepped into the hall out of sight without another word, and then cracked the door back open. "I can't be who you need. I am not who you want."

The door shut again, and I fell against it face first, like running into the side of a pickup truck. Me on one side. Mahlee on the other side. I burst into a crying storm of rage and sadness. "But ... you are ... my Mahlee, you are who I need, but I'm not who you want."

Open Door to Death

I curled into a ball, whining, sobbing and shaking. Staying the rest of the night in this hotel would only make me sadder, make me madder. I sat up, forcing myself to stand, and moved to the window, and picked up my PF Flyers, setting them near White Beard on his chair. The gray from outside had now gone black, but across the street next to a light pole, a brown dog sat on his haunches watching something.

Ruff. Ruff.

He barked at the commotion stirring in the alley, below my second floor window. I heard a scream like a bellow from a hollow broken place, and then—*kabang-slam.*

I slumped to the floor shaking, unsure what to do. I peeked over the windowsill. A man wearing a long black coat tugged on the arm of someone, and he shoved that person inside the backseat of a gangster-type car like I've seen in movies.

I charged out my door, down the long hallway, to the creaking staircase, and hurried to the front desk of the hotel. "Where's Mahlee? Do you know? She was … she was cleaning my room."

The small man who stood only inches taller than the counter spoke. "Mahlee's out back. She's with Carl." He pointed down the hallway to his right. "She's off for the night. I'm sure she'll be here tomorrow."

I raced down the hallway of the first floor, barreling from the building into the shadows. I caught a glimpse of the car skidding its tires over the bridge. "Mahlee? Mahlee?"

A nudge on my leg made me look down. "Hey, boy. What are you doing?"

Ruff. Ruff.

I talked to the wiry-haired dog about God. "Did you know that God could leave you all alone? Alone." I let tears leak from my eyes, and the brown dog licked my hand. "Boy, you best get going. I'm trouble. You don't want to stay too close to me."

I sighed, shuffling in my bare feet to the back door, my body shivering from the cold. "God, why? Why can't I have a family like other little girls and boys?"

Ruff. Ruff.

"Go on, boy. You better get home."

Creak. Creak.

The man from the front desk called to me from the alley door. "Are you okay? If you're looking for Mahlee, she'll be back."

I knew he was wrong, I knew it with all of my heart.

The deskman called, "There's a snowstorm headed our way. Mr. Marion called to check on you. Says to make sure you're safe and warm. If he knew you were out here, and barefooted, I'd lose my job."

I sighed, following him down the hallway that felt like the tunnel of death, not saying a word, inching my way up the stairs. At my opened door, I told the man goodbye.

He called to me. "Be sure and lock your door."

Inside, I looked under the bed, in the bathroom, and behind the chair, stepping over the clean towels on the floor. Clean except for a few drops of what looked like blood from my head. I touched my bandage on my brow, the dampness was drying. "White Beard? Where did you go? You didn't follow me out the door, did you?"

I hurried to the window, turning my head from side to side. I saw a shadow of a cat sauntering into the woods across the road, toward the bayou. I had to get him, he's all I have left.

Ruff. Ruff. Ruff.

The brown dog galloped like a horse down the trail, and I slapped the windowpane. "No, leave my kitty alone." I slipped on my shoes, grabbed my coat, my satchel and ... turned the knob on the door to my room. I stuck my head into the hallway, trying to figure out how to get past the front desk. To my left, a door to a spiral staircase. With my room at the end of the hallway, I have a quick exit to the cold night.

Ca-click.

I tiptoed out to the swirly stairs like a ghost in the night. My hair damp from earlier, my feet now warm—but my heart broken into slivers of pain at seeing Mahlee, at getting her back. And then, at having to let her go, again. The storm coming into town and the storm in my life were colliding faster than I could keep up.

Broken Hallelujah

I'm trying to hear above the noise in my head, even though the silent shadows lurk inside these woods. Every step crunched on the ground, and I'm crying out in my own silence to God. I pray He gives me strength, the kind my grandma had, the kind my friend, Mahlee, still has, and the kind that can show me the way to find my kitty. "God, I should have left my kitty back in Texarkana, but since I didn't, will you help me find her?"

Swish-swish-pa-thud. Crackle. Pa-kit. Snip.

The land sloped lower with each step and the whisper of water trickling, rushing, moving and splashing along with the wind let me know the bayou intersected my trail, but when and where—I had no idea. "White Beard? Where are you? Here, kitty. Kitty. Kitty."

Swish-swish-pa-thud.

A short shadow darted past me, my heart sped up, my gasps grew, and from my left the ghostly image dashed across the trail. I held my breath listening, trying to figure out what creature circled me. I knelt down on one knee, focusing now, on the light peeking from my right, a glow cutting the darkness in half.

A *swish-swish-pa-thud* stopped on the trail a few feet from my nose, and the shadow of an animal blocked the way, but only for a second. He leaped into the darkness between the trees faster than the wind rushing up my overalls pants. "It's just a deer. Don't get scared."

Talking to myself, I'm reminded that I don't trust my feelings. When I was three, maybe four, living with my grandma, I trusted her arms and her smile. When my daddy snatched me from her at five, I became lighter than a breeze; however, trusting him and no one became the next part of life together on the rail.

Now, I'm the captain of my ship, without a ship, or … I put my hands on my mouth. "Stop talking like a crazy girl. You have to find your cat."

The light off to the side led me to the river, and the water made a splatter sound like broken glass tumbling from a bathtub of sorrow. "Where is my cat?"

I marched ahead, ducked between two skinny trees with four zillion arms, feeling hairy moss sweep my face like a scouring pad. I bent my head back, gazing at the branches reaching for heaven. Whispering another prayer, not sure why I bothered, considering how tattered my life seems, I included God in my search. "God, please help me find my cat."

I stepped into a clearing where a small house, the size of a classroom, rested on stilts. "There he is … on the porch. White Beard. I'm here."

A wooden rocker sat behind him, and along the side of the house, I could see two windows. No shades or curtains. The light from inside popped out to the ground like two spotlights, and creeping toward the house, I whispered, "White Beard, come here. You keep running off. I can't lose you, too."

He arched his back, rolling over three times, then stretched. His paws went over his head and he yawned, as if he'd fallen asleep for hours and was waking up. He'd been gone for only minutes.

I sat on the steps, petting his head. "What am I going to do with you? You need to stay with me."

Meow. Meow.

"Come on, kitty. Let me save you from your sorrow since I can't save myself from mine." The audience of trees rubbed their branches together applauding my idea, and their screeching sounded like weeping, as if the cries of the lost were rushing down the river.

I touched my kitty's nose. "Maybe we should go back to Texarkana and let the O'Malleys know what happened. I don't know where we're going to stay. I need Mahlee—she's gone somewhere, even though I don't know if she went on her own.

Ruff. Ruff. Ruff.

The wiry long-legged dog barked at my kitty and chased White Beard from the porch, trailing him around the other side of the house. "Stupid dog. Stop chasing my cat."

I charged around the corner, stumbling over a log, and the moon parted a lonely cloud. Standing, I got my balance, realizing I was a few feet from the river. "Phew, I could have fallen in." I sucked in a big breath of courage and inched close to the house, calling for my kitty.

Pla-splash. Splash-pla-tikkle-splash.

The water poured past me, and I circled some trees back to the porch, not sure where the dog ran my cat off to this time. I listened to the eerie sounds of frogs competing for solos, and the sour taste in the air made my mouth water like I was standing in a rainstorm, which hadn't started yet. "White Beard?"

I plopped down on the bottom step, hoping the people inside would go on with their life, and I could pretend I lived inside—with a family, one with bedtime stories, warm beds, and plenty of cake.

I jumped to my feet and marched in circles around some trees on the side of the house. "Kitty, come on boy."

Nothing. Not a bark. Not even a meow. Just croaking.

I gazed at the light peeking from the side window, and shimmied up the small trunk next to the house. Pressing my fingers against the windowpane, I hoped to see, wished to see, and yet, not sure what I wanted to see.

A family of boys sat on benches at a long unfinished wooden table. Some of the boys were freckled, tiny and thin. One boy was fat, and three looked alike. They clanked spoons in their bowls, and each talked to the one next to him. No one seemed to listen, but every one of them talked and laughed. They must be sharing their most important tales from the day.

I sucked in my loneliness and let go of the glass, sitting on the branch, wishing I were sitting outside of Taddy's window in Texarkana. I leaned forward and peeked inside for one last glimpse, pressing my nose on the pane. I counted heads. "One, two, three, four, five ... six, and seven. This family has no girls. Maybe they would want me."

I squinted my eyes and giggled while watching the two boys on the far end pretend to have a sword fight with their spoons. Oh my, it was the cotton-haired boy, Tak, and the red-haired boy, Timmons.

I fell from the branch, screaming, even though I tumbled only a few feet to a patch of weeds. "*Ouch*! I've got to stop being so nosey. It only gets me in trouble."

The hand on my shoulder turned me over, and pulled me to my feet. "You are so right. What are you doing out here? No one comes here. No one bothers us. This is my place. Mine. Not yours." Crush towered over me, his hot breath angry, his words slicing me apart.

"I came for my cat. A stupid dog chased my cat to your porch."

Crush shoved me. "Tell me why you're here. I don't have time for your nonsense. And if you tell anyone about ... about

86

them boys inside, you'll never chase a cat, or climb a tree, or peek inside of someone's window again."

"Why? What are you hiding?"

"Nothing. Nothing."

"Sure, you are. Or you wouldn't be scared of me."

Crush grabbed my shoulders. "I mean it. I could lose them all if anyone knew I took care of them."

"What? Lose who?"

"The boys."

"Timmons and Tak?"

"No, they are my real brothers, but the other five are from our clan down the river. We lost our parents in the flood of '45, and I've been taking care of the boys who had no one, who needed someone."

"You? You don't seem like the caring kind."

"I care enough to feed them. To work for Mr. Marion. To keep them dry. Warm. And safe. Some of the town folk wouldn't like a teenager being in charge of them. No one can take them from me."

I sniffled, my chest caving in and out.

Crush touched my chin. "Why are you crying?"

"I don't know. It just seems every road I take leads to a dead end, and every trail I take leads to sadness." I found myself telling Crush about myself, without meaning to, wishing my words would stop up like a beaver dam—but they burst from me like lava from a volcano.

Crush wiped my tears. "Are you cold?"

"Maybe."

"Come inside. Warm yourself by the fire. Then you have to go back to the hotel. Mr. Marion is going to help you get home. He's bringing his brother, the sheriff, over to meet you in the morning."

"No, I am not meeting a sheriff."

"Mr. Marion wants to get you back to your family. He's like a father to me. You should trust him."

"I don't need his help. Or yours."

A voice from the trail spoke. "You might need God's help."

I twisted my head to see a boy with wavy hair, who clutched a giant Bible, bigger than the ones people put on tables for decoration. "And who are you?"

"I'm Toby Raike. I came by to do my practicing."

"Practicing?"

Crush answered for Toby. "He's our Hollywood actor-preacher."

I smarted off. "He's too young to be a preacher."

Toby Raike smiled. "I'm not too young. I'm twelve and a half, and I'm old enough to know a sad, broken hallelujah when I hear one."

"Oh gosh, you don't talk normal."

"I can. I might. But not tonight."

"Stop with the silly words. I'm leaving. I don't have time for preachers, even baby ones."

Toby touched my forehead. "I pray your head heals, but mostly I pray your heart sings with hope someday."

I backed up. "I'm gone. I can't be here. I have to find my cat."

Two more voices piped in. "It's her. It's our new friend."

Timmons and Tak rushed to me, holding my waist and hugging me. My heart melted at seeing the two little boys and they were happy to see me. No one gets excited when I'm around these days.

Tak took my hand. "Come meet the others."

Crush interrupted. "She might need to be on her way. If she can't keep her mouth quiet, she doesn't need to meet anyone."

I slugged his arm like a sister might. "I can stay a second. I want to meet the other boys. I can keep a secret."

I soaked up the warmth inside the two-room house, and met Tripp, Thor, and Thicke, the triplets, who have pitch-black hair. They snickered at me, and walked in a circle around me as if they were doing ring-around-the-rosy.

One of them told me their age. "We're ten. I'm the oldest by three minutes. I'm Thor."

I met Thomas whose glasses hung crooked over his nose. He held his head high, and smiled like a smart kid who got the good genes.

"I'm proud to make your acquaintance, ma'am."

"You don't have to say ma'am. We might be the same age."

"How old are you, ma'am?"

"I'm eleven."

"I'm eleven, too, but in three months and 21 days, I'll be twelve."

Theodore, the chubby one, sat in the corner on the floor with his legs crossed, holding a flat piece of bark with what appeared to be white and black piano key markings. He caught me staring, and flipped the bark upside down, hiding his pretend musical instrument. He watched me like a hawk, but he never said a word. His eyes told me trust is a problem for him, too.

I inched over to him. "So Theodore, how old are you?"

"Who wants to know?'

"Never mind." I walked to the fireplace and held out my hands, letting the chatter from the boys bounce to my heart and back to theirs.

Toby clapped his hands. "I'm in the mood to preach. Let's have a study."

Scr...aatch. Scr...atch. Meow.

"It's my cat." I hurried to the door, and bent down to greet my kitty, only for the wiry dog to charge me, knocking me over. "Dumb dog! I'm about tired of you."

Tak called the dog. "Here, boy. Bingo. Sit. Sit down."

The four-legged creature sat next to Tak and licked a paw. If a dog can grin, this one did.

"I guess this dog belongs to you boys."

Thomas pushed his glasses up his nose. "Yes, he's the town dog by day, but he sleeps out here at night. He loves ice cream."

The boys chuckled, and so did I.

Toby announced. "I'm canceling tonight's study, too many distractions for you boys tonight. Everyone meet me by the cemetery at sunset tomorrow next to Diamond Bessie's grave. If it's sunny. I want us to spend time learning about the shade we find in the cross of Jesus."

I mouthed. "Shade? At a cemetery? And who is Diamond Bessie?"

"She was a poor lost soul who was murdered in Jefferson. But come to our study, and you'll hear me preach about life from Jesus."

"I don't think I'll be there."

I'd left the door open and the cold air rushed in. White Beard stuck his ears inside by the crack, but ran when he saw Bingo.

I slung my satchel over my shoulder, charged out to the porch and jumped from the steps, determined to catch my cat before sunrise. I rounded the house, darting between a few trees, and barreled the other way to trick him. "White Beard. I'm getting a rope if you keep this up."

My foot slammed into something on the ground, sent me tumbling forward, and I rolled up against a warm something. White Beard pawed at the ground like he was trying to bury it, and Bingo whined, a howl of bark.

Owhoooo! Owhoooo!

I wiped the dirt from my face, and saw—saw the eyes of a man in a suit, lying on his side next to the tree, and his right arm was bent the wrong way behind him. His legs were crooked like noodles under spaghetti sauce, but this was ... was no spaghetti sauce, it was blood! The man's nose bled, and he didn't seem to be breathing!

Suitcase to Soda Street

Jumping to my feet, I wiped my hands on my overalls. "No more. No more dead people. No more death." I reached for White Beard.

Meow. Meow.

"Look at you. You're covered in blood! We have to get away." Shuffling crunches on the ground grew louder than my terror of screams. I was not alone. I spun around. "Who's out there?"

"It's me, Tak. Did you get your cat?"

I choked on my fear. "Yes, he's fine. You better get Crush … there's something … something …" I swiveled Tak away, giving him a not-so-gentle shove, putting my kitty down with my other hand. "Go get Crush. And get him now!"

"I'll get him, but first, I have to get Bingo. Come here boy, come on." Tak twirled in a circle, not stopping. "What are you pawing at? Come here."

I yelled, "No, stop. Don't go over there."

Tak charged for the dog, but in three small steps he halted, hollering, *Aaah!* "Who is sleeping on the ground? It's too cold for camping."

I pulled Tak to my side, holding him close, feeling his body shake in trembles. "Come with me. Let's get Crush. He'll check on the man."

Leaves crunched behind me. "I'm right here. What are you two up to? Tak, get inside the house. You know the rules. Never leave Timmons behind, and Timmons will never leave you behind. Go on, now. Get inside." Crush ordered Tak, while inching closer to me.

Tak pointed. "But, did you see … see the man? He's camping …"

"I saw him. Now go on, and make sure you stay inside."

"Yes, sir."

Shaking, I slumped to the ground next to a patch of trees. Crush hovered over the man on the ground, touching his shoulder, rolling him over. I could see the lifeless face. I whispered, "Who is it?"

"I expect you know."

"What? I have no idea who he is. I came out here to find my cat." I charged Crush, slamming my hand into his back. "I've never seen this guy before. What are you accusing me of?"

"Nothing, yet. If I recall, you're the only one wandering down our trail tonight. I heard you tell Tak you had to get away. So what do you have to get away from? A dead body?"

I wiped my brow. "If your dog hadn't chased my cat, I wouldn't even be here. I don't know who he is, and you better get help, or call a doctor."

Crush shook his head. "Too late for a doctor. I've seen this man with Carl at the Kornbread Kafe. He's one of his hands." Crush clinched my arm with his fingers. "Tell me. What did you do with the gun? This man's been shot."

"Shot? Did you hear a gunshot? It's not like I have a gun."

"What's in your satchel?"

I hugged my bag. "I don't have a gun. I've never seen this man before."

Crush pulled the man's jacket open. "He's been here for a bit."

"I'm not a killer. This happened way before I got here." I stepped up to the dead man's shoes, looking down at the shadow of a man who'll never have a tomorrow. "What are we going to do?"

"To do?" Crush pushed me away. "You need to go to the hotel and you need to go now. Act like this didn't happen, and pretend you never saw any of this. Pretend you didn't see us, either. Remember to forget about the boys, and the house."

"I can keep a secret. I never wanted to be in your town. It's only because you ran over me in the pickup I'm not long gone."

"I never hit you. You slammed into the panel of the truck, because you were running down the tracks in the rain. You are not bringing good luck to us."

I swung my satchel to my other shoulder, gathered up my cat, and mouthed. "Luck? I never came to your town promising anything. I'm not in charge of luck. I'm not in charge of anything."

Crush stormed to the house, rushing up the steps, turning to make sure I was leaving. "Go on, get. I'm getting the law so they can come get this man."

"If you get the police, then everyone will know about your boys."

Crush barreled at me, charging like a bull on the loose. "Do you think you can outsmart me with your wisecracks? I'm nearly fifteen, and I've been on my own for a few years. I have more than one place to keep my boys safe. You move along. I have this under control."

I swiped his hand away. "Sure, you do. I'm not the one with a dead man next to my house." I snorted, turning to the trail. "I hope I never see you again." I screamed those words, but Crush never heard them. He'd already slipped inside the house.

I paused on the trail, unsure if the person who shot the man lurked in the mossy bayou. I inhaled the cold air, the ache in my lungs tightened, and I gazed back at the house. In the window, two little boys' faces peered into the night. Timmons and Tak were glued to the window. I couldn't help but hope they were looking for me.

I ran down the path the same way I'd come and headed to the hotel. Hurrying, I charged along with a gait of fear, hearing every croak and every creak and howl in the woods. Getting to the warm bed sounded like the best idea now. I was scared and brave, and not as shocked as I should be at seeing a dead man on the ground. Death should never feel so common, nor blood on my shoes feel normal. The wind made my nose drip. Snot trickled over my lips, and I used my sleeve to wipe away the sticky mess.

White Beard clung to my shirt as if, for the first time, he was afraid of the dark. My breaths turned into long gasps, and I stopped for a second, collapsing in the damp sand. Sadness hung over me, and sorrow lingered in my thoughts. "There's the street light. I can go to Room 19, take another bath, and clean off the dirt and ugly from tonight."

I stuck my kitty inside my satchel to make sure he didn't escape and charged across the brick road to the back of the hotel, scaling the metal staircase to the second floor. I twisted the knob, back and forth, and forth and back. "It's locked."

I charged down the steps, rounded the hotel, and hurried to the front door. The glass entrance with two windows on each side would allow me to get up the stairs to my room, but the clerk behind the counter caused me to pause. I pressed my nose on the glass, glaring at him. "If he'd go do something down the hallway, I could slip by."

I grabbed White Beard from inside my bag and hovered near the window in the darkest shadow, away from the corner streetlights, hoping for a chance to rush inside. Time ticked faster than my heartbeat, faster than a second hand on a clock.

Whoop. Whoop. Whoop.

The police car siren caused me to hold my breath, and the car flew by the hotel, turning left, heading to the alley near the trail. I crouched down, hiding in plain sight, but in the nighttime shadows, somehow knowing Crush contacted the police meant no one was looking for me.

I sighed, not knowing if Crush had said I'd been at his house or not, not sure what to do next. Staying in Jefferson might not be the best idea, except a part of me longed to find out what Mahlee's wrapped up in. I whispered to God, something I'm doing more of these days. "Hey God, if there's a way Mahlee will let me be in her life, will you see she changes her mind about leaving me?"

Running to the middle of the street, swinging my arms, I shouted in whispered squeals, facing the hotel. I stomped my feet on the bricks, my madness growls roaring like a small lion. I pounced in a circle and faced the building across from the hotel, gazing at the balcony. I read the sign: The Choctaw Trading Store. I wished to see some of my friends at Wheelock Academy, girls who would love to shop at this store.

A few cars puttered down the road at the end of the street, crisscrossing, their headlights shooting a beam of light into the night. They disappeared, leaving me alone, and the lights in the trading store blinked off one by one, and the street lanterns lit the sidewalks like stars. Turning, I saw the sparkles from the chandelier in the lobby of the hotel, and they were shooting beams like a dozen spotlights.

My entrance to safety was through the front door of the hotel, but the little man stood guard. If he saw me I'd get tossed smack dab in the middle of a man's death in the woods, and land smack dab in front of a cop.

I talked to the half-moon appearing like an open door to heaven. "God, I'm talking to you again. Are you listening? I'm tired of all of this. I never picked this life. It picked me. What am I to do? If I go inside the hotel, White Beard's covered in blood. Have you seen my overalls? They're coated in mossy dirt and blood, too. How will I explain this?"

Honk. Honk.

I jumped to the sidewalk, and the person behind the wheel of the pickup shook his fist and drove away.

I peeked inside the window of the hotel, and two people blocked my view of the clerk. A man wiggled, and his slacks hung. His jerky shoulders made me nervous. The lady scratched her neck with a fitful rub until her skin turned red. They must be leaving town, which is something I should do, but Mahlee's got me twisted up like a knot. I want to leave. I want to stay. No, I have to leave.

Sighing, I plopped down to the sidewalk curb, crossing my legs, and hugged my satchel. I sat for minutes, it felt like hours, but the time crept like seconds, rushing like a waterfall of confusion. My cat rolled into a ball on top of my bag. I whispered in his ear, and he twitched from my breaths. I blew words into his head. "You have the perfect life. You can go anywhere you want."

Tap-top. Tap-top. Tap-top.

I sat up taller.

Tap-top. Tap-top. Tap-top.

Shoes on bricks. Feet in shoes. People in those shoes. I unfolded myself, picked up my cat, and flung myself to the shadows by a nearby parked car

Meow. Meow.

"Sorry, White Beard. Be quiet. We're leaving as soon as those people do. In a minute, we'll hide out somewhere until I figure out something. Or we could sneak inside the hotel where it's dry and warm, but then I'm trapped like a caged lion in a boxcar."

I ducked lower into a two-foot space by the bumper, hovering close to the ground, watching the two people on the sidewalk.

The lady with the itch mumbled, waved her hands, explaining herself. "This is your fault. We planned the week to escape, and now, all you want to do is sleep. I want to ride a boat on the Big Cypress Bayou, and learn the history about the steamboats. This quaint cafe around the corner makes the best chocolate cobbler. One of the housekeepers told me, she's had it twice in two days since arriving here. But no, you wanted barbecue, and taffy for dessert. We can have barbecue anytime. You never do what I want. You are so selfish."

The man dropped the suitcases, and he placed one hand on her shoulder, and one beneath her chin. "Honey, you're upset. I'm sorry. You're letting my habits get to you. I simply took a late nap. A short one. We can ride the boat tomorrow."

She moved his hand from her face. "Your nap was … too long. I sat there counting your snores from across the room. I even counted your breaths."

"I thought you were reading a book."

"I was. But … I got hungry."

"Food isn't the answer for our pain, and you know we deal with this sorrow each year. We'll have another baby someday. The doctor told us we're young and healthy. We have to give it time. Let's stay. Going home will remind us of losing … losing little Kade. I miss him, too. But …" He broke down, wiping tears from his face.

I wiped my eyes, too.

The lady wrapped her arms around the man. "You're right. It's so hard. It's been three years, but every time his birthday comes around, I remember the first time I saw him. His black hair, those blue eyes. I can't imagine how cute he'd be now, if he had lived." She wept like a broken faucet.

I cried with her. She wanted a baby, and got one, only she lost her baby for some reason. I wanted a family. I got Grandma. Got Mahlee, too. Grandma died. Mahlee ran off and left me. Maybe the lady might want me. I popped up, only to shake my head. She's not about to want a girl my age. I'm too old. I come with a lot of history, but she likes history. Besides, I may not even like them. I'm just feeling sorry for myself.

The couple whispered mushy words, talking at the same time. The man hugged his wife, "I love you. We'll have a great week. Let's check back in." Minutes later, they danced inside the hotel, ready to finish their getaway.

I dragged my feet down the sidewalk, away from the hotel, and White Beard brushed up beside my leg. I had no idea how far I was from Texarkana, unsure how long it might take to get home. I gazed up at the clouds rolling past the moon. "God, can you get me home?" I ran my fingers through my hair. "Is that what I should do? Should I go back to Texarkana? Or should I search for Mahlee? She's hard to talk to. Hard to like, but I do love her. I do. God, I hope you love me enough to get me home. Sorry, I'm bothering you so much. I don't have anyone else to talk to."

A few blocks later, I shuffled down the middle of the tracks, sidestepping in the bushes around the train depot. I wished for a ticket, for a chance to ride in the passenger car, but with only a few dollars in my satchel, walking home was my only answer. Or catching a boxcar ride.

White Beard weaved between my legs as I marched inside the tracks. His stride kept pace with mine, except when he didn't, and he got tangled in my legs. "Kitty, you are causing me to stumble. Stop playing. It's late. We need to make some headway and find us a spot to hide, to sleep, and to not get caught."

I shivered as a curtain of darkness dropped, blocking my view. "I can't see where I'm going. White Beard, you better be following me. I'm not chasing you anymore. I'm tuckered out. My head hurts. My arm, too. And my heart." I felt a tickle on my nose. "Was that a snowflake? Did you see that? God, you better not let it snow. Could you let the moon come back out? Wait one more day before you let it snow. Please, just one."

Gathering up my cat, I cut to the middle of the rail, hurrying to wherever. The wind blasted from the side, cutting through trees, whistling a goodbye, a good-riddance tune.

Snowflakes floated from above, landing on my nose and eyelids, tingling my nostrils, making me blink. "It's snowing."

White Beard wiggled in my arms, and leapt from my grasp. He darted into the trees after something, and I misjudged the angle of the slope on the hill. I lost my step, and rolled to the bottom of the ditch, landing with my head on my satchel. I sighed, ready to give up. Ready to sleep under a tree. Ready to fall into the river and drown. Ready to be ready, to stop chasing after cats or family or anything. It's not like anyone would miss me.

I moved through the thicket, pushing slick branches away, as icicles formed on limbs higher than my head. The snowflakes coated my hair as if they were forming a cap around my ears. "When I catch you, I'm sticking you inside my satchel, and you're not coming out to play until we get to Texarkana."

My shoes crunched on frozen leaves, and "whoa" I tumbled forward, landing on a puff of icy dirt. "This weather's turning colder than ice cubes in an ice box." I twisted my face, leaving my right cheek sticking to a fresh pile of snowflakes. "There's a street lantern. I'm still in town? Goodness, I have no idea where I am."

Dusting myself off, wiping my face, I marched to the street sign. "Soda Street." Where have I seen this name before? A flashback of scenes ran through my thoughts as I twirled around the pole. "What is it about this street? Soda Street. Soda … Street."

A blur of a cat scurried to the two-story house on the corner across from me. "White Beard?" I charged to the front of the house, wiping snow from my sleeves. What is it about this house? It's empty. The windows are broken, the boards are falling from the side, and on the porch rail is ... my cat. "White Beard, stay there. Don't jump. Don't move."

I hurried to the front yard, and lights flickered inside. I wasn't sure if my eyes were playing lantern tricks on me, or if a real light was on in the front room. I charged up the steps of the porch, leading to the double doors, where broken windows let snow fly inside. "Stay! Don't move!"

I paused mid-step. "What was the number on the front of this house?"

I spun around, went back, and gazed up. "Four. A zero. A crooked one. 401 Soda Street? I know this address. I do. I do. I know it." I pointed at White Beard. "Stay, I'm thinking. Don't you move."

White Beard tends to do the opposite of what I say, almost like how I react when grownups talk to me. He pounced through the broken window into the house, licking his paw while sitting on the windowsill.

I shook my fist. "I see you sticking your neck through the window. Stay put."

I marched back up the steps, and tumbled on a wiggly slat. The jarring of my foot must have jarred loose a memory, because I remembered Grandma's will, the one where she left a house to Mahlee. "Oh my! This is the house. No, it can't be. But it is. Is it? Or am I confused? This must be the house. It has to be!" I ran to the yard, standing in a blanket of snow, staring at the numbers. "I just know this is the house!"

Meow.

I glanced at my kitty, and he took my squinting as a cue to disappear inside.

Ghosts in the Night

I twisted the icy doorknob, and the creaking under my feet made me shake. I was afraid the porch might crumble beneath me, and now this majestic door won't budge. I pushed hard, opening the entrance to a dungeon of flickering lights. I poked my nose inside, whispering, "White Beard, where are you?"

I opened the door wide, and layers of snowflakes flew in like mini tornadoes behind me, the wind rushing up the lofty staircase. Shivering, I wrapped my arms around myself. "The night's getting colder. Here, kitty, kitty." A twinkle of light on my left drew me to the front room, and I peeked inside.

I rubbed my hands together, blowing on my fingers. "No way. A fire? In here? In this abandoned house? In my Grandma's old house?" I scooted to the flames, and knelt on the hardwood floor. Crossing my legs, I fanned the warmth toward my face. "This is perfect. This is … wait, not perfect! This means someone else is here besides me!"

I jumped to my feet, moving slowly to the sidewall to gaze upon the room, to make sure I was alone. I could see my breath in the air. I needed to leave, to get out. I mouthed, "Someone put logs in the fireplace, and might be … might be..." I rushed back to the fire, warming my hands. "Or maybe I scared them off."

I rubbed my eyes, shifting my satchel on my shoulder. I have to get my kitty. I have to find him. I shambled to the foyer, the wind whipping through the broken window. "Kitty. Here kitty, kitty."

Meow. Meow.

I bit my bottom lip, and White Beard's meows cascaded down the staircase to my ears. Stumbling toward the stairs, kicking a piece of cloth on the floor, I bent down. "What's this? A handkerchief?" I clasped the fabric, wiping my nose, smelling fear in the room. My arms felt numb, my skin tingled, and a sensation made my legs ready to run from the house. I had to get White Beard first, so I charged up the stairs. "Kitty, I'm coming for you."

Landing on the second floor with a flub, the face down tumble caused me to drop the handkerchief. I watched the cloth float like a feather to the hardwood floor below.

Kabam.

I whispered, "What's that?"

I pushed myself up, bent over the rail in time to see the front door bouncing in forceful slams. A final boom closed the dungeon off from the front yard. I slumped to my knees, peeking between the rail, waiting to see if someone had rushed in with the snow. I waited for movement and held my breath, my heartbeat louder than my thoughts. Convinced the gust of wind thwacked the gateway closed, I peeked into the room to my right. "White Beard?"

Scuddle-tink. Scuddle-tink.

Clanking tinks rattled my ears inside the dark room. "Who's there?" Leaping back to the top of the stairs, I pulled the door to, holding the doorknob with both hands to keep the ghost inside. I shouted with silent words, "Don't hurt me."

The clanking metal screeches leaked from under the door, and shrieks echoing in threes rose up. "Leave us be. Leave us be. Leave us be. We be three. Ghosts to haunt. Ghosts to haunt. Ghosts to haunt."

My mouth hung open, my heartbeat in my throat, and I soared down the stairs. "Let me out of here. Yikes! Ack!!!"

At the bottom, I careened head first, crashing against the closed front door. "I'm getting out of here." I grappled for the doorknob, my shoes slipping on the handkerchief, and the door wouldn't budge. I rattled the knob with both hands, listening to the words "we be three" bouncing on the walls upstairs. "Let me out of this house."

I charged into another room the other way, and the moon's glow sent a blue beam like smoke through the windows where glass once hung.

Ka-plat.

I tumbled over an object, one that exploded with arms like an octopus. The monster screamed at me, "How old are you? You are too old to be afraid. Tonight you die."

I dove between its legs, crawling like a baby. I got to my feet, ran into a wall, felt a door handle, and opened it. I rushed inside, only to find another ghost, which stroked my hair. "This is my closet. You better …"

I barreled from the tomb, escaping from the person or monster or ghost. Screaming, I shouted at the moonbeams in the room, and anything else lingering. "Leave me alone. I never hurt anyone. I am cold. I'm … Annie Grace Kree."

I stopped in my tracks, surrounded by ghosts circling me like death. I held up my hands to surrender. "Take me now. I'm too tired to run. Too tired to hide. Too tired to live."

Two small figures stepped into view from the fog of the moon's glow. One spoke in a quiet voice, "Shoelace? You've forgotten your name? You called yourself Annie Grace Kree."

Clearing my throat, I asked, "Tak, is that you?" I twisted my head sideways trying to get a better look.

"It's me."

The other small person touched my arm. "Shoelace, what are you doing here?"

"Timmons?"

"Yes, it's me. Your friend."

Tak tugged on my satchel. "We're staying here tonight. Crush brought us here. He said he had to deal with important stuff, and we hid when we heard stomping on the porch."

Timmons yanked my sleeve. "We should go to the fire. It's warm in the other room."

The other ghosts stepped into the light, faces of boys I'd met, the noses and eyes of not-so-scary ghosts. "Wait, so you guys were trying to scare me away?"

Theodore giggled. "We had no idea it was you. Crush found the fire burning when we got here, so he told us to be careful, to remain alert."

Thomas smiled. "We make pretty great ghosts, don't we?"

I frowned. "You do, but I was afraid I'd die in my grandma's house."

Tak squeezed my hand. "Your grandma's house?"

"Yes, this ... was hers. It's been in the family." I followed the boys like a puppy on a leash, "So are you sleeping here?"

Tak skipped, "We are. Want to stay? I like you. You are lost, aren't you?"

"I might stay. I might not." I found myself sitting on the floor gazing into the faces of Timmons and Tak. Two brave boys. With no parents.

Thunk-thump. Thunk-thump.

"What's that?" I hugged my satchel, and twisted like a top on the floor.

Three pretend ghosts scooted into the front room trying to stop, but instead fell over each other. The triplets piled up like charcoal, their faces blushed with matching grins. Thor gave me a small wave. "Hi, Miss Shoelace. We hid in the bathtub upstairs. We thought you were a burglar."

I didn't wave or smile. "You could have caused me to have a heart break-out."

Thomas mocked me. "A heart break-out?"

"That's right. My heart nearly broke from my chest."

Ha! Ha! Ha!

The boys giggled and snorted, and the sounds echoed through the chambers of the dungeon, and the room started to feel like a home.

Kabam.

"What was that?" I pointed, scooting backwards on the floor.

Kabam.

The booming sound caused all of us to stand at attention.

Tak hugged my leg. "What is that noise?"

The triplets answered together. "We don't know."

Theodore called to the sound, pushing his hat to one side on his head, a hat I hadn't noticed until now. "Who's here? Who is in this house? You better get. We have guns."

Timmons whined, "We do not."

Tak shushed him.

I held Tak's hand, and his grip cut tight into my fingers. I assured him. "Don't get scared. It's probably the wind."

A man's voice bellowed from the foyer. "It's just me. I've been hiding in the closet next to the stairs. I'm just a wanderer. I started this fire to keep myself warm. I was starting to think this house was haunted."

I blinked my eyes hard. "Archie?"

The man inched closer. "Hey, little Shoelace."

"I'm not little, remember?"

Archie cut his eyes to the fire. "Can I warm myself, the closet was freezing?"

Tak smiled. "You were with all of our quilts. You could have covered up."

Timmons giggled. "But the fire's better."

I waved my arms like a crazy girl. "Archie, I thought you were with the circus."

"No, I was tagging along for a ride. I'm looking for work in Uncertain, Texas. I'm hoping to find pearls and strike it rich in the swamps at Caddo Lake. The circus might be an option if the swamps don't pan out."

I shook my head, not sure if I believed Archie, not sure if I cared. I found myself relaxed with him, and listening to his voice calmed my insides.

Archie glanced at the boys. "So is it okay if I sit near the flames?"

Theodore nodded, but rubbed his nose like he was about to add his two cents.

Archie stepped closer. "Thank you. The snowstorm has covered the town in white tonight. We may need to huddle here by the fire to stay warm."

The triplets sat down, keeping their gaze on Archie. Thor rubbed the mole on his neck. "So you know Shoelace? Are you two riding boxcars together?"

Archie shook his head, and blew on his hands. "Not all the time. What is your name? You match the other two boys in hair and color."

"I'm Thor. I'm three minutes older than the other two. Do you and Shoelace go way back?"

Archie rubbed his ear. "We met in Oklahoma, and we seem to travel the same way even in Texas, but that's all. We happen to be on the same journey."

I sat down on the corner of the fireplace, and Timmons and Tak snuggled on each side of me.

Yawning, Tak whispered, "I'm sleepy."

Thomas agreed. "Me, too. Let me get the quilts."

The rest of the clan followed Thomas, and they returned with enough quilts for everyone. We unfolded them, and one by one, the pallets became a bed of warmth for all of us. We snuggled near the flames, but far enough to keep from blistering.

"Oh no!" I popped up. "Has anyone seen my cat?"

Archie leaned on a wall with a quilt over his legs. "Not me."

Crush's voice rippled from the shadows "I have your cat. He's shaking, and he's left a puddle of red in the snow by the streetlamp. You might check him out, and see if he's hurt. I had to come in the back, the blasted front door is jammed again."

I ran to retrieve my cat, rubbing my hands over his fur. "Thank you for saving my cat. He's not hurt, he had blood on him from your house."

Archie moved away from us down the wall. "Blood? Why would there be blood on the cat?"

I patted the front of my overalls. "I have blood on me, too. I need to change into clean clothes. It's nothing. Just a little leftover blood from fishing."

Crush nodded, going along with my lie. He warmed his hands by the fire. He turned to Archie. "Sir, who might you be?"

Archie clasped the quilt with both hands. "Just a wanderer who loves to wander. Saw this place, and needed out of the weather. Made us a fire, too."

Crush listened without saying a word, nodding each time Archie made a point.

Tak whispered in my ear, "Crush isn't mean. He's just hard like a jawbreaker."

I smiled at Tak. "I know. I know."

Crush broke the silence. "Shoelace, I have one question for you. Why are you following us?"

I stormed up to Crush ready to argue. "I'm not following you."

"It appears you show up wherever we are."

I shouted. "Or you show up wherever I'm going."

Archie handed his quilt to Thomas. "I best be on my way. I'll find another spot to sleep tonight. The storm in this room might be colder than the one outside."

I hurried to Archie. "Why? This room's big enough for all of us. My fight isn't with you, it's with him." I pointed to Crush.

Crush shuffled up to Archie. "And who are you, really? I saw you hanging around the bridge today. What brings you to Jefferson?"

Archie rubbed his chin. "I'm on a search for the pearl to save a life."

I puckered my lips. "You're going to save a life?"

"Yes, time's short. I need to …" Archie stopped mid-sentence, giving Crush a glance, giving the boys a sly grin, and coughed into both hands. "Never mind. No need to weigh you down with the burdens I carry." Archie skittered from the room. "Bye, see you soon."

I argued. "It's snowing. Where will you stay?"

"I'll find a spot. There's bound to be a place for me." He pulled his coat closed, slipping into the other room.

I started to say bye, but Crush added a complaint no sooner than Archie disappeared. "There's something wrong with him. He's up to something. We don't need any more trouble. The cops told me the man we found dead at the river was seen with the new housekeeper at the hotel, and they were arguing in the alley earlier today. The sheriff's worried the woman knows something. She might be involved."

I swallowed hard, afraid Crush meant Mahlee, and pretty sure he did.

Crush placed his arm on my shoulder. "So why didn't you go back to the hotel?"

"You're not the boss of me. I don't answer to you." I waved an arm. "So why did you bring the boys here?"

"I told you I have more than one place to keep them safe. And look, now you've gone and broken in."

"Broken in? The door was unlocked. Besides, this house doesn't belong to you. It belongs to … it belonged to my grandma."

Crush tipped my chin up. "So you do have a family."

I swiped his hand away, and White Beard growled, scatting spit-scats, like he was too cold to fight.

"You better keep your cat from scratching me."

"Then you better move away."

Knock. Knock. Knock.

Crush twisted toward the door, and I twirled too, letting White Beard slide from my arms. The boys all sat up, their glaring eyes on the foyer.

I heckled Crush. "Aren't you going to answer the door, Crush? It's probably Archie. He may have changed his mind. It's freezing out there."

He sighed. "He might have, but the door's jammed. I'll have to pull it open."

I bumped into Theodore, knocking his hat off. "I had an engineer's hat like this one. Where'd you find yours?" I picked up his hat, handing it back to him.

"A little girl wanted to take our ghost tour at the Jewish synagogue. She didn't have any money, so she gave me her hat. Me and Crush take turns wearing it. We hold ghost tours in the basement for the local kids. We charge a nickel a scare."

"You do this on purpose? You scare people for fun? No wonder you were so good at scaring me."

Thomas pushed his glasses up. "We usually don't have a ghost night in this house. Just down the street. The synagogue basement is perfect for making hair stand up on your arms."

"Wonderful, you act like ghosts on purpose."

Timmons giggled. "It's fun. I hide in a suitcase and scare the girls."

Crush bellowed. "Enough talk. Settle down. No need to tell her our business."

Knock. Knock. Knock.

Tak ran to the foyer. "I'll get it. I'll get the door."

Crush charged behind Tak. "You're too small to open the door. It's stuck, remember?" Crush caught his shoe on a quilt and slammed to the floor. Gathering himself, he hurdled to the front foyer, his grunts told me he was doing his teenage tough-boy thing.

Being nosey, I rushed to the edge of the room. Crush jerked the door wide open, and a gust of wind sprinkled with snow blew in. And a lone suitcase sat on the rickety porch—alone.

Suitcase to Packing

The clan of boys sat on their knees in a circle around the brown suitcase, not asking questions, and watching Crush while he considered whether to open the suitcase. Crush spoke to no one, but to all. "We might need to leave it closed. The snow's falling like a quilt in layers and there were no footprints on the porch. It's like the others, but different."

I paced behind the boys, while staying close to the fire. I was unsure why Crush didn't pop the latches on each end. "Hey, Crush, are you afraid of a suitcase?"

Tak hopped to his feet, and put his fingers over my lips. "Crush remembers."

I frowned, whispering in his ear. "Remembers what?"

Timmons unfolded from the floor. "He remembers watching our ma and pa hold onto a suitcase in the flood. How they went under the water."

Tak finished the story as if it were rehearsed. "Our ma and pa drowned two years ago when I was three. I don't remember much, except Crush saved me and Timmons. We were sitting on top of a suitcase in deep water. Timmons had wrapped me inside of his coat."

Timmons gave me the rest of their story. "Our pa tried to swim over and save our baby brother, Tink. They went under. So did our ma."

I shook my head. "I'm sorry. That's so sad."

Tak spoke up. "But I have Timmons."

Timmons agreed. "And I have Tak."

They ran to Crush, hugging his legs, spouting off. "And we have Crush."

113

Crush hugged the boys, whispering big brother words into their hearts. I watched, unsure if this lone suitcase sitting in an empty room had anything to do with *Crush remembering*. I darted to the middle of the circle. "So let's open the suitcase."

Crush shoved me. "Trust me. This has nothing to do with you."

"You're right, but you're the ones in my grandma's house."

Crush charged me. "We keep receiving suitcases. They show up at the house on the river. On the trail. Even at the synagogue where the boys hold their tours. At the oddest times. We have no idea why."

"Tours? I'm not so sure they should be called tours. Scaring little kids isn't nice."

"It's a way to feed ourselves. We have a dozen or more suitcases now. Nothing is ever inside of them, either."

I squinted my eyes. "This is too weird. Who would send you empty suitcases?"

Crush shook his fist at me. "I don't know, but it's got me on edge. That's why I have trouble with strangers. I can't trust anyone, especially strangers like you who wander in, or men like Archie."

I screamed. "Archie never did anything to you. He's simply a man without a home."

"And you're a girl without one, too."

Thomas crawled to the suitcase. "Why don't we put the suitcase over by the wall? I don't like all this fighting."

Crush agreed. "Great idea. Later, we'll put it with the others at the synagogue."

In one split second, Crush went from remembering to being his bossy self. He gave out orders. "It's getting late, time for sleep."

114

Rescue of Undaunted Spirit

Thomas and Theodore, along with Timmons and Tak wrapped their arms around Crush, talking at the same time. "Night. Night. Goodnight." They rushed to the pallets and piled in together.

The triplets curled up, and Crush knelt near them. "Stay close. Watch each other. Don't get separated."

I grabbed the quilt Archie left behind. "Come here, White Beard. It's just you and me."

Crush sat by the suitcase, letting an arm fall over one end. He pulled some covers over his legs. "Boys, we'll leave at sunrise. The snow could be deep, but we'll make it home."

I tucked my hands under my head, turning to face the dancing flames. The flickers appeared like a river of rushing water, whipping in the fireplace. White Beard curled up on the bottom of my quilt, purring, and I peeked at Crush whose head bent sideways on the suitcase.

The boys cuddled tight, all bundled up as if they were in one big bed. Their feet were tangled, their arms crisscrossed. One by one the snoring filled the room, and heavy breathing kept rhythm with time.

I sat up, unable to keep my eyelids closed. I sprang to my feet, ready to snoop. I'm not sure how long my grandma lived in this house, or if she knew it was run down when she left it to Mahlee. I grabbed my satchel and a quilt, and wrapped up in the fabric. I made my way back to the foyer, in time for a burst of cold air to shoot at me like a gun through the side window.

Slipping my bloody overalls off, and my shirt, I pulled out clean clothes from my satchel, digging them out from under my poem can. I dressed and tossed the filthy clothes out a broken window. Sitting on the first step of the staircase, I tried to figure out my next move. I wrapped up tighter in the quilt, breathing under it to warm my nose. I curled up like a broken toy without a toy box, without the glue to fix the cracks.

Sobbing, I couldn't forget the kindness of Mr. Marion, or the soft bed at the hotel. I couldn't forget the dead body, either. I couldn't get past the ugly of the last few days, let alone the last few years. I rolled onto my back, putting my feet on the staircase rail. "God, do you even know I'm here?"

A padding sound on the floor made me jerk.

"Who's there?"

Tak scooted up to me. "It's me. I heard you praying. I wanted to tell you, God knows where you are."

Tak's soft words cut through my pain.

He patted my arm. "God loves you, too."

"I'm not sure He does. I'm hard to keep up with."

Tak sat on the floor near me. "Toby tells us all the time how much God loves everybody."

"Tak, you're wiser and braver than any five-year-old I've ever met."

He sniffled. "I'm not brave. I just pretend. It's like pretending to be a ghost when I'm not. I wish I had a pa to teach me how to fish. Crush tries, but he's a little grouchy for a pa. He can fish good though."

I hugged Tak without thinking. "I'm glad I ran into Mr. Marion's truck." I touched my head. "Except for getting these stitches."

Tak ran a finger over them. "You might have a scar."

I laughed. "I'm one big scar. Look at my arms."

He nodded. "Scars can be pretty. They show we lived through something."

"Tak, are you sure you're only five?"

He held up five fingers. "Yep."

I opened my quilt wide to let him cuddle up next to me, and we snuggled together without words, letting the night settle in, letting the sleep come.

**

Knock. Knock. Knock.

Startled, I sat up, realizing I was still snuggled with Tak, only we were no longer on the step, we were on the cold floor by the staircase. The sun lit the house, and the light ushered in a new day.

Tak moaned, and pulled the quilt over his head.

Knock. Knock.

I got to my feet, and inched to the front door, peeking through one of the broken windows, seeing a landscape of pure white, so bright it hurt my eyes. I jerked on the door with all I could muster up, after seeing a skirt, figuring the person at the door was a woman.

Crush appeared from the front room, joining me. "Move out of the way. Let me do it."

I bumped him with my hips. "I can do it. I don't need your help."

He stuck his head part way out the broken window. "Gladys Winston. What brings you here?"

The woman's voice cracked. "Remember, call me Susan. My middle name is easier on the ears than Gladys. I've brought a warm breakfast for you and the boys, but you need to get me out of this cold."

Crush pushed me hard enough to send me tumbling backwards, and he waggled the door open. "Morning. Come in. So how did you know we were here?"

Tak jumped up like a bullet. "What? What's going on?"

I tapped his head. "Nothing. It's someone with food."

Susan strode inside talking faster than snowflakes falling. "Mr. Marion phoned me. He noticed a smoke signal rising from the chimney, and he ordered you breakfast."

Tak danced in a circle around me. "I'm starving."

Susan smiled. "Well, I've got pancakes with scrambled eggs in this basket, and milk. Lizzy Beth has blackberry muffins."

I licked my lips. "Blackberry? I love blackberries."

A shadow, shorter than Tak hid behind Susan's long coat, and I propelled myself to an angle to see the brown eyes peeking from the porch. "My Lizzy Beth? Could that be you?"

A smile as long as any bayou flashed in front of me, and the basket tumbled to the floor. The smiling girl raced to me. "Shoelace … Hi, you are my Wheelock friend."

I embraced Lizzy Beth with a new touch, one reserved for half-sisters, those who don't know they are even family. I cackled with joy. "Lizzy Beth, I had no idea your adoption brought you to Jefferson. Right here. And I'm right here, too."

Tak and Crush gathered up the muffins, blowing dust from them. Tak announced, "They are good to eat even with the dirt."

Crush laughed. "Yes, anything Susan bakes is great. Period."

My little sister smiled, "Hi, Tak-Tak." She reached for a muffin and handed it to me.

"Thank you." I could barely keep my eyes from popping out of my head. I'm in Jefferson. Mahlee's in Jefferson. And Lizzy Beth, too. I couldn't breathe, but did, to keep from passing out.

Crush pushed me aside. "Let's shut the door. We're letting the heat out."

I smarted off. "Really. Haven't you noticed most of the windows are broken? This door isn't our problem."

Crush whispered into my ear, not letting the others listen in. "I agree. You might be our problem."

Snarling, I thought about praying, but hitting Crush sounded like a better idea. Lizzy Beth grabbed my free hand, pulling me into the front room. "Come with me."

I bit into the muffin, soaking up how it felt to hold hands with my sister. Soft. Small fingers. Cold. I sniffed the top of her hair. Clean like shampoo.

Tak carried the muffin basket to the boys, and everyone cuddled close because the fire needed a new log. Susan sat her oversized breakfast basket in the middle and the wild haired, starving faces dove in like alligators.

I stayed close to Lizzy Beth, afraid to let her out of my sight, I kept staring at her black hair, her blue dress, and her brown stockings. I couldn't believe she was this close, and I was in the town she lived in.

I tugged on Lizzy Beth's adoptive mama's arm. "Susan, I remember seeing you at Wheelock Academy when you picked Lizzy Beth for your daughter."

She patted my head. "I don't remember meeting you. I forget things easily. I figured you knew her from the orphanage by how you both reacted at the front door. Did you get adopted, too?"

I nodded. "Sort of. Sort of, not."

Tak handed her the answer I wished he'd not shared. "This is Shoelace. She ran into Mr. Marion's pickup. She rides in boxcars."

I was thankful Susan wasn't listening to Tak, and was busy helping pass out pancakes. "Did everyone get some eggs?"

Thomas held his plate up. "I'd love some more."

"Absolutely, Eat up." Susan waited on the boys, keeping their plates loaded.

Thomas announced, "Hey, we have Marion Kane Syrup in the kitchen. I'm sure there's a jar left." He scurried like a rabbit to the other part of the house.

Lizzy Beth moved to my cat. "Kitty. Pretty kitty."

I followed her. "Do you like cats?"

Susan snatched Lizzy Beth into her arms. "She might be allergic. We watch her around dirt, and animals. We don't want anything to happen to her. She's been through some hard times."

I backed up, ready to mouth off, but kept my words inside. I didn't want to risk losing this moment with my sister. Lizzy Beth's eyes sparkled with a deep glow like marble. Her skin tanner than mine, her hair long and black like my daddy's hair.

I asked Susan a nosey question. "Where do you live?"

"Over by the library, but I spend most of my time at the Kornbread Kafe on Polk Street. I run the restaurant by myself since my husband had his accident." She coughed. "But, I have the best chocolate cobbler in town."

I smiled. "Accident?"

Lizzy Beth whispered, "He hurt his eyes."

I nodded, not sure what she meant. "Susan, I heard you do make a great cobbler."

She smiled, hugging her Lizzy Beth. "I also make the best bologna and cheese cornbread sandwiches. You might need to try one."

I nodded. Susan put Lizzy Beth down, and my sister ran to Tak to get a swipe of syrup from his plate. She stuck her syrupy finger into her mouth.

Susan corrected the little syrup swiper. "Lizzy Beth. Manners. We don't put our hands in other people's plates."

120

"Yes, ma'am."

I moved toward Lizzy Beth, running my fingers through her long hair. "You have silky hair. You are so pretty. Prettier than I remember."

Susan snarled. "Don't get her hair dirty. I just washed it last night."

I looked at the crusty dirt on my hands, wiping them on my overalls. "Sorry. I didn't mean to contaminate her." My harsh words felt hard, even to me. "I'm sorry ma'am. I'm just tired."

Tak threw out a comment. "You get grouchy like Crush."

Everyone giggled except Crush.

Susan turned to Crush who was smacking on a giant bite of eggs. "I'll swing by after a while and get my dishes. Place them on the back porch, and after the lunch run at the café, I'll get them."

Crush swallowed. "Thank you ma'am. We appreciate this."

She ruffled his hair. "Be sure and thank Mr. Marion. He's the one who saw the smoke signal."

Crush answered with food in his mouth. "Yes, ma'am."

Susan held Lizzy Beth's hand, but she pulled away from her new mama and rushed to me, hugging me hard. "Bye, Shoelace. I miss you."

"I miss you, too. I will see you soon. I will." A knot in my throat sent me running upstairs. I rushed inside the bathroom, crumbling like a broken girl whose wings were snipped to keep her from flying. "God, please, if you ever did anything for me. Let me see Lizzy Beth again."

Crush hollered. "Hey, Shoelace, we're headed home. Tak wants to say goodbye. Will you be okay here? Or should I let Mr. Marion know where you are?"

I cracked the door open. "Don't tell Mr. Marion where I am. I'm figuring out where to go. Are the boys about to go to school?" I stepped to the top of the stairs. "I want to tell them bye, too. I'm coming."

"No, they're not going to school. Schooling' is for regular folk. My boys learn all they need to know from me. I teach them to read and write, to chop firewood, to hunt game, and mostly to fend for themselves."

At the door, the boys waved goodbye, and Tak hugged me. "Will you see me more? I want more …"

"I don't know. We'll see." I held my kitty, hugging him tighter today than yesterday.

After the boys left, I muddled over to the front room. Crush had put more logs on the fireplace, but I had no idea where he got the timber. The quilts were gone, probably back in the closet, and the food basket was gone, too. "Goodness, these were the neatest boys ever. I could learn a few things from them."

I plopped to the floor, realizing I'd not eaten much, only a muffin. Jumping to my feet, I ran to the back porch, digging through the basket. Nothing left. Not even a crumb.

Back inside, I rummaged in the kitchen cabinets, hoping for something, and found not one, but dozens of jars of syrup. I twisted the lid, and stuck two fingers into a jar, pulling out a stringy mess of sweet goo, licking my hands. I opened a drawer, hoping for a spoon, only to see … to see a revolver.

"Whose gun is this?"

I picked up the pistol, my fingers sticking to the barrel. "Maybe I need this gun for protection." I dug in the drawer, found some bullets, stashing a handful into my satchel.

Knock. Knock. Knock.

I padded to the foyer, leaning, taking a peek out the window. A woman towered above the doorframe like a ghost caught in the middle of a haunting, a ghost wearing raggedy brown work boots.

The handkerchief from last night was still on the floor and it became a cloth to wipe syrup from my fingers. "Now, I have syrup on both hands." I placed the gun between my knees, wiping my fingers clean. Clutching the gun with one hand, I stuck the hanky in my pocket.

Knock. Knock. Knock.

"Coming. Just a minute." I called to the door, hoping the person knocking heard me. With a final jerk I opened the door, and found myself gazing into a face from my past, one haunting my present. "Mahlee? What … what ... are you doing here?"

"I might ask you the same question. What are you doing in my house? And what are you doing with my gun?"

Death of Me

I waved the gun in the air like a teacher using a pointer on the chalkboard, tiptoeing backwards. "You left me alone in Texarkana, then you show up in my hotel room, then you run off, and now here you are again. Are you taking me with you?"

"No, I'm not here to get you. It's too mixed up. I came for my gun. I heard some noise, and figured someone was inside. That's the only reason I knocked. Get out of my way. I don't … I can't stay with you."

I handed her the gun. "So you can go on a search for your gun, but not me? I don't get you. I don't understand why this is happening."

Mahlee mumbled. "I don't have anything to prove to you. When I met your daddy some years back … well, he saved me from those men who attacked me. I rode the rail with him, and you. Your daddy gave me a chance to live, but I always knew my past might destroy the present. By leaving, I'm giving you a chance to live."

"What? You are the only mama I have or even know. I figured we'd always be like cereal and milk, but instead you slip away from me more than you stay. I'm drowning without you, but you can still have me, just say you're sorry." My voice snapped like an icicle breaking from the roof of a house, and my eyes pleaded at the empty gaze coming at me from the porch.

Mahlee bolted at me, and twirled around as if she was looking for someone. She closed the door, and offered me a growl. "You have no choice. Give up on us. I'm not here to get you. I'm not." She covered her mouth, choking on her words. "I only came for my gun. I'm on my way to work at the hotel. I have to hurry, or I'll be late."

"Late? You never worried about being anywhere on time before. Or working." I touched her cold hand, and she pulled away. I called to the wind. "Where did my Mahlee go? Why are you running away?"

"I'm not running. You won't understand."

"So you keep saying."

Mahlee pounded her chest with the butt of the gun. "Be quiet. I have to be careful. There's a man in the car waiting for me, and he won't wait long before he's charging up here to get me. I have to go."

"Since when do you have a man? I thought you loved Ernie."

"I do love Ernie. I did. But he's out of the picture. I've got a new life here in this town."

I pounded my fist in her stomach. "Just a few days ago, Ernie was your fiancé. How do you up and move on without even blinking? That's not fair. You have room for a new man, but not for me?"

Mahlee bent my arm backwards, turning me in a circle. *Ouch!!*

"Stop. You're gonna break my arm."

Mahlee pushed me to the floor. "Then stop bothering me and get yourself moving on down the tracks."

I dove at her knees, taking Mahlee to the floor, the gun plunking, sliding to the wall. I hovered over her with my arms flapping. "The Mahlee that my daddy found wouldn't up and leave me or hurt me, especially now my grandma is gone."

"Girl, that's it. I've had enough. You're in my house. Get out." She grabbed me by both arms like she was sweeping the floor, and dragged me to the door. She pulled hard on the handle until it opened, and kept yanking on me, as my satchel flung against my shoulders. Mahlee threw me outside onto the porch.

I slugged on the door with my fists. "I'm not finished telling you off." I stuck my head inside one of the broken windows, yelling, "Let me in." No answer, but I kept pounding on the dungeon door. "Let me in. I'm … I'm …" I crumbled to the rickety porch, weeping mad icy tears.

Screek.

The black car revved its motor behind me, and I gawked at the driver bending himself from the front seat. His loafers sunk with each step in the snow, and he shook a foot with each stride.

I screamed, "What do you want? Leave my Mahlee here with me."

The squinty-eyed cane pole of a man cackled. "Who are you?"

"I am no one to you."

He stomped toward me. "Do I know you?"

I frowned. "No, I'm not worth knowing."

The grumpy driver snubbed me with a half-grin. "I never forget a face. I have seen you before, somewhere."

"No, you haven't. I'm out of here." I dove past the bushes like a deer set loose from a trap, bolting around the side of the house next to the road, stomping in the snow. At the back of the house, I stopped, and peeked to the side to see if the man followed me. No sight of the cane pole stalker.

I called to Mahlee at the back door, sticking my head inches inside. "I've got more to say to you." A flutter of wings behind me caught my attention, and a flock of redbirds perched themselves on the branches of the trees and on top of the gazebo. I yelled, "Even these birds have something to say."

No answer from inside, but I waited, afraid to move too close, fearing she'd hit me, or go crazy like she does every Halloween. That's the terrible-horrible night when she remembers giving up Lizzy Beth at birth because she couldn't take care of her.

I lingered on the porch for a minute, noticing the plates and dirty silverware scattered on the wooden slats. I figured White Beard had dug through the basket. My feet itched, my hands twitched. I couldn't wait for Mahlee to come and listen to me. I barged through the back door and into the house, tripping over my own shadow.

Meow. Meow.

"Kitty, not now."

I felt like a ghost, like my heart had exploded with hate. "Mahlee? Where are you?"

From somewhere deep in the belly of the giant house, a voice howled words of disgust. "No, you are not staying. This is not an option." Mahlee's lumbering footsteps came closer, grew louder. "I will not put up with this."

I froze in place, falling backwards, becoming a part of the kitchen wall, sliding to the floor. I shouted, "God, Mahlee hates me. Why? What did I ever do to have no one want me?"

Mahlee hovered over me. "Stop your crying. I've been looking for my bullets. Have you seen them?"

I vaulted to my feet, unable to control my whining. "I have them." I pulled handfuls from my satchel, shoving them at her. Some of the bullets tumbled to the kitchen floor. "When did you get a gun anyway? And why do you need bullets?"

A sniffling wheeze like raw emotion leaked from Mahlee. "I have to protect myself … and … I cannot let you die."

"Protect yourself? What's going on with you? Why are you keeping secrets from me?"

"I've told you, this is beyond your understanding. You have to leave. I came to Jefferson because your grandma gave me the house."

"Sure you did. So you need a gun to decorate the house?"

"Things are more mixed up than you know."

I shook my head, my hair whipping against my face. "You make no sense. You are hiding something."

Mahlee clumped in her boots on the linoleum, charging at me. Picking up bullets, she tossed them into her skirt pocket. She rushed through the next room where the moonbeams shot from windows last night, and hurried to the front of the house.

I trailed her. "Wait. You forgot these." I held six bullets, but she didn't turn around. I stuck them inside my satchel. "Don't leave me, please?"

Barreling through the maze of rooms, I caught up with Mahlee as she swung the front door open. I dove at her, grabbing her skirt, not letting go, and my face got buried in the snow like a plow.

She halted, swinging her arms. "Shoelace, these are my last words to you." She paused, as the nosey man stepped from the other side of the house.

Mahlee assured him. "I've got this. This girl's mine. Don't worry."

He moved to the side of the car, kicking a tire. "I'll be right here if you need me."

Mahlee towed me right back into the house, shoving the door to, in one giant thrust.

I wiggled, trying to get my arm loose from her grasp. "Stop, you're hurting me."

She tossed me against the stairs.

Pa-lump-fa-clump.

I touched my head, the throbbing inside my brain felt like my heart had jumped behind my eyes. "My ear is bleeding. You ... you are not in your right thoughts." I screamed more words, a garble of sorrow and pain flying from my gut, emptying myself.

Mahlee stooped to her knees, whispering one long sentence. "Listen. Don't speak. I never wanted to cause you any pain. I had no choice, but to come here. I'm going to fire this gun in a second, because the man outside expects me to get rid of you. Especially since he's seen you. If I let you live ... you could die."

I sobbed. "Mahlee, I'll leave. I'll leave. Don't shoot me." My hands went over my head, and I rocked.

"I'm not going to shoot you."

I peeked from under my arm. "But, you said ..."

"I'm going to fire in the air to make him think you're dead. If I don't, he's got his own gun. He's simply in charge of driving me to and from work. He's in charge of keeping me here in Jefferson, too."

I sat up tall. "Keeping you here?"

"No, I said he's in charge of keeping me from being late for work."

"That not what you said."

"It is. You heard wrong." Mahlee gulped, "Listen, I came to get my gun. I've got to go."

"I'm sorry. I just need a mama." I wiped the last of my tears from my face before the waterfall started again.

"Listen. And listen good. There's a secret room where your great grandpa gave piano lessons to the children in town who couldn't afford lessons. Your grandma told me about the room one night when we sat on the porch at the manor, drinking sweet tea."

I sniffled, "Why do I care?"

"Find it. If this man drives by the house, or sees you again, you've got to hide in there. He might harm you."

"Harm me? Have you seen my ear? I can barely hear from it."

"Get into a closet for now. Stay there for longer than you think, and then find the piano room. After you feel safe in a day or two, get out of town."

I swallowed the snot thickening in my throat. "I can't ... I can't leave or live without you."

"If you have me, you won't live."

Mahlee cloaked my neck with a warm, long, and soft hug, and a tender kiss on my cheek. "Goodbye, my sweet daughter."

"Daughter?" I trapped the kiss on my face with my fingers, and trapped the word daughter in my heart.

Mahlee hopped to her feet and pointed the gun at the plaster.

Honk. Honk. Honk. Honk.

The horn from the car blasted a bleep louder than the train passing by on the tracks nearby, and then Mahlee shot the gun off.

Pffft. Pffft.

I held my ears, and fixed my eyes on the two bullet holes in the wall, since Mahlee didn't give me time to get inside of a closet. Somehow, I expected blood to pour from the holes. I wailed. "Mahlee, I need you. Mama, I love you."

She clomped to the door, stuck the gun into her heavy coat, and gave me one last glance, her eyes red. She used both hands to unhinge the door, and bolted to the blanket of snow, leaving me imprisoned inside. With blood on the wall, and blood on my ear, and sadness pouring out, I cried like a baby who had fallen from her cradle.

A white mist came toward me. "White Beard, what do you have in your mouth? Did you kill a redbird?"

My kitty dropped the cardinal at my feet, meowing as if he knew death was what I wished for. I crawled to the window in time to see Mahlee in the passenger seat of the car with the cane pole man. She was leaving behind a daughter who might as well be a dead redbird on the floor.

Staircase Songs

I crawled from the foyer like a toddler without hope. Mahlee told me I'd *live* without her. She's wrong.

Kneeling at the fireplace, I stared at the embers of orange poking through the logs. They were a reminder of the flame of love I still held in my heart for Mahlee even when I wanted to kick her. I stuck my hands over the heat, and White Beard danced around my legs. "Sorry, kitty. We've gotten ourselves in a pickle."

I embraced him, swooping him close to my neck, listening to him purr. "We need to move your dead bird and bury him. It won't be long until we smell the stink."

I sighed, and clung to hope, wishing to be a redbird so I could fly over the land to see what Mahlee is doing. I felt like a broken bird, without a branch, without a tree, without a tomorrow. I yelled, "My life stinks sometimes."

A cold chill ran down my back, and I hurried to the back porch for firewood, remembering I'd walked right by it coming inside. My heart burned with questions and thumped with cluttered pangs. Wrestling with my 'vestigation, I tossed a log onto the fireplace, and smoke shot up the chimney with sprinkles of orange ash. The icy log crackled, warming the room.

I then dug around in the kitchen cabinets, wishing for something to drink. Out the window on the neighbor's back steps sat four glorious bottles of milk. I chided, "They wouldn't miss one jar. I could take one and leave a dime."

I bolted out the back door, off the porch, past the garage, and darted behind a shrub, bending low and clasping a jar in my fingers. I dug in my satchel, found some change and left the coin, making a milk purchase from the neighbor's steps.

Ding-a-ling. Ding-a-ling.

What kind of bell is ringing on the street? I rushed between my grandma's house and the milk-store-house, in time to see a chunky young man riding a bicycle with newspapers in a basket. He threw a paper like he was tossing a baseball, and it slid to the yard, parting the snow on the neighbor's walkway.

I've never read the paper much except when the Phantom Killer was getting famous in Texarkana. I trekked to the paper, clutching it to my side. Thirsty for love and starving for comfort, I felt like reading the paper since my grandma did every morning.

Back inside, I scooted the suitcase from the wall, the one belonging to the boys, used it for a seat, and unfolded the paper. The headline read: "Plantation Owner's Top Hand Found Dead by the Cypress Bayou."

"No! No way! It's already in the paper?" The swig of milk in my mouth spewed to the *Jimplecute* newspaper, and the words smeared on the page. The body I'd tumbled over last night was the same man in the story. It had to be. Had to be.

I paced around the room, stopping every couple of sighs, to swallow some milk. "What do I know about Crush? Or Archie? Mahlee's acting weirder than ever and she has a new man. What do I know about him?"

I hustled in awkward two-steps. I put my hands over the fire, warming them from holding the cold milk jar. "What if the murderer is the man driving the car for Mahlee? She warned me about him, told me to hide in the … the secret room."

I spun around, placed my milk jar on the floor, only to swing my red shoe into the jar, kicking it over. "Secret room! I

need to find it!" White Beard lapped up my spill, and I
scrambled like a rat stuck in a maze, pounding the walls in the
rooms. Each one. Up. Then down. Repeating my pounds,
hoping to find the secret room.

Puh-puh-puh. Puh-puh-puh.

I found nothing behind the bookshelves in the dining
room. Retracing my steps, I pounded, hit, and slapped, then
ran my fingers over the cracks in the plaster. Going over my
path again, I found not one odd door, or hinge. Some of the
paint on the walls crumbled at my touch, but no magic
entrance. "Maybe Mahlee lied about a secret room. Or my
grandma told her a tall tale."

Charging to the kitchen, opening and slamming cabinets,
checking closets, and dragging all the quilts from the one deep
closet beneath the back of the stairs. I 'vestigated the house
one last time.

Creak. Kaboom.

Spinning around in the foyer, I whispered, "Who is here
now?"

Tiptoeing to the front room, I picked up the suitcase to use
for protection, and leaned on the wall near the wide doorway.
Someone was in the house, or something, and the creaking
came from near the kitchen.

I waited, hovering, ready to slam the suitcase into the
intruder, ready to smack the person in the gut, or head, or
whatever.

A voice rattled words, first low, then muffled. "My help
comes from the Lord, I know this because … He is my
strength in times of trouble."

I squatted, listening. Footsteps and … something else.
Maybe it was two people.

Pad. Pad. Pad. Pad.

A dog's black nose came through the door's entrance, followed by his whole snout and his pointy ears.

I whispered, "Bingo? What are you doing here? You're gonna chase my kitty, aren't you?" I hugged his neck, and he licked my cheek. "Awe, you can be nice."

The voice in the other part of the house soared, singing, "It is no secret what God can do, what He's done for others, He'll do for you."

I clutched the suitcase, swinging, and standing tall.

Bam. Bam. Bam.

Ouch!

"What the … who is attacking me?" The singing intruder rolled on the floor, his arms wrapped around his belly, his brown sack sailing across the room, his Bible landing at my feet. He screamed, "Stop hitting me. I'm … I'm …"

I knelt over him, dropping the suitcase. "Toby Raike? What are you doing in my house?"

Toby whined, "Can you help me up, please?"

I extended my hand. "Sorry. You scared me. What are you doing here? This is my house."

"Your house? This house has been empty as long as I've lived next door."

"You … you live in the house next to me?" I glanced at the now empty jar of milk by the fireplace. "If you have a house, why come to a cold and empty one without furniture or food?"

Toby coughed. "I'm skipping school, and can't be home. My grandpa might not like it. The housekeeper comes every morning, and she'd let him know."

"What? You're a wanna-be preacher boy and you're lying to your grandpa? A preacher shouldn't ditch school."

"If my grandpa doesn't know, I didn't lie."

"I didn't know you had a home. I thought you were like the boys. Like me."

"Like you?"

"Never mind."

"Shoelace, we're all orphans and God adopts us into His family." Toby picked up his Bible. "I do live next door. Hey, whose paper?"

"I borrowed it from your yard."

"Where did you get the milk?" Toby pointed at the now empty jar on the floor.

"I borrowed the milk. Actually, I left a dime for it."

"I see. You trespassed to get the milk, and I'm trespassing to practice my preaching." Toby tapped my belly. "I don't think you're returning the milk, either."

I pushed his hand away. "Stop that."

"You accused me of lying and all the while you're stealing from neighbors."

I slugged his arm. "And you're trespassing."

"I'd say we're even. I've made sure this house has regular people over, like Crush and his boys, and me. I'm the master of this house. This is my pretend Hollywood home." Toby giggled, moving to the fire.

"Hollywood? You have a big imagination." I scooted next to him. "That's my fire."

"I'd say you have my firewood."

I sighed, stepping to the side. "Did you put the wood on the back porch?"

"Yes, during the winter months, it's for Crush and his boys."

"That's nice of you, but why are you skipping school?"

"Like I said, I have to practice for my preacher service tonight at Oakwood Cemetery. Now it's snowed, so we might have it here."

I shoved him. "You might need to ask the owner."

"Stop pushing and hitting. I'm not your enemy." Toby turned on his preacher talk, smiling, "So is your family moving into this house? It needs some paint, and new windows."

I rubbed my aching ear. "Not exactly. I'm sort of without a family right now."

Toby nodded. "So are you running from something? You can always run to God."

"Really? Can't you talk like a kid? I'm kind of running to something. Or I was until it threw me away."

"You are talking in circles like Crush does when I pray with him. Shall I counsel you?"

"What? I could counsel you on a few things."

"You probably could, but I'm trying to get my plan in place so I can work my plan. I want to be a Hollywood actor like Stuart Hamblen, and be famous. Or I might be a preacher, depending on which works out best for me."

"Who is Stuart Hamblen? It sounds like you have no idea what you want to do."

Toby moved his hair from his brow. "Mr. Hamblen is on the radio and he's an actor, and writes songs. I have options. I can be like him, or I can be a preacher. That's probably two more than you have."

"I have a plan, too."

"Sure you do." Toby paced to the other side of the room, raising a hand. "Lord, you're the river of love, flowing with grace, filling my heart with life. May we run to you in times of trouble." He cradled the Bible to his chest with his other hand.

I watched the flickers in the fireplace, trying not to stare, but my one good ear was unable to block out the words. I glanced at Bingo. He was now curled up next to White Beard like they were friends, unlikely friends, but content just the same.

The intensity of Toby's preaching squawked to a high pitch. "Listen, my people. Jesus took a thief to paradise with Him that day on the cross. He saw two criminals hanging on crosses next to him, but only one got saved. Repent. Turn to Jesus."

White Beard and Bingo raised their heads to inspect the noise, and my own ears wondered what Toby might be saying. I stomped over to him. "Stop practicing with screams. No one likes a preacher who shouts. And why would Jesus take a thief with Him? And where is paradise?"

"Paradise is in heaven." Toby held up his preacher hand to explain. "Jesus was talking to a bad man who recognized Jesus as the Savior."

I nodded, like I understood, but my ears burned with questions.

Toby went on. "I love to pray and to preach. To tell people to repent of their wicked ways."

"You need to tone it down. Pastor Cody, back home, speaks in sentences we can understand, and he shows us kindness. You could learn from him."

"I can learn. I can. I'm used to Pastor JW. He's my pastor at the Methodist Church, and he's sort of loud."

"You're a Methodist?"

"I am. What about you?"

"I'm a member at the Creek Church in Texarkana, it's for hobos."

Toby puckered his lips, like he trapped the words from insulting me. He sighed, "So I need to be quieter?"

"Yes, much." I placed my hands on my hips, "What do you know about this house?"

"I know there's four bedrooms upstairs with two bathrooms, and two fireplaces. I know it's been empty forever. I know the kitchen is bigger than most, and the house needs plenty of repairs. Why?"

I rolled my eyes, bit my lip, and blurted out my request. "I need to find ... to find the secret room." I hoped Toby might know where the hidden door might be.

"What?" Toby dropped his Bible to the hardwood floor.

Plop!

Scat. Meow.

Ruff! Ruff!

I twirled around to see my kitty and Bingo circling their warm spot on the floor, where they cuddled like long-lost friends in a new bundle, relaxing after the boom on the floor.

"Hey, Toby. You frightened my cat."

He put his arms up like a singer praising God. "I didn't know anyone knew about the secret room, except me."

"Why would you be the only person who knows?"

"Because this is like my home when I'm not home."

I grabbed Toby by the collar. "So there is a secret room?"

"Yes, of course. Many of these old homes in Jefferson have passages and secret rooms." He shoved my hand off. "If this is your house, why don't you know about the secret room?"

"Because I've never lived here, I only got this house after my grandma died. She ... she left it to me." I lied to a preacher. Maybe it won't make God too mad since this preacher might be an actor.

Toby grinned, "Would you like me to show you where it is?"

"Would you, please?" I spit out nice words, since Toby might be good help. He's from this town and knows things I don't. I might use him, and then drop him like rock into the river of goodbye.

"Come with me." Toby shuffled to the foyer, facing the staircase.

"Why are we stopping here?"

He knelt to the floor. "Did your cat do this?" Toby cradled the feathered body of the redbird, moving him to the side.

"Yes, White Beard does what cats do."

Toby sighed. "We'll need to have a funeral. I need funeral practice, too."

I tapped his shoulder. "You are a preacher-boy with no focus. Where's the secret room?"

He pointed to the stairs. "Right here. We go this way."

"This is it?" I twirled around. "The front door's behind me, the fireplace room is to our left, and the other big room to the right. So the secret room is upstairs?"

He shook his head. "No, watch this."

"Watch what?"

Toby bent down, and flipped not one latch, but two, then three, and finally four—hidden locks under the lip of the first step on the staircase. He yanked on my arm. "Push the spot in the middle between the two center latches, and then watch the center of the stairs rise, revealing your ... secret room."

I knelt, placing my hand right where Toby pointed. "Here? Do I just push?"

"Just push."

Clitter-creak. Clitter-creak.

The center of the staircase opened up, like a stone rolling away from a tomb, like an entrance to a hiding place. It was not letting someone out but letting me inside.

"It's dark in there. How did you find this room?"

Toby smiled, "I was practicing my preaching, and sitting on this first step when I dropped my Bible."

"You could use a smaller one. Your Bible is scary."

"Big is not scary. Big is heavy." Toby snickered. "That day I kicked one of the latches, and checked out the others. I had been reading about walking on water in the Bible, and nearly fell out when the stairs creaked upward. The secret room is off to the left behind the fireplace wall, a small room with one window. The glass is covered with a pillowcase to keep the room secret."

"How do you know?"

"Because I put it there, to protect the piano."

"Piano?"

"Yes, the upright piano was there when I discovered the room. I can play the piano and the fiddle. What about you?"

"No, I only have hobo skills."

"Hobo? I thought you were home."

"Not exactly. This was home for my grandma, way back. I am searching for a home." My throat tightened at saying *home*.

"You might want to seek help from God."

"Can I try you, instead?"

Toby nodded. "Maybe, God might have sent me to you."

"Really? Now you're talking weird again."

"I talk like I think, and I think like I talk. I would make a great actor or a most convincing preacher. Either way, I love God. You do, too, don't you?"

"I'm trying, but He's making it hard."

"At least, you're trying." Toby inched forward, sliding into the shadow of the dark room, and then like a burst of sunrise, a beam of light shot into the secret room from the left, lifting the darkness. "Come on in, I took the pillowcase down. You can see now."

I entered, slowly, focusing on the details. "I see the piano."

"This is the room where music plays, and lives change, and hearts sing."

"Stop talking weird, or I'm shutting you up in this room."

"You can't lock me inside, there's a button to get out."

"But if the latches are hooked, it wouldn't work."

"Oh, but it does. I tested them one day, and the latches pop just like a soda pop cap flying from a bottle."

"What would you have done if that hadn't worked?"

"There is a window."

"Yeah, but it's smaller than a bread box."

"I didn't think about that. It's good the latches unhook. A long time ago, the people hid slaves in secret rooms during the Civil War."

"Really, do you think so?"

"I don't know, but that's a good story."

"You know, you should stick to the truth if you're going to be a preacher."

"I might be an actor, remember?"

We both laughed, and I touched the top of the upright piano, remembering my friend Skip who played at my daddy's funeral.

Toby patted my shoulder. "This piano's always been here. It must be yours now."

Ding.

I tapped a key.

Ding.

I tapped the same key.

Dong.

I tapped one to my left, and poured myself out like a spilled jar of milk, sobbing and shaking, and letting the sunshine warm my heart. "Toby, I need your help. I have to tell you why. I have to find my … my … my Mahlee. Will you help me? I'm going to need a tour guide."

The Secret to the Answer

I smacked on the peanut butter and syrup sandwich, the piece Toby gave me from his lunch sack. I slurred my words, "I hope my life story hasn't made you change your mind. I'm lost and needing to find Mahlee, and I need to see if we can still be a family. Will you help me? If you just put a hole in your heart, you'll know how I feel."

Toby pinched the crust from the edge of his bread. "I believe you. It's only ... well, you run away from things. You sound a lot like this Mahlee you speak of."

"I'm not like her. I'm not." I swung my feet on the piano bench, thinking hard about pushing Toby from his end. But he did share his lunch with me. I mouthed. "I don't run. I ride the rail. Riding is different from running."

Toby wiped his hands on his pants. "How is riding in boxcars not running?"

I glanced at my red tennis shoes. "I don't use my feet. So it's not running."

"What?" Toby slobbered, and wiped peanut butter from his finger. "You need them to jump into those boxcars. You might fall one day, like your daddy. Gosh, I absolutely hate trains."

"Why do you hate trains? I love the bump-bump of the wheels, and the sights. I've seen mountaintops and orchards. I've rode over rivers, and down slopes. Trains have the best view. Why do you hate trains?"

Toby gulped, "My ma and pa died on a train two years ago when it left the tracks. A dozen people died in the wreck. That's why I live with my grandpa."

I looked at Toby with new eyes. "I'm sorry. You have a hole in your heart, too."

"I do. I miss them so much." Toby sniffled. "So why do you need this Mahlee? She doesn't seem keen on keeping you in her family."

I handed Bingo my crust. "I ... love her, even though she's not lovable."

Toby nodded, "I guess God feels this way toward us. We're not always lovable, but he never stops loving us." He stared off into space, tilting his head.

"Hello, Toby ... come back. So will you help me 'vestigate and find out the secret to why Mahlee keeps running away from me?"

"Sure, but you have to promise me something. You can't tell my grandpa I skip school."

I reached for Toby's hand ready to shake on our deal, when a chug-chug motor sound made me twitch. "Did you hear that?" I looked out the staircase door opening. "I heard something."

"It's probably a car going down the road."

I shook my head, and fear ran through my veins causing me to jump. I told myself to calm down, and snatched the lunch sack from Toby's lap. "Do you have anything else to eat?" I stuck my nose into the bag, reaching for some orange sticks. "Carrots? Who eats raw carrots?"

"I do. They are good for your eyesight. I want to see life. I want to see how things come together. I want to see the good. To see God. I simply want to see."

I tossed the carrots at Bingo's paws, and he snubbed them, too. "You're weird. Weirder than my best friend, Taddy."

"Taddy? I know a Taddy." Toby shook his head. "Naw, it wouldn't be the same one. So do you think I'm weird-weird?"

"No, not weirder than Crush. I mean it as a compliment. In the nicest way."

"Sure you do." Toby jumped to his feet and walked to the window where the sun shot in. "The snow's melting. Maybe the winter will turn to spring faster this year."

Chug-a-lug. Chug-a-lug.

I climbed onto the piano bench arching my neck, trying to see through the foyer, but the angle was off. "I hear a car engine."

Toby darted from the room to the front door. "I hope it's not my grandpa. Maybe he knows. Maybe he's talked to my teacher."

I charged behind him, bumping into him as he stopped by the side window. He pushed me back and put his finger to his mouth. *Shhh!* "There is a car. And it's parked. The driver is pointing his finger at the woman in the passenger seat. She's shaking her head, and he's pounding the steering wheel with his other hand. They're arguing about something."

"Move out of the way."

"No, use the window on the other side of the door."

"Fine. I will." I stuck my nose into the empty spot where glass once sat, sucking in cold air. "Oh no! That's the man from this morning who drove Mahlee here, when she got her gun. When she pretended to shoot me!"

"What? You left the part out about the gun."

"Sorry. I wasn't sure I could trust you. I didn't think you'd help me if you knew there was a gun involved."

"Why are they back?"

"I don't know, but we better hide. They're getting out of the car."

Ducking, we both sat with our backs against the front door. The cla-plunk of doors slamming told me we better hurry.

Mahlee's deep gurgles sounded like fear trapped without an escape. She rattled, "I took care of the girl. I did. No need to return here, the cops might show up."

The man's voice argued, "You're acting like you have more on your plate than keeping our Boss Man happy. I'm glad I checked on you at the hotel. The clerk told me you were taking a walk. Why were you headed back to this house? Tell me. Is it because you're hiding the girl?"

"I was just taking a walk for lunch."

"Sure, you were. In this snow?"

The doorknob jiggled, and Mahlee's voice sent shivers down my spine. "Let me help you with the door."

"Woman, get out of my way. Where is the girl?"

"She's gone. I told you. I shot her."

"Shot her? Then she's not gone. Get your story straight. I didn't hear a gun go off."

"That's when the train rumbled by, so you probably didn't hear it."

Toby and I rushed under the staircase, and he pushed the button causing the staircase-door to close, but it was going at a snail's pace.

"Toby!" I yelled in a whisper. "It's going too slow. They're coming inside."

"Grab onto the rope, the one dangling above your head. Yank on it, and the stairs will come down faster."

Bingo brushed by my leg as I yanked on the rope. I reached for his hair standing up on his back. "Boy, stay in here. Get back." I pulled harder, the stairs lowering.

Toby grabbed Bingo by the neck, keeping him with us, and the stairs snapped into place like Lincoln Logs. We were sealed inside the secret room, hiding from the world.

I sat on the floor under the sloping staircase. "Phew! That was close."

Toby marched up behind me. "I'm a preacher. I should have stayed out in the foyer to reason with them."

"Reason with them? Mahlee has a gun, and her man has one in his belt. They aren't looking for your kind of help."

"But she's the reason you want my help."

"If we talk to them now, you wouldn't get a chance to go to Hollywood or to preach." I glanced around the room. "Darn. I forgot to get my kitty."

"He'll hide. You know how cats are. They sneak around, disappear, and can be right in front of you before you …"

Thud-plunk. Thud-plunk.

We huddled under the stairs, and watched the rope hanging on the makeshift ceiling wiggle. I pointed to the rope. "They're in the house. Listen."

Toby put his ear to the side of the wall. "I can hear them. They're arguing again."

"What are they saying?" I rose, and put my ear on the plaster. "They're fighting like wild dogs."

Toby nodded. "Mahlee is calling him out, saying he robbed a bank. That he tied her up. Now Mahlee is telling him, it's time that he made it right. He can do something about it."

I rubbed my chin. "What does that mean? What else are you hearing?"

"I can't repeat the rest of what she's saying. Seems he and two others took advantage of your Mahlee several years ago. She's being held against her will even now."

"I knew it. I knew it. I knew it."

Shhh!! "I can't listen if you're making more noise than them."

"Why are you hearing what they say and I can't? I'm not hearing one blasted thing." I rubbed both my ears, and remembered Mahlee tossing me into the stairs. "Darn. I had my bad ear on the wall." I twisted my head, placing my right ear up to the cold plaster.

The familiar panic of Mahlee's screams caused me to shudder. She hollered, "What? What are you doing here? We ... we just came back for something."

My hands clinched together, my feet ready to sail from the secret room. "Toby, we have to save her. It sounds like she's talking to someone else."

Toby shook his head. "They want you. Don't you get it? You. And now you've gone and got me mixed up in this. With a criminal record, I may never get my pastor ordination papers."

I slugged Toby in the arm. "What are *ordy-nate* papers?"

"They make me a real pastor."

"Whatever. I don't need your help. I can do this without you."

Pffft! Pffft!

Toby hugged me like a brother, shaking. "Those were gunshots. Someone ... someone is shooting."

I almost embraced him, but instead pushed Toby away. "Listen. See if you hear anyone talking."

"I can't hear a thing. Nothing. No talking. No yelling. Nothing. Just us."

We squatted on the floor, and Toby hugged Bingo. I rocked like Mahlee does when she's lost in her world without answers. I shivered, and touched Toby, who jerked. He shot me some questions. "Do you think they left? What is going on? Would they shoot you? Or me?"

I blinked my eyes hard. "I don't know. Her man might. He sounded pretty angry."

Toby closed his eyes, whispering. "Lord, keep us safe." He shook his head, opened his eyes and announced. "We have to wait. We can't let anyone know we're in here. Give them time to leave."

**

The sun hiding behind the trees caused the secret room to grow shadowy, and Bingo danced in circles like a doggy needing to run to the woods for a potty break. I peeked out the window. "The street lanterns are on. It's late, and we haven't heard anything out front in hours."

Toby sighed. "I know, and we're going to have to chance opening the door. My grandpa will come in from work, and he'll send a search party if I'm not home for supper."

I moved to the side of the piano, while Toby tapped the button on the wall. The staircase rose upward, allowing the musty smell of cold air to rush inside the room. I whispered, "I don't hear anything."

Toby motioned for me to wait, which I didn't, and I stepped next to him. He held my arm. "You don't listen too well. Do you?"

I tiptoed into the foyer, moving ahead of Toby. "Oh my! It's White Beard. He ... he isn't moving. His neck is bent backwards. No! Not my cat!" I rushed to him, kneeling on the floor, cradling my kitty. "I love you. You're mine. Or you were mine. Who did this? Why? Why?" I sobbed tears bigger than the snowflakes. "God, why did you take my kitty? If you take one more thing from me, I'm going to die."

Toby hurried to my side. "God didn't take your cat. Either Mahlee did or the man."

I shrieked. "What do you know?" I turned on the ugly words. "My Mahlee would never kill my cat. It had to be her man. He won't get away with this."

Toby shuffled his feet, waving his arm at me, but his words would not come. He coughed, choking.

Argh! Argh!

I shouted. "What? What do you want?"

"It's … it's a body, over by the fireplace."

"A body? No! Is it Mahlee?"

"You best come and see."

I charged into the room, skidding to a stop, clutching my lifeless cat. "It's Mahlee's man. He's dead, isn't he?"

Toby loomed next to me. "Watch the blood on the floor. Don't step in it. What are we going to do now? I have to call the police."

I twitched, and my heart pounded like a hammer inside my chest. "We can't, not until I can get gone. I have to find out if Mahlee did this. I have to disappear, to pretend I'm gone, and to search for answers.

"Then we need to pick up the house, and remove any sign of your being here. Then I'll call, disguise my voice, and tell the police about the body."

"We need to bury my kitty, and the little redbird, too." My sobs trickled like a waterfall of sorrow, dipping a lightning rod of pain into my soul.

"Can't it wait?"

"No, not one more second."

"Fine, I'll help you. We'll have two funerals in the backyard."

Sniffling, I hugged my kitty. "I'm going to miss you. I've never had a cat before. You were the best pet ever."

Toby whispered to the smoke in the fireplace as if he thought I didn't or couldn't hear. "If I'd known this was how the day was going to unfold, I would've stayed in school. I'm mixed up in something, and I'm not so sure I like knowing Mahlee is a murderer."

I shouted. "She's not a killer. I'm going to prove it."

The Pearl Holds the Answer

Toby and me made our plan, and buried White Beard and the bird in little graves by the gazebo in the backyard. I marked both spots with pieces of broken logs from the porch.

"Bye, Kitty. Bye, little redbird."

Toby called to me from the porch. "Hurry. I've got to get home, and I'm moving you to a place where no one will look for you."

"What? I have the secret room. There are quilts in the side stairs closet. I can wrap up in them, and hide next to the piano."

"No, it's too dangerous. The cops will search this entire house for clues. They'll probably come to my house and ask questions, too. My grandpa could tell them how I come over here to practice my preaching. I'll have to lie about today, and this will be my first time to lie for someone. I'll have to repent for saying I don't know how a dead man got in this house."

"I'm not making you lie. I'm asking you to wait until you say the truth. Give me time to figure something out." I hurried to him. "I'm staying here."

"You are not."

"I am."

Toby followed me into the house, growling. "Look, I told you I'd help, but it's my way, or not at all. I'm the one going out on a limb for you, but I have faith that somewhere inside of those overalls is a girl who can, and will make her life matter."

I twirled around. "Stop judging me. I am making my life matter. I'm getting my Mahlee back. She may not be my birth mama, but somehow God let her into my life, and I'm keeping her. He can't have her. And neither can anyone else. I'm sure she's not involved in this."

Toby marched beside me as we moved to the front room, where I stared at the man we'd covered with one of the quilts. Toby touched my shoulder. "Stop whining. I've got a brilliant idea."

Tap-a-tap.

I tugged on Toby's arm. "Was that the kitchen door?"

We both spun around facing the foyer, waiting for the shadow padding on the hardwood floors to show. A voice called. "Hey, Shoelace. It's Crush. We've been looking for Bingo all day. Have you seen him?" He bustled into the room, stopping like a statue tilting over in a cemetery. "Oh my! Tell me that's not another dead body."

Toby wiped his nose. "It's complicated."

Crush inched closer. "If Shoelace is in the picture, I'm sure it is."

I growled. "This is not my fault."

Toby defended me. "It's not. We … we don't know how it happened."

Crush leaned over to look under the quilt. "It's another one of Carl's men."

Toby explained, "I came in to practice my sermons, and two people came inside, and we hid. The gun went off, and we found this … this man lying here."

Crush shook his noggin. "So that's all you've got. There's more to this story. Cough it up."

I swallowed hard. "It's all we're telling you."

Crush shouted, "I'm getting out of here. Where is Bingo?"

I answered Crush like he was asking only me. "Bingo ran across the road to the woods earlier. He was cooped up in here

154

with us, and was ready to go out, and we let him. So he's not here."

Crush ambled over to me. "So you're over-explaining about a dog you just met, a mutt you barely know, to convince me of … what?"

Toby stepped between Crush and me. "She's just nervous."

"Why? What's to be nervous about?"

I stuttered. "I'm not nervous. I'm … I'm not anxious either, or scared, or worried, or upset, or …"

Toby put his hand over my mouth. "Enough. You're not helping." He turned to Crush. "She's upset about the dead man."

I licked Toby's fingers.

"Shoelace, stop acting like a toddler." Toby wiped his fingers on his shirt.

Crush peered at me. "What are you two up to?"

Together we answered, "Nothing."

I rattled off more explanations, a revised version of the day while Toby gave up and sat on the suitcase by the wall, hugging his Bible. I inched up to Crush. "I can tell you what happened. This man came in here, and I was hiding. He argued with someone, and then I heard the shots."

Crush wiped his mouth. "You show up in our town, and now there are two dead mean. In less than a day. Who are you working with? Is it Archie? Or someone else? And why are you not calling the police? How long has this man been lying on this floor?"

Toby stumbled over. "Maybe we should pray."

I slapped his shoulder. "Praying isn't going to bring this man back."

Crush put both of his hands on Toby's shoulders. "Toby, what's gotten into you? We don't even know this girl, and so far she's caused your grandpa trouble, and now you ... you're in a room with a dead man, with her."

I squinted my eyes. "You're grandpa? Who is your grandpa?"

Toby slurred his words. "He's Marion Kane Raike, and he's the syrup man here. He owns the factory west of town and he also makes jams and sorghum. Back in '27, my grandpa traded some sacks of potatoes with a hobo for his syrup recipe, and then opened a business."

"You are Marion Kane's grandson? You? Oh goodness, now I've gotten in deeper than deep, and the dent on my life isn't going away anytime soon."

Toby smiled. "I knew who you were. I saw you when you were asleep at the hospital."

"Why? Why didn't you tell me?"

"I wanted you to like me because my name is Toby, not because I'm Marion Kane's grandson. I don't have many friends, since I'm always talking of going to Hollywood and also being a preacher."

Crush bolted at Toby. "Really? Do you think this is the time to talk about your family history? Remember, there's some explaining to do about how this body got on the floor. I'm not so sure Shoelace didn't have something to do with his death."

"I didn't. I was hiding."

Toby took up for me. "She was with me. We were both hiding when two people charged into the house, fighting." Toby turned to me. "We have to include Crush. We have to tell him what's going on, and we have to do it fast. I have to get home before I'm missed. We won't be having church at the cemetery tonight anyway, and I have to make sure my grandpa doesn't come over here."

Crush stomped in a circle like he did the day before. "I wish someone would tell me what in the heck is going on here. My boys are frightened about the first murder, and now this. They wanted me to bring Bingo to the river, to have a watchdog with us. Now, you two are up to something, and I'm ready to knock you both out. Tell me what's going on here."

I sat on the floor, and Toby sat across from me. Toby patted the wooden slats. "Crush, sit down. Let me catch you up. You have to promise to believe me, to trust me on this, and not to rat on us."

Crush crossed his legs, joining us on the floor. "Toby, tell me all of it, or I'm going to get your grandpa."

Toby shared the pieces of my story with Crush, about losing my daddy, my grandma, and the days I rode the rail. Broken pieces of my life that didn't sound real. He jumped to the part of how someone might be holding Mahlee against her will. I got lost in his words, and squinted, staring at a small white bead near the dead man's boot at the edge of the quilt.

I reached to my side, stretching out like a worm, ignoring Toby and Crush. "What's this?"

Toby hollered in a preacher tone. "Shoelace, I'm trying to convince Crush you're a nice person, with a not-so nice family. At least, pay attention."

"I will. And my family is nice. Sometimes."

Toby tapped his knee with his knuckles. "We don't know what Mahlee's tangled up in, or if she's in danger."

I added my two cents. "I'm sure she's in trouble, and I have to help." I grabbed the white bead. "It looks like a pearl."

Crush rolled his eyes. "It's no pearl. It's just a pebble, and you're going to owe me for this. I'll help hide you, but you're going to become a ghost. My boys need to think you're gone. They aren't good with secrets, and maybe, Toby and me will help you investigate your Mahlee story. I hope you're telling me the truth."

I folded my arms. "I am telling the truth. Besides, being a ghost sounds like a great way to sneak around. I've always wanted to be a ghost."

Toby raised his voice. "You're a ghost in a town full of ghosts. Many of our people are not who they seem to be in daylight."

Crush laughed, bellowing out his creepy words. "Watch out for the ghosts in Jefferson. The ones on the railroad tracks. The ones in the alley, and especially the ones at the cemetery."

"You're just trying to scare me."

"I am not. But they sure will."

"Stop it. You don't scare me."

Toby clapped his hands. "Stop it. Both of you. Shoelace, we're moving you to the Jewish synagogue. Remember, we do have a dead body here to deal with."

Crush echoed his words. "It's pretty warm in the basement since there's heat in the building. And we can slip in and get you tucked in for the night."

I touched his arm. "Why the change of heart? Why are you on my side now?"

"I'm on my side, and I know what it's like to be alone. It's not your fault you get in the way more than most. At least, I hope I'm right."

I giggled, not because Crush was being funny, but because no matter what I try to do, getting in the way comes easy.

Toby corralled us. "He changed his heart, because he knows Jesus would do the right thing, and we have to mirror Jesus."

Crush scowled. "It's hard being friends with a preacher."

Toby spoke up. "Let's get going. Get your satchel. I'll put the suitcase by the wall, and I've got the newspaper. Crush, grab that jar."

I tucked the pearl into my satchel, thinking about if Mahlee could be a killer. One second, I thought she was, and then the next I didn't. Either way, I felt safer with Crush and Toby than with her right now. I quizzed them. "Where's the synagogue?"

Toby pointed toward the backyard. "The building is a few blocks up the hill, next to my church, not far from the library, or Susan's house, or from downtown."

"Susan's house? That's where Lizzy Beth lives."

Crush smarted off. "I bet you're related to her, too."

I didn't answer, because telling him I had a half-sister might make it worse. I'll keep my sister secret tucked inside my heart like a pearl.

Pam Kumpe

It Doesn't Look Like Rain

Crush clunked in front of us in the road as we walked away from the house. "Why am I carrying this jar?"

Toby responded with a firm tone. "I didn't want my grandpa's milk jar to be found. Just toss it in the bushes." Toby grabbed the jar and sent it sailing.

Crush gazed into the sky. "It's gonna rain, and this snow's melting. Those clouds tell me they're ready to dump water on us. I hope it's a light rain. The water rises near the Polk Street Bridge first, which is too close to my house, too close for safety."

I stuck my tongue at Crush since I was strolling behind him. "You think you know more than anyone else, don't you?" I shouted at his hind side.

He spun around and stepped next to me. "Not more than some, but more than you." He chuckled like a laughing hyena wearing blue jeans.

I picked on Crush. "So what's your plan? What will you be when you grow up?"

"I am grown up." He kicked a clump of snow like he was playing kick ball.

"You are not. You're a boy."

Crush grabbed me by my shoulders. "You need to learn some manners."

"Me? Look at how you love to manhandle me. Using force isn't the way to treat a lady."

He let go, shoving me. "Lady? You are a child wearing red tennis shoes, with nappy blonde hair, dirty fingernails, and wearing overalls like a boy."

160

I glanced at my fingers. "I haven't had time to take a bath, or a place to take one." I clicked my tongue on my teeth, ready to hand Crush a lashing, but the truth he spoke hurt.

Toby tapped my arm with the newspaper. "I like your shoes, and the overalls. You fit the part of a hobo. You have hobo style."

I smiled. "If I didn't know better I'd think you were practicing your acting on me."

Clapping his hand on the back of the Bible, Toby laughed. "You get the award for seeing right through me."

Crush stomped ahead, moving faster than us. "We only have two more blocks to go."

Toby skipped up next to Crush, leaving me in their shadows. "Crush, we need to call the police as soon as we get inside the basement. There's a phone on the wall by the stairs."

"Hello, you are talking like I'm not here." I pushed my way between their shoulders. "So I'm a ghost now?"

Crush snarled, "You are to me. If you want to live, you better stay in the shadows, and never let anyone see you in the day. At least, not until these murders are cleared up." He gave me a stare and his green eyes cut right into my brain.

"You think I know something about these murders. Well, I don't. I only know Mahlee knows something, and was nearby on both of them."

Toby pulled my arm, stopping me in a snowy patch. "Both of them? Why did you say that?"

Stuttering, I cleared up my words. "I meant she was at the second one. I didn't mean to say the first one." I glanced back at the two-story yellow house with the body inside. "Are you sure we are safe?"

Toby pulled my face back forward. "You will be. We can pretend this is a scene in the movie where the hero gets ready to solve the murders."

"I'm a hero?"

Crush cackled like a rooster who was mixed up on what time it was, bobbing his head like one. "Ha-ha! She's no hero."

I pelted Crush with my satchel. "Stop making fun of me. I'm not going to put up with it."

"I don't think a ghost has any choice."

Toby corrected both of us. "You two act like best friends."

We snorted together in the cold sunset. "We're not."

Crush ordered, "Up there. We just have to go one more block, and then left on Market."

Toby announced in the wind. "I do know the way. I live here, too."

Chug-a-lug. Tip-a-lug. Chug-a-lug.

The yellow lights on the car inched down the hill, and Crush pushed me into a bush, and he and Toby tumbled over me. I pushed them off of me. "It's only a car. It's not like they're after us.

Toby reminded me. "You can't be seen by anyone."

The car wriggled through the ruts in the road, pulling into a driveway.

I dusted the snow from my knees. "I'm not someone you can just toss away, Crush. You treat me like I'm an intruder. I didn't mean to hit the truck with my face, or be at your house, or step over a dead man at the river, or find the one at my grandma's house today. It's just … trouble follows me. I can't seem to shake it."

"Exactly! That's why we're getting you out of the way. I somehow expect you're up to no good, but Toby … he has faith in you. He's sure you're a good person. But I think you're a person who is up to no good."

"So you're helping Toby, not me?"

"Exactly. He's my friend."

Toby hushed Crush with taps on his arm. "Enough. Crush, you don't have to let all of your thoughts fall out. We can give her the benefit of being in the wrong place at the wrong time."

I shouted. "Exactly!"

We kept time with each other's steps, and not one of us spoke the rest of the way. Toby pointed, and we darted behind the synagogue, sliding on icy patches in the shade. Toby skidded in his loafers. "There's the basement entrance. Crush keeps a chain linked on the latch, but it's not locked. It's designed to keep the daytime ghosts away before we hold our tours at night."

Puzzled, I ran my hand through my hair. "Toby, should a preacher boy be hanging out where ghosts lurk?"

Toby unraveled the chain. "We don't have real ghosts. The boys pretend, remember? It helps them put food on the table."

"I know. I'm only teasing."

Crush shook his head. "Watch your head, the pipes are low until you get to the other end of the basement. The synagogue is built on the side of the hill, so the ceiling's lower at some parts."

We stepped inside the darkness, the smell of dirt reminded me of being inside a coffin. "Did either of you think to bring a lantern? Or a flashlight?"

Crush spouted an eerie whistle. *Ooowee! Ooowee!*

"Stop that, Crush."

Crush bumped me. "I'm not whistling."

Toby giggled like an owl hooting in the dark. "It's me. I was trying to scare you."

I swung in the dark, unable to touch him. "Then stop. You did scare me."

Crush announced, "Here you go. Let there be light."

Slwalop-click.

"Light? There's electricity in here?"

Toby nodded. "Yes, the stairs over there lead to a door, one you're never to use. We keep our suitcases for our tours over behind a stack of old cradles and desks. No one comes down here, unless they're hunting for light bulbs."

I skipped to the suitcases. "So are these the ones you keep getting, Crush?"

He sighed. "Yes, we don't know why, and they're always empty."

"You left the other one at my grandma's house."

"I'll have to get it later, once the body's gone, and everything quiets down."

Toby patted me on the back. "Stay here. There's some old curtains stacked by the light bulbs. You can use them for bedding. There's a bathroom in the corner."

I lost my footing, wobbled backwards, and stumbled over a stack of old newspapers. "I don't want to stay here alone. I don't want to be a ghost. I don't … I can't. I'm just a kid."

Crush used his deep teen voice on me. "Now, you're a smart kid, one who knows her way around towns. We will keep you with food, and check on you in the morning. The cops will be all over your grandma's house, so you need to stay here."

Toby plodded up to me. "Let me pray for you."

I smarted off. "Will it be a real prayer, or your acting prayer?"

Crush answered, "Toby only prays real prayers to God. He's not playing when it comes to talking to the Man upstairs."

I apologized. "I'm sorry. Kids don't usually pray for other kids."

Toby took one of my hands, and Crush squeezed the other. I glanced at Toby, whose kindness seemed real, not fake, and then I gawked at Crush, tilting my head. "So do you pray?"

"I've been known to. Just ask Timmons and Tak. They love to pray and have me tell them how ma and pa are in heaven with God running things."

I felt a lump fly up in my throat, and figured God could help with some answers. "So pray already."

Toby whispered, "Dear Jesus, we thank you for having a plan for our lives, even when plans seem to get lost in the secret rooms of despair. Be with our friend, Shoelace. Be with Mahlee, too, and if she's guilty of anything may she turn herself in to the police. In the meantime, keep Shoelace safe tonight. Amen."

I didn't have to open my eyes, since praying with them closed doesn't come easy for me. I sent up a whispered prayer. "God, keep Mahlee from shooting anyone else tonight, until I can find her. Please."

Crush whispered in my ear, "See, you think she's guilty. Don't you?"

I whined. "I don't know. I hope not."

Toby and Crush slipped into the shadows outside, and the clanking told me the chain was hanging on the latch of the door. I rattled the door leading to the side yard, and jiggled the handle. "Hey, how will I get out? Hey … you have me locked inside even with it hanging over the latch." I raised my voice to a ghostly scream. "I can't get out. I can't."

Toby's whisper drifted through the crack in the hinge. "All you have to do is push."

I shoved the door hard with a thrust, and tumbled to the cold icy snow. I wiped my hands, and stood up. "Oh, so you didn't lock me inside."

Crush thundered to the road next to the towering tree near the front of the synagogue. "I have never in my life known such a scaredy-cat of a ghost." He shouted in the street like a chicken hawk, which was ready to snatch up a meal. "Why can't we have a quiet night in Jefferson?"

Toby shook his head. "He's making too much noise for my liking."

I ran after Crush. "I'm sorry. I'm not brave. I don't have anyone who even cares if I live, so if I came up missing no one would care."

Toby called me back to the hill. "Come on, you two are going to bring the neighbors into the road, and then we'll have some explaining to do. I have to get to supper. My grandpa is going to have my hide."

Chug-a-lug. Chug-a-lug.

Orange lights careened at us from around the block, spinning on the ice. Crush pushed me, "Get out of the way. Hurry, run."

I charged to the yard, rolling to my side. "Crush, get out of the road."

Crush spouted out brave words. "He has room. He can go around me. I'm on the side."

Toby bolted to him. "Crush, stop playing chicken with the car."

Crush twisted, raising his hands like he was about to say something, but …

Ka-splat. Thug!

Pride and Joy

"Oh no!" I screamed like an eleven-year-old, and not like a ghost.

Toby hightailed it to Crush who curled up like a snail under the bumper of the fancy car. It skidded close, but not near enough to cause one scratch on him. Toby knelt, folding his hands. "God, we thank you for protecting Taggart from certain death."

I wrinkled my nose, breaking my stride, bumping into Toby. "Taggart? Who is he?"

Crush stuck his nose in the air, and emerged from his snail curl. "I'm Taggart, that's my given name."

"Goodness, I thought Annie Grace Kree hurt my ears, but Taggart is worse. I like Crush much better than Taggart." I rubbed my belly holding in my giggles, thankful for no bleeding or broken bones on the snail-boy.

The man behind the wheel swung open his driver's door, whizzing to investigate his bumper caught in the hollow of the tree.

I wailed, prancing up behind him. "Sir, you care more about your car than my friend, Crush. You nearly hit him with your car." I sucked in the freezing air, shivering, spitting my words. "A decent man would check on a person before a tree."

Toby stepped beside me. "Amen."

I muttered my complaint to the backside of the man's coat. "Are you listening to me?"

The wrinkled man swung around, pointing his finger at me, his jacket swinging open, revealing a chain to a pocket watch. The chain draped over his pooching belly. He growled,

"This is a steel top, two-door 1947 Cadillac. I've only had it for a week. I bought this beauty in Texarkana, and now look what you three have done."

"Texarkana? Are you from there?" I squealed, like I'd just met someone who might have known my grandma.

"No, I live here. I own the Clementine Plantation west of town on Highway 49." The squatty man wearing his Sunday suit on a Tuesday night ran his hand over the injured black car.

"It's just a car, sir."

He bore into my face like a monster loose in the woods. "A car? Maybe to you, but not to me. I've worked hard. This is my pride and joy."

Boom. Boom. Boom.

"Did you hear that?"

The wrinkled man checked under the bumper of his car without answering me. I listened, knowing I heard thumping.

Kabam.

I jumped, twisting in a circle to find Toby christening the front of the man's car with his Bible. "Sir, there's a boy in the front seat, and he's leaning sideways. You better check on him. He should be your pride and joy."

Crush motioned to me, waving his hand, shooing me off. "Scram. Get out of here, you need to hide."

I ignored him, and trudged to the passenger side of the car, peeking inside, hearing booming sounds coming from the back. I paused, and the noise stopped again. I shook my head, guessing it was nothing.

I pulled on the passenger door handle. "Hey, this door won't budge." The shadows of sunset cast darkness like death, and I couldn't see into the car for the reflection. "This kid's not moving. Please tell me he's not dead." I put my hands to my ears, spinning in a circle, crying and weeping. "No more death."

Toby tugged on my shirt. "Come with me. Come now." He whispered in my good ear. "It's imperative that you become a ghost, and do it now."

I sobbed. "But, it's a kid. Crush caused this accident by being stupid in the road."

Crush jerked on the passenger door. "It's jammed, and won't open."

I yelled, "No kidding."

The man pushed Crush out of the way, wrestling with the door. "It won't open. That's my ... that's my..."

A woman waving her arms showed up from the house across the street, along with other ladies in skirts and men in straw hats. The woman announced, "I reported the accident. I hope everyone's ... everyone ... is ..."

Bweep-bip. Bweep-bip.

The woman pointed. "Oh wait, there's the ambulance now."

Toby stepped up to the woman. "We're all good here, except the boy in the car."

She twirled Toby around looking him over. "Toby Raike, are you hurt? Are you?"

"No, ma'am. I'm just a witness."

The driver hollered to Toby. "I know your grandpa. He's probably wondering where you are. You best be getting home."

Toby swallowed, "Yes, sir. I'm headed there shortly."

I put my back against the synagogue wall, hiding behind a hedge that was full of prickly brown arms. The ambulance rolled up, shining its lights on the side of the car, and the wrinkled man crawled across the front seat to get the boy. He cradled the lifeless boy, running over to the ambulance.

Toby rushed to their side. "Can I pray for him before I leave?"

The ambulance man didn't respond, but the man who belonged to the boy did. "Get out of the way. You kids shouldn't be playing in the road. I've got to get to Soda Street. Seems I've lost another work hand to a shooting. And now this?"

The boy whose brown hair stuck above the sheet murmured, and the grouchy man touched his head. "Son, are you? Are you hurt?" The ambulance man blocked my view for the most part, but I could see him using doctor tools.

The boy answered from the ambulance, "My head hurts." He listened to the boy's heart, and peeked at body parts under the sheet, checking to make sure he wasn't broken.

I swallowed hard, and scooted up to Crush who was standing by the tree. "Are you hurt? Anywhere?"

Whap!

I yelled. "You don't have to slug me."

"It made me feel better." He scowled. "I shouldn't have played around in the road, especially since I'm responsible for Timmons and Tak, and the other five boys. I'm just so stupid sometimes."

I touched his arm. "We all can be. Even me."

He smiled. "I already knew you could be."

We giggled in the midst of the sadness, in the midst of the little boy's pain, in the midst of our watching and wondering.

Toby ran up to us. "Did you hear what he said? That's Mr. Carl, and he's headed to … to your grandma's house, Shoelace. Someone called the police. They must have found the body, or Carl wouldn't know anything about where to look."

"That's Carl?" I shivered, ready to become a ghost for real. We huddled together behind the tree, and I offered my advice. "I'm going inside the basement. I'm not coming out until you let me know I can." I jingled the chain, forcing it from the latch, and squeezed into the basement room, switching the light off, wishing to sit in the dark alone, to think.

Clink. Clank. Jink.

The noise on the door told me either Toby or Crush put the chain over the door, to make things appear secure. I slumped to the floor, sitting on my heels. I heard the sirens blare and fade, and the talking outside ended.

Toby and Crush most likely disappeared to their homes, and I prayed the boy in the car had only a bruise. "God, I hope you can see me sitting here in the dark. Running away isn't turning out so good. Should I stay here and try to save my Mahlee? Or should I go home? Give me a sign."

Tingle. Jink. Clink.

I stopped praying. "What? Who's there? Toby? Crush?" I fumbled for the light switch, and turned it on. "Who's there?"

Clank. Jink.

I pushed on the door, and slammed my shoulder on the wood with a bam, real hard, shoving, and cramming my body against the door. I hollered, "Toby? Crush? Are you out there? The door won't budge. The chain's hung again, and I can't get out."

A shuffle on the other side sent tremors through my bones.

A voice seeped under the door, a muffled edgy tone like a wisp of smoke with claws. "What are you doing inside this basement? Did those boys hurt you? Are they forcing you to stay here?"

I shuddered, wondering, and worried that Toby and Crush locked me inside this time.

The jingle of the chain rattled. "Are you in there? Hello?" I mumbled to myself. "Why would they do that? Why?"

The clanking of the chain sent chills up my spine like a ghost was about to be released into the room. I threw up, choking on leftover peanut butter, a sour taste that burned my throat. I cried, "Toby? Crush? Where are you? And why did you lock that chain?"

The Escape to Pretend

I clutched my satchel, storming to the stairs, jumping on them. Reaching for the knob, I twisted with every ounce of strength left in me, but tumbled to my knees when my fingers slipped. "Open up. Open up." I twisted, turning and pulling hard on the knob, and I wobbled, losing my grasp. I tumbled backwards down the stairs to the damp dirt. "Darn ole door. I have to get out of here."

Soaring up the stairs, I twisted and twisted and sighed, unable to make the door budge. I plopped my head forward. *Thud.* I rested my head on the wood, unable to hear the voice outside the basement, but sensing fear crawl up my legs like goose bumps.

Creeeeaaaakkk.

The door swung into the room, away from me. "No way, I should have pushed the door? It was unlocked all along?"

I skittered into the darkness, bumping into a counter, feeling of the flat part, sliding my hand over it, finding a faucet at a sink. I extended my hands out like a blind person trying to get to another wall, to get to an opening to somewhere. My shoes shuffled from what felt like smooth tile to rippled carpet. "So a synagogue has a kitchen? And carpet?" I shook my head and stubbed my toe on something, then touched a tall wooden chair. It had a padded seat.

Reaching forward, I felt of a slick table. I ambled to my right, slamming into a wall. *Ouch!* I ran my hand along the plaster, and my fingers sensed hard objects like cold stones, but they were plastered to the wall. "Is this a fireplace?"

Clunk-clunk.

"Rats, I've knocked something over." Fumbling in the dark, making my way over to another wall, but not knowing where my steps were taking me, I scooted my shoes ahead anyway.

Bam.

Ouch! "Another wall?" I groped forward, knocking over furniture.

Crash-clap.

More groping. More fidgeting. More touching.

"Is this a lamp?" I picked up the neck, setting it on the flat part of what felt like a table, the one my knee plowed into. I found a light switch and lit up the room. "Finally, I can see."

I focused my eyes on the stones on the wall, which turned out to be bricks and yes, a fireplace. Above the mantel hung a picture of a lady from a million years ago, with a wide Easter-type hat on her head. She must have liked blue. I bet she enjoyed watching me stumble in the dark.

Across the room, on the other side was another fireplace, and in the center of the room was a huge table the size of a small fishing boat. It sat below shimmering crystal glass dangles on a chandelier. Eight empty chairs surrounded the table. "This doesn't look like a synagogue."

I rushed to the door near the first fireplace, and twisted the knob, swinging the door wide, ready to step into somewhere, to find an outside door.

Jingle-Jingle.

I jumped back and the female ghost rattled her jail keys at me. She floated at me, soaring into the room, pulling my arm, and asking me questions. "What are you doing in here? And why were you in the basement?"

"It's a long story, the chain wasn't supposed to be locked. Was it locked?"

"It was latched shut with a padlock. I saw Toby and Crush running behind the synagogue."

I realized my ghost was none other than Susan, Lizzy Beth's adoptive mama. I squealed, "Did they lock me in there?"

"It seems so."

"How do you know? Were you spying on us?"

"No, my neighbor who lives across from the synagogue phoned me to tell me about the wreck. I live two houses from her, down Market, and she keeps the neighbors in the loop." Susan put her keys in her pocket. "So tell me what you are up to. You are trespassing, you know."

"Well, we were playing in the snow, and they showed me the basement, and then the car crashed into the tree, and then they must have forgotten I was inside." I swallowed hard, trying to convince her with my sad eyes.

"Those boys hold ghost tours here with the children and scare them. We've run them off plenty of times, but they keep bringing suitcases inside, and hiding them in the basement."

I glanced around the dining room with two fireplaces. "This doesn't seem like a synagogue."

"This is the quarters where the nuns used to stay. There's a couple of bedrooms upstairs."

"Nuns? I thought this was a church for Jewish people."

"It is. Or it was. It's been a school, and a synagogue, and for a time the Catholics used it. Now it's an empty building and people practice dramas here, and the town folk hold plays to bring in tourists. It's … it's like a playhouse or a theater." She pointed across the way to another part of the building. "The synagogue is through that hallway, and there's a double door entrance out back, too."

"Well, thanks for filling me in. I have to go now." I swung my satchel over my shoulder and started to leave, but offered up one more question to Susan. "So who gave you keys to get in?"

She shook her keys inside of her skirt pocket. "I clean the building and cook for the actors when they practice. I simply let myself in."

I stepped toward the entryway to leave. "I have to go now. I have to be somewhere."

"Stop, little lady. We need to talk. You're going to freeze out in the weather. Come home and spend the night. No need for you to go back to the house on Soda Street, no need for you to shiver in this cold when you can spend the night with us. I expect you're passing through, and passing through has gotten you stuck here in the snow."

I paused, my heart tired, my feet aching, my joy sapped. "I could stay one night. One night to rest before I pack up and leave this town."

"So you are passing through?" Susan rattled her keys.

"I am ... I'm passing from house to house it seems, after landing here."

Susan touched my shoulder. "Marion shared your little mishap with me, when he had lunch at the café today. He comes by for my cornbread and bologna sandwiches."

My tummy growled, and I licked my lips. "I'm sort of getting hungry. What's for supper?"

"Chicken and dumplings."

I patted my stomach. "Maybe I should go. I don't want to be a bother."

"No bother. I don't want you in this cold or in that basement. You didn't get to Jefferson by accident. God brought you to our town and you need a warm bed, a bath, and a hot meal. Besides, Lizzy Beth hasn't stopped talking about you. She's enthralled with you, and doesn't quite understand why you're not at Wheelock." Susan lifted my chin. "Why ... why are you on your own?"

I inhaled, my breath backing up in my lungs. "I was visiting Wheelock with my grandma, with Tin Can Mahlee, and my best friend, Taddy." I coughed. "Well, he used to be my best friend."

"Best friends do have times when being friends is like sadness tucked inside of a back pocket. When you revive the friendship you discover the reason you stopped being friends will be forgotten."

"I'm kind of mad at Taddy. Maybe we'll make up someday."

"Where is your grandma?"

"She's in the grave. She died when we left Wheelock for Texarkana, and her heart gave out on the train. I'm pretty much alone now, except for..." I didn't finish my sentence. I couldn't let Susan know anything about the last few days.

She swiped my hair out of my eyes. "Life's fallen in on you, my sweet girl. Isn't there someone who is looking for you?"

"No, not one person. I'm … I'm … used to being on the rail. I'm made for being alone."

"No, you're made to be with a family. You don't really ride boxcars, do you?"

"Yes, I do when I'm not running into the side of pickup trucks." I sighed. "It's been a sad day, too. My cat died. Everything I touch seems to die."

"You've touched the heart of my Lizzy Beth, and she's never forgotten you. She's thriving. She's made our house a home since we adopted her. The accident shook her up—well, me, too." Susan gasped, her hand covering her mouth. "Sorry, it's been hard. My husband's eyes were scorched in a kitchen fire at the café, but he may see again."

I found myself patting her arm. "I'm sorry. I didn't mean to make you sad."

"Sad is a part of life, but joy comes in the morning, and in unexpected meetings. That's why you're coming to our house. We can use some laughter. Lizzy Beth would be happy to have a friend over for the night."

I shuffled my feet, and shifted my satchel on my shoulder, nodding a yes. My heart beat with hope, but my feet wanted to run. I was afraid to go, but more afraid to stay behind. I needed to see Lizzy Beth, one more time. Even if it's for just tonight.

Pretend Family

Near the front yard at Lizzy Beth's house, I ran my fingers along the picket fence. "Bingo? What are you doing on the porch?" I rushed through the gate, hurrying to the steps, and I ruffled his ears. "Good boy."

He licked my eyes, nose, and forehead.

Susan patted him on the head. "Bingo lives everywhere. He's the town dog. Did you know he loves ice cream?"

"I've heard." Chuckling, I trailed behind Susan, while Bingo sidestepped with me into the tiny living room.

Tootle-too-twang. Twang-too.

Lizzy Beth sat on a man's lap, but I couldn't tell who he was because his head was wrapped in a white bandage. Lizzy Beth turned to look at me. "Shoelace, what … what are you doing?" Her toddler voice cracked with excitement, and the man playing the harmonica stopped blowing into the instrument. She patted his arm. "Papa. It's Shoelace."

"I remember a Shoelace. She's a pretty blonde we met at Wheelock Academy. She stuck out like a shiny penny as the prettiest girl there, besides you, Lizzy Beth." He held out his hand, sitting in his chair, as Lizzy Beth ran to me. "I'm Boyd. I'm the eyes and ears of this house."

I smiled, not sure if he was joking or being serious. I shook his hand. "Hi, sir. Glad to meet you—again."

Susan clapped her palms in fast taps. "Mr. Boyd's eyes are healing nicely. We just know he'll see every color of the rainbow soon."

Boyd rubbed the gauze on his eyes. "I'll be happy to see anything. But I can play the harmonica without eyes, thankfully."

A woman in a blue skirt and matching top, wearing her hair pinned back, came into the room holding a potholder. "Mam, the dumplings are ready."

Susan nodded, pointing at me. "We'll eat in a bit, but first this one needs a bubble bath."

I laughed. "That's two bubble baths this week. I could get used to this."

Lizzy Beth skipped around me, following me as her mama tugged on my arm. Susan pointed to the door at the end of the hall. "Shoelace, the bathroom's in there. Let's get scrubbed up, and then we can have a nice meal."

Lizzy Beth danced in circles, ready to play. "Can she sit by me at the table?"

Susan patted her daughter's head. "Sure, let's get her spotless first."

I giggled. "You just want me decontaminated."

Susan let a burp and giggle escape all at once. "Sorry, that struck me as funny. I'm over the top when it comes to having everything clean."

Lizzy Beth kissed my face. "I love you, Shoelace."

I wrapped my contaminated arms around Lizzy Beth, engulfing her in tears of happiness. But laced in layers of sadness. "Lizzy Beth, you're the sweetest girl ever. You have a voice like an angel."

Boyd hollered from the other side of the wall. "She's our gift. We are so fortunate to have her. I hate that I've lost my sight, but I saw her shiny black hair, tan skin, and those marble chocolate eyes before …" He choked. "I can't wait to see her smile again. We are so grateful that we were able to adopt her."

Lizzy Beth jumped like a rabbit. "I love my new mama and new papa." She bounced on her toes. "Can Shoelace stay? Can she?"

Susan shook her head. "She's here tonight. It's a party time for you, and for her."

I waved my hand. "Party? I've never been to a party with dumplings, with a sleeping over, and with a bubble bath."

The room burst with chuckles, chatter, and the sound of Boyd playing his harmonica. The *tootle-too-twang* gave my heart a chorus of hope. I sat on the edge of the tub, kicked my shoes off, and Lizzy Beth scooted off to listen to her pa.

I pretended this was my house with the fence, with the green sofa, the rocker, and the flickering fireplace. With a mama. A papa. A maid. With heat. With love. Even with running water.

My daydreaming was interrupted when Susan reached behind me to turn off the faucet. "Shoelace, hop in the tub. Bubbles are floating in the steam. Here's two towels for you. Do you have a change of clothes with you?"

"Yes, ma'am. I do."

"I will wash your jacket, and clothes for you, if you like. They'll be dry for the morning if I put them by the fire. I'll wash those shoes, too."

I smiled. "Thank you. Are you sure I can stay here tonight?"

Lizzy Beth stuck her head into the bathroom. "Yes, you can sleep with me."

Susan nudged me like I was a dirty pig on her clean floor. "Hop in, and let the bubbles wash away your worry."

"Yes, ma'am." Susan shut the door, carrying my clothes. I dove into the bathtub, ducking under the hot water. I rose like a whale blowing bubbles into the air. "I wish I could stay here forever. This is great. My kitty would have loved it here."

I sat back in the tub, sticking my big toe into the dripping faucet. "I should have left my cat at home. He died because of me. I hope Mahlee doesn't die because of me."

Tears erupted, and I couldn't wipe away the sadness or bring my kitty back. I had no idea if Mahlee was involved in the murders, either. I swallowed the lump of panic, shouting at the bubbles. "My Mahlee is no murderer. She isn't. She can't be. No! I will never believe she is. Never!"

Tap. Tap. Tap.

"We're ready for supper. Are you all right in there?" Susan called to me through the door. "Do you need anything?"

I hit the water with my hands. "Sorry, ma'am. I was playing in the suds. I got carried away. I'll be right out."

**

After supper, Susan tucked me into the soft sheets. The lace bedspread dressed up Lizzy Beth's room, and the sheets were softer than any I've ever slept on. Lizzy Beth wiggled her toes, and I tickled her. "Your feet are freezing."

Susan tapped our feet, walking by the bed. "Night girls. Sleep tight. Don't let the bed bugs bite."

We giggled like sisters, only my laughter was laced with a dash of leftover sadness. Having Lizzy Beth love me coated my heart with hope, and I never wanted the night to end.

She played with my hair. "I like you. Can you stay?"

"I don't think so. But I'm here now."

Lizzy Beth pointed to the wall by the headboard. "I have my dream catcher. No bad dreams at this house."

I swallowed hard. "I left mine at home, the one you gave me."

Yawning, Lizzy Beth touched my nose. "You need a home like me."

She didn't wait for me to answer, and turned over on her pillow, twisting and snuggling under the sheets.

I touched her shoulder. "Night, Lizzy Beth."

"Night night, Shoelace."

Wearing one of Mr. Boyd's T-shirts, I cuddled close to Lizzy Beth, soaking in her baby powder smell and memorizing her smile. She may be my half-sister, but she's made me whole. "Goodnight, Lizzy Beth. Your mama's cook makes great suppers. Best dumplings ever. Best rolls."

"We have a good cook, but Mama makes better food." Her words became a faint whisper.

Susan cracked the door open. "Is everything good in here?"

"Yes, Lizzy Beth is almost asleep."

"She falls asleep faster than I can get the light out sometimes."

"Thank you for having me."

"My pleasure."

I snuggled with my pillow as Susan left the door cracked, allowing the light from the hallway to slip inside.

I dozed. I tossed and turned. I slugged my pillow. My mind wouldn't shut off, and my thoughts were stuck in replay. Curling into a ball, I squirmed. I sighed. I punched the pillow some more.

Creak. Tweak.

Bingo pounced to the bed, twirling in a circle to find a place for his head. "You're one lucky dog. You have a whole town that wants you. I'm surprised Susan lets you on the bed with those dirty paws, though."

Bam. Bam.

I whispered, "What was that?" I kicked the covers off, stepping to the wood floor. Bingo crawled to my pillow, while I crept to the doorway. Listening to see what made the booming sound, I peeked into the hallway, and tiptoed to the entrance to the front room.

I glanced around the door jam and saw Boyd in his rocker. He slammed his fist on the table next to his chair, whispering low, but sounding mad at Susan. "I know you want to keep Shoelace, but with all we're facing since my accident, and not knowing how my eyes will do, this is not a good time to have two girls. I don't see how we can keep her. We don't know for sure she's an orphan. Someone could be searching for her."

Susan responded, "Did you see her? She's carrying her whole life in that satchel."

Boyd whispered, "In the morning I'm contacting the sheriff. Marion said they wanted to talk to her and hadn't gotten the chance. She's been hanging out with the Crush boys. We need to keep her away from them."

Susan argued, standing in front of Boyd. "If she stays here, she's away from them. The Crush boys aren't so bad, they just need some soap and water." Susan embraced Boyd around the neck. "Honey, it's someone for Lizzy Beth to play with. Losing three babies over the years, and having three rose bushes out back to remind me of their precious lives, only makes me want to save Shoelace. She could be ours."

In the not-pretend world where nothing works out for me, no one wants me. Tonight Susan does, and she can't have me. I sighed, crossing my legs, and leaned on the wall. I knew what I had to do. I had to get my clothes from the chair by the fireplace, get dressed, and skip out. Cops mean jail. I had to give my final goodbye to Lizzy Beth, and make my escape from this house.

I hurried to Lizzy Beth's room, and crawled into the bed next to Bingo, snuggling up to my sister. I pretended I was wanted. Pretended I was loved. Cried about pretending. And hugged my sister, kissing her ear. "I love you, Lizzy Beth."

The lights in the hallway went out, and I waited for the Winstons to fall asleep. Popping up, I grabbed my satchel and dug inside, pulling out my harmonica. I blew into the side of it, and a *tang* sound caused Bingo to raise his head. "It's okay, boy. Sorry."

I touched the wooden toy box next to Lizzy Beth's rocking horse, and gazed into the shadows. Dolls sat on the dresser. Pretty ones. All belonging to Lizzy Beth. I whispered, "Lizzy Beth, I hope your life is better than pretend, better than mine. I love you."

I placed the harmonica on the dresser. "This is for you, so you can play with your papa."

I walked to the bed, kissing Lizzy Beth's chocolate hair. She wiggled, a sleepy exhale of contentment. She pulled the blanket up, and Bingo crawled to the edge of the bed, kissing my ear as if he knew I was leaving.

Digging inside my satchel, I retrieved my grandma's cat apron. "I'll put this on the sofa for Susan. My grandma would hate to have her apron sit without being used." I sighed, "It's time to leave and not get caught."

Pam Kumpe

Pages in a Book

I made it to the front room where a small fire crackled,
sending warm heat into my face. Holding the apron, I tossed it
to the cushions on the sofa. My overalls, jacket, and T-shirt
were folded with my socks on the end table. Even my tennis
shoes sat warming by the fire.

Clip. Clip. Clip. Clip.

Ducking behind the end of the sofa, I hid from the noise
until I was sure it was Bingo. I whispered, "Bingo. Go. Get." I
shooed him with my hand, hanging onto my satchel, while
getting dressed and slipping on my jacket.

Bingo clipped to me, his nails hitting the hardwood floor.
He disobeyed me like I disobey adults. "You are a dog without
any training." He put his head next to my leg, rubbing his ear.

I plopped down on the sofa, slipped on my shoes, and tied
them. Bingo gave me an eyeball gaze, and I petted his ear.
"You have to stay here. I have to go. I can't be here when
morning comes. No sheriff is gonna take me to wherever."

Bingo rested his nose on my knee as if he was pleading
with me to stay.

"I have to go. I'll see you around town. You tend to pop up
at Crush's house by the river, at the Soda Street house, and
now here. Maybe you're following me."

Bingo's ears went back as if he heard a noise in the house.

"What is it boy? Did you hear something?"

I knelt to the floor, and crawled to the front door, turning
the handle.

Twik-tweak. Twik-tweak.

186

"Shoelace? Bingo? Where did you go? My bed was lonely."

I gulped, releasing the handle, and sat back on my legs. "Lizzy Beth, I'm right here."

She quizzed me. "Come sleep. I'm sleepy." She twisted her head sideways. "You got dressed? Is it time to play?" Her toddler eyes wanted answers.

I took both of her hands and wrapped her into my arms, swinging her in the air. "I love you, Lizzy Beth. Never forget me. Never."

With those final words, I carried her to her bed. "I'll be right back. I forgot my satchel."

"Hurry, I'm cold."

I shot to the front room, grabbed my satchel, swung the wooden door wide, and rushed to freedom. Scurrying off the porch, I jumped to the ground, charging ahead, crashing into the picket fence. "Darn ole fence." I tumbled over the top, catching my satchel on one of the slats.

Ouch!

From the porch, Lizzy Beth wailed. "Where are you going? Come back. Come back. You can't leave. I just got you."

I dusted the snow from my knees, wiped my hands off, and ran across the street to the backside of the two-story building, and I hid in the hedge. Breathing hard, the cold air caused my chest to ache, and I scolded myself. "What are you thinking? It's freezing out here."

Whiz-woe. Whiz-woe.

My heart stopped, and I became a statue. Something was in these bushes, and I was not alone. I reached behind me to the breathing sound by the wall, and touched the furry monster.

Ahhhhh!

Crawling through the snow, my overalls became damp from the slush, and fear rattled my insides. I tumbled from the bushes, rolling down the slope of the side yard, clumping into the road.

"There she is. She's running away." Susan hollered in the background, her voice high-pitched and sad. "Shoelace, we can help you."

I galloped like a wild horse into the alley, ducking next to a spiral staircase. The furry monster rubbed his body up next to me. Shivering with fright, I'd wished I'd stayed inside the house with Lizzy Beth.

Ah. Uh. Ah. Uh. Ruff.

"Bingo?" I grabbed his snout, kissing the not-monster. "You are … you are following me. You make a great monster."

Bweep-bip. Bweep-bip.

A police car sped up to the front of Lizzy Beth's house. "Darn ole Mr. Boyd Winston. He probably called them. He wants to get rid of me, so he's getting his wish. I'm gone."

I hurried around to the inside part of the yard, the one taking up enough dirt for three houses. I rounded to the front at the other end, coming to tall stairs made of concrete, and pillars on each side. "What is this? This is not a house."

A whispered call came from the porch. "Hey you. Over here. Hurry. It's me, Archie. Come on. Slip in. They'll never look for you inside this library."

"Archie?" I took a step, and stopped. "Did you break into the library?"

"No, little friend. I was reading a book when everyone went home."

I argued. "So you had no idea they were leaving?"

"I had an idea, and that was to stay behind some bookshelves, so I could be warm for the night. Get in here before the police snatch you up. We'll be safe in here."

I marched up the steps with Bingo going ahead of me.

"So you've found you a dog? Where's your cat?"

I wiped my nose, trodding inside as Archie took one last peek into the shadows before shutting the double doors.

"My cat's gone. He died today."

Archie ruffled my hair. "Sorry, losing is hard on our hearts. But losing reminds us how alive we are."

"I don't feel so alive. I'm just cold." I shivered from top to bottom.

"You appear alive to me."

"I'm a ghost. I was alive, but now I'm a ghost, and I'm a dead ghost."

"You talk in sadness, instead of speaking of the beauty before you."

"Beauty? My grandma's gone. My Mahlee is missing. And my cat is buried in the backyard a few blocks from here with a bird. That's not beauty."

"A bird?"

"Yes, White Beard caught himself a bird before he died."

"Tough day, huh?" Archie rubbed his chin. "I have to ask. Did you bring a smile to your grandma?"

I sighed. "Well, yes. Except when I was in trouble, but even then she smiled through her growls and punishment."

"Did your Mahlee ever seem happy when you were with her?"

"Not so much. But she made me happy when I was with her, especially when my daddy used to disappear, leaving us alone in towns."

"How about your cat? Did he bring beauty to you?"

"Yes, I loved my kitty."

He motioned for me to follow him up the stairs. "Beauty rises up like a second story library loft, where the pages of our life can be written with hope. Without the sorrow, we won't appreciate the beauty. With the beauty, we can live during the sorrow, and find a way to survive. God can give us the strength to fight back to living."

I rubbed my eyes. "I'm not into fighting anymore. I feel like I might need to give up."

"Giving up isn't what your grandma would want, now is it?"

"No, sir. She would want me to live." We stomped up the stairs.

"Then what's your next step? What can we do to make that happen?" Archie guided me up the long flight of stairs to the second story.

"I'm not sure."

He opened the double doors leading into the loft, a room with chandeliers, half-moon windows, and tables with cloth on them. Archie announced, "It's warmer up here. We can use these tablecloths for blankets."

I followed like a puppy on a leash, without choices, with a friend who might be a criminal, who might have a past, but who doesn't mind being with me. Who loves to give me advice.

I slipped into the room behind Archie, taking in the size, noticing how the windows let the light from outside in. "They must have parties up here." I scooted to one of the windows, watching the police car leave from Lizzy Beth's house. Their porch light went off, and the street quieted down for the night. I whispered, "They didn't care if I left, did they?"

Archie moved next to me, putting a hand on my shoulder. "People travel through and people come and go. Times are hard, and hard times make people give up on others too fast. Maybe praying to God for his help and guidance might be a good idea."

A flicker of light lit up the window in Lizzy Beth's bedroom, and her face popped into view. She pressed her cheeks on the glass, watching with big eyes, with a hopeful gaze. And for a second, a brief one, I considered returning to her. I couldn't go back, because they won't let me stay.

Archie asked, "So who is she?"

"She's my … my friend."

"I'd say you brought beauty to her heart. I can tell by how her eyes search the night for you. I can tell by how you can't stop staring at her. Is she a good friend?"

"No, she's more than a friend, she's like a sister."

"Oh, the beauty. Marvelous beauty."

I sighed, wishing for more than a window view. I turned to Archie. "Do you think God listens to me? I've run away, and now I'm hiding out inside this library. I keep messing up my life story, and I'm sure He's disappointed in me."

"He listens to the heart of His children. He comforts us when we can't see the answers, when we lose sight of the beauty, too."

"That's too deep for my tired ears."

"It does seem God brought you in from the cold."

"No, you brought me inside."

"I'd say, God made sure I was here to open the door. That's all."

I turned my back to Archie, pulling tablecloths from the tables, and making a pallet. I sat down with Bingo, whose breaths kept time with mine. I called into the shadows to Archie who made his bed down the wall. "Hey Archie, where are you headed next?"

"I was headed to Uncertain for the pearl digging, to get rich, but I heard two men talking at the general store. It seems a rich plantation owner hired the entire circus to come to his property for his nephew's birthday. They're setting up west of town. I got hired today. I'll be working with the elephants. I start in the morning."

I sat straight up. "The circus is here? The circus?"

"Yes, for a few days. They will hold the private party on the first day, and then open the doors to the public for a couple of days."

"I can join the circus." I jumped to my feet, practicing my wire act on a wooden slat. "I'm joining the circus tomorrow, too."

"You better get some sleep then, because a ghost will need to be alive and rested if she wants to go with me in the morning."

I collapsed like a tired girl with a new idea, and whispered, "The circus. I will be a performer."

"That you will be. That you are. But who is the real Annie Grace Kree, who hides behind a hobo name like Shoelace?"

"Hey, how did you know my given name?"

"You told me once, but I don't remember the time and hour."

Rubbing Bingo's soft wiry hair, I shook my head. "I'd remember telling you."

"You're tired, and you must have forgotten. Get some sleep. Tomorrow's gonna be full, and there's no telling what the next page in your life will hand you."

I called to Archie, "Will you pray an out loud prayer? I'm scared."

"Sure, little one." Archie inhaled a deep breath. "Dear God, we're here in this warm place, and we thank you for libraries with second floors. Help us to trust you. I'm with a fragile soul who is caught in the gate of sadness and sorrow. Help her to see the beauty of tomorrow. And please, go with her, and go with me, too. In Jesus' name. Amen."

I whispered, "Amen." My tears trickled to Bingo's snout, and he tilted his head up, licking my cheeks. "Boy, you won't like being with me. It comes with bumps, and lots of stumps. I won't be a good master. I'm a broken heart that the world has forgotten."

Archie called to me with a voice like lightning. "God has not forgotten you. Tomorrow is a new day. Filled with elephants, and plenty of surprises."

A Circus of Memories

Tangled in the tablecloth, I unraveled, popping up to see the new day explode into the library loft. "Archie? Where are you?" I called to the empty party room, wondering if he'd gone downstairs to the book part of the library. Wondering how late I'd slept, I wiggled from the cloth. "Bingo? Where are you?"

Stomping, I kicked the tablecloth from my legs, rising to my feet. "Am I alone again? Every time I find Archie, or he finds me, hours tick by and then he disappears. Archie must have taken Bingo with him." I tugged on my satchel, slinging the strap over my shoulder, shuffling to the doors leading to the stairs. Hurrying to the foyer, I glanced at the floor. "Another handkerchief? Archie loses them faster than I lose him. This is the third one he's left behind."

I tossed it into my satchel, shaking my head, mad at Archie for deserting me. Now I'll have to find the elephants by myself.

I slipped outside, deciding which direction to walk. To my left, a bronze fountain sat in the crossroads with some sort of goddess on top of it. A dog could get a drink, or a horse, or even a person. The fountain reminded me of the one in Texarkana, except the one by the Grim Hotel doesn't have a goddess on top. I sighed. "I've got to find the Clementine Plantation and check on joining the circus, in case I don't find Mahlee. Or in case I can't get rescued from this town."

Counting the bricks under my shoes, I roamed the streets, passing a church, a gazebo, the Jimplecute Newspaper office, and a bakery. "I'm hungry. Breakfast. I need food." I rounded the corner of the brick building, my nose tingling from the smell of bacon sizzling somewhere.

I pressed my nose on the glass in front of the cafe. At most of the tables, plates with eggs and bacon sat ready to be chewed, while the men and women sipped on coffee. To my left, by the wall, was an upright piano, and a man … a familiar man, who sat at the table next to it. He hunkered over his coffee cup, talking to the air. He mouthed words to the empty chair across from him.

I scooted my nose along the window to see if he was speaking to a short person. Nope. He's talking to a photograph of a woman sitting in the grass with a picnic basket.

A woman strolled from the kitchen, a woman who would love to keep me. "It's Susan. This must be her cafe."

Before I could run either way, Susan darted through the glass swinging doors, stomping in her loafers wearing my grandma's apron. She ran her hands down the front. "Look what some sweet girl left me." Susan hugged me. "We lost you last night. Did something happen for you to leave?"

I put my hands in my overall pockets. "No, ma'am. I heard Mr. Boyd though, and he wanted to turn me over to the cops. I don't need no cops, but …" I inhaled. "I could use some breakfast."

"Perfect. Come inside. Sit with Marion. He could use someone besides a photo to talk to."

"What? Why is he talking to a photo?"

"It's his late wife, Naomi. They were close. She used to play the piano for lunch, and her favorite song was 'Shall We Gather at the River.' Last year, a boating accident got her, right after Toby's folks died in the train wreck. Marion's a strong man, but losing her nearly got him. He misses her so much."

I danced away from Susan. "I'm not sure he wants to see me, but I could sit at another table."

"Sure, just come inside. Lizzy Beth's in the kitchen. I'll get her."

"Lizzy Beth is here?"

"Yes, she'll love seeing you … as she says … more."

The bell on the door jingled, and Mr. Marion glanced up at me. He motioned for me to sit. "Did you know I've had everyone looking for you?"

I swallowed hard. "Hi, Mr. Marion. If you want to know why you couldn't find me, you might ask Toby and Crush. They locked me inside the basement at the synagogue."

Susan patted my shoulder. "I plan to talk to them about that, but you're slipping off from my house wasn't too bright, either."

I grinned, pulling out a chair.

Mr. Marion smiled, but his glare told me he was not happy with me. He touched my arm. "Now, why would they go and lock you up?"

"I don't know, but I'm clobbering them both."

"Would this have anything to do with why Toby came home so late last night?"

"I don't know. I wasn't with him. I was trapped with a bunch of suitcases, and a monster."

"Well, you must be a ghost who travels through basement walls." He folded his hands around his mug. "We need to talk."

I obeyed him like he was a father who might dish out punishment. "Yes, sir." I hung my satchel on the red-backed chair, and took off my jacket, sitting down.

Mr. Marion put the photo inside his shirt pocket. "Tell me. What put you on the tracks the other day in Lodi?"

"I was … going somewhere."

"Now, why didn't you stay at the hotel? You were warm and safe."

"I had to search for my cat when he snuck outside, and then he ran into the woods."

"Is that how you ended up at the Cypress Bayou with Crush? You know, the police found a man shot out there."

"Yes sir. I met the rest of the boys there, too. Just so you know, I had nothing to do with shooting any man. I don't even have a gun."

Susan placed a glass of milk in front of me, and I looked into her kind eyes. "Thank you, Susan."

She held my chin up. "I'll get you some eggs and bacon. Growing girls need their strength."

"Thank you, but I can't pay you. I only have a little money."

Mr. Marion nodded. "I've got this covered."

I grinned, afraid of him, but still glad to be with him. "Thank you, Mr. Marion."

"No problem. Back to our talk." He watched Susan skirt to the back of the cafe. "So you don't know anything about how a man ended up behind Crush's house?"

"No sir. I only fell over the body."

"I suppose you know the police found another dead man, and he was inside your grandma's house."

"How do you know about my grandma's house?"

"I've been talking to Toby." Mr. Marion sipped his coffee. "It appears the second man was shot, too. Two dead men in two days. And you've been here for … about two days. Is there someone you're traveling with who might be a danger to our folks here? Or to you?"

I sat up taller, sipping milk. "No! I'm alone."

"Really? Crush told me about a man named Archie. Toby mentioned him, too. I've quizzed them both, and while Toby was confessing, I found out he didn't go to school yesterday. I'm not sure what he knows, but he's still praying confessions this morning in his room before I drove him to school. If you've gotten my grandson mixed up in this, now is the time to tell me. I can help. I want to help you."

My ears burned, and my throat ached with truth, but it stuck to my tongue. Stuck to some lies twisted around my tonsils, too. I didn't know what to say. "Mr. Marion, I'm not sure what I know, but what I know is … Toby didn't kill anyone. But Crush, he could have."

Mr. Marion slammed his hand on the table, and his fork fell to the floor. "Crush wouldn't kill anyone. Never. He's too busy being alive for the other boys."

I scooted my chair back, realizing I'd pushed Mr. Marion too far. "I'm sorry. I have to go. I can't be here. I can't be involved."

Mr. Marion reached for my hand, a firm grasp, and I sat back down. He wrinkled his bottom lip under his front teeth, sighing. "You're already involved, and I'm not mad at you. I'm afraid for the boys. I'm upset my Toby knows something, and is keeping a secret from me, too."

I swallowed part of my lies. "He's protecting me. Crush, too. They are afraid the person who killed those men might be after me. Especially since I saw the second dead man alive before he died at the house yesterday. Plus, Mahlee warned me."

"Mahlee? Are you talking about the new housekeeper at the Jefferson Hotel? Did you know she's missing?"

"Missing? She can't be. Not her. Not my Mahlee."

Mr. Marion sighed, "Wait, you know her?"

I coughed. "Yes, she's my mama on the rail, or she used to be."

Mr. Marion's hand went to his forehead. "I thought you were alone."

"I am. She left me."

"I've learned the first man was her driver. He drove her to and from work, and so did the second man. It all seems connected. Now no one can find her. And two men are dead."

"Mahlee can't be missing. I just saw her. How do you know for sure? Who told you?"

"I talked to my brother, the sheriff, and he made the rounds questioning people. No one's seen Mahlee since she left walking for her lunch yesterday."

"No, I saw her yesterday. At lunch. Something must have happened to her after the shooting." I shook with fear, feeling safe might never come to me again.

"What do you know about the shooting?"

"No, I meant … well, you said a man died. I'm mixed up." I rubbed my eyes, shaking my head as if I got my facts twisted, afraid Mr. Marion knew more than me.

"I see." Mr. Marion rubbed his ear. "It's best you stay with me, until we figure out what to do."

I found my head nodding yes. "Promise me, you won't turn me into the police. They'll send me off somewhere."

"I want to talk to you and Toby after he gets home from school. I promise, I'll do what's best for you. I don't want you to get hurt, or my grandson. I need to get my facts in place."

Susan showed up with my plate of food, and I gobbled it down, chomping on yummy eggs, and she filled my glass with more milk. I ate without answering, without saying another word, knowing Mr. Marion might be a way to stay alive for now.

Clip-clop. Clip-clop.

Lizzy Beth danced over to the table. "Shoelace, I thought you ran away. I want you to come home with me. Come with me. We can play with my dolls."

Hugging her neck, I kissed her nose. "I can't stay. I have to go with Mr. Marion."

"But, if I could get a sister, I would pick you."

"Me, too. Me, too."

Bam-bing. Bam-bing. Dong. Dong.

Lizzy Beth moved to the windowpane. "What are those?"

Mr. Marion gathered her up, and put Lizzy Beth in his lap. "It's the circus parade. See, there's elephants. And clowns. Oh, look, a lion in a cage."

Lizzy Beth cocked her head sideways. "It's like in a cartoon."

I stood in my chair. "Yes, only better. Mr. Marion, where are they going?"

Mr. Marion's voice turned kind. "They'll be setting up at Mr. Carl's, not far from here. At the Clementine Plantation. After school, I'm taking Toby and Crush, Timmons and Tak, and the other boys to watch them set up the Big Top."

I found my mouth begging. "Can I go with you? I love the circus."

Lizzy Beth mocked me. "I love the circus. I want to go."

Mr. Marion smiled. "Lizzy Beth, you'll need to ask your mama, but Shoelace, I can arrange for you to ride with us, especially since we have more talking to do."

I took a bite of bacon. "Since when do they set up a circus at someone's house?"

"It's not just any house. It's Carl Clementine. His ranch is the biggest in the county, and his two-story mansion sits right across the highway from my syrup factory. They're having a birthday party for his nephew today, even though his nephew got hurt last night in the car wreck. They released him around midnight with a bump on his head."

"Car wreck? I saw an accident. Mr. Carl nearly hit Crush."

"I expect you did, since Toby mentioned he was with you yesterday for most of the day."

I rolled my eyes. "Mr. Marion, you seem to know a lot about everything."

"It's a small town. News travels fast."

Lizzy Beth watched the tall man on stilts wobble past the window, her eyes glued to the parade. A band marched by and the drummers beat on their drums so loud, Lizzy Beth's words became a whisper. "I want to be tall like that man."

I giggled. "You need to do some growing."

"I will grow." She looked at her tiny hands. "I will."

I touched her fingers. "They're perfect."

Mr. Marion agreed. "Best hands in town."

I quizzed some more. "Mr. Marion, why are they having a private circus for one kid?"

"Oh, he's not an ordinary kid, he's the heir to the estate. Carl is leaving his fortune to the boy, even though he's only a youngster."

"Gosh, and he gets a circus, too?"

"It seems so."

"I would love to be in the circus, but to have one on my land would be pretty neat, too. Who is this boy?"

Mr. Marion stood Lizzy Beth on the floor. "His name is Thaddeus William Day Jr."

I choked, spitting the last bit of bacon from my mouth. "Taddy? Here? An heir?"

Mr. Marion patted me on the arm. "Do you know this boy?"

I held my neck, gagging. "No, my food got stuck in my throat. So what time ... what time are we going to the plantation?"

A Birthday Party to Scream

Pa-tut. Pa-tut. Pa-tut.

Timmons and Tak sat on each side of me. Tak next to Mr. Marion who steered the pickup along the bumpy road, while Timmons clutched the door handle with both hands to keep from sliding from the seat.

Tak put his hand in mine. "Have you ever seen a lion?"

I smiled. "A couple of times. Way too close for my liking though."

Roooaaaarrrr!

Timmons mocked Tak. "We live with a lion." He contorted his head to the side, looking back at Crush and the other boys sitting in the bed of the truck. "We live with Crush. He's a lion. He's always roaring at us."

Mr. Marion nodded. "Crush can bring a growl to the day; he takes good care of you, though."

Tak whined, "I like Crush. He's like a papa. Just grouchy."

Mr. Marion stuck his hand straight out the open window, turning the truck to the left, bumping down a ravine and up a driveway. We rolled up the hill to a castle house, one with four columns, two on each side of the steps leading to a second floor.

The warm breeze swirled dust from the floorboard, and the sunshine melted most of the snow today, just in time for the circus birthday party. In time for me to search for Mahlee, in case she's here. In time for me to look for Taddy, too.

I pulled myself to the dash, tilting my head as we drove by the porch. Carl towered in a white suit, holding a white cane. I mouthed. "Mr. Carl's ready for a party."

Mr. Marion nodded. "Yes, all the children get cake and can stay for Thaddeus' birthday party, too."

I put my hand to my lips, ready to correct Mr. Marion. I wanted to let him know Taddy's birthday is not today, it's officially Saturday, February 22.

Mr. Marion waved to Carl, inching the truck toward a patch of trees where other vehicles were parked. He tapped the steering wheel, "With his nephew here, Carl's going to put on a grand show. Many think he's a tyrant, but there's a good man hiding inside."

Tak and Timmons pointed, yelling. "There. Park over there. There's the elephants."

Squinting from the sun's glare, I made out Archie, who cleaned the side of the trumpeting elephant with a long brush on a handle. The trunk of the beast swooped around the brush, yanking it from Archie's grip, and Archie stomped and pulled. He slipped in the mud puddle he'd created, screaming ugly words at the elephant.

Mr. Marion cruised to the shade of a pine tree, putting the truck in park. He used his fatherly voice. "Tak and Timmons, stay with Crush. Don't leave his sight, and don't get in the way. The elephants and the workers will raise the Big Top after a while; make sure you're not under foot."

Tak pushed me. "Hurry up. Get out of the truck." He turned to Mr. Marion, responding to his orders. "Yes, sir. Can we ride one of them?"

Mr. Marion answered, getting out of his driver's seat. "No, no riding. Only watching. We'll come back for the circus tomorrow, and then, maybe you can ride one."

I pushed Timmons. "Open the door."

Timmons jerked on the handle. "This door sticks, give me a second."

We tumbled to the soggy ground, one on top of the other. Our giggles felt real, but my real goal was hidden inside my heart. My worry for Mahlee pressed in like the clank of hammers on stakes, and I wanted to pound the truth from anyone whom I could question. I had to find her, to see if anyone knew where she went.

Ca-pank. Ca-pank.

Dozens of sledgehammers clobbered the circus stakes around the red and white tent rippling in the wind. It was as if it was ready to rise by itself.

Crush leapt from the back of the truck, laughing. "The Three Stooges have arrived in style."

I dusted myself, holding onto my satchel. "Not funny."

"You are clumsier than most girls."

I wrinkled my nose. "At least I got to ride up front."

Crush shook his head, helping one of the triplets from the back of the truck. Theodore and Thomas jumped to the ground and hurried to where Archie and other circus hands bathed the elephants. The triplets kept step with each other, and headed toward the cages where the lions and tigers pranced inside.

Roar! Roar!

Mr. Marion journeyed up the driveway toward Mr. Carl, and I vamoosed to the first tree with bark, scaling the branches to get a view of the grounds. Glancing to the highway, I watched the parade of cars and trucks roll in, with families ready to catch a glimpse of the circus tent and the animals.

Boys jumped from the seats, and girls romped to catch the sites. The grownups shook hands, and chatted like they'd not seen each other since last year. Most likely it was only three days ago at church.

Crush held Tak's hand and Timmons held Tak's fingers, and they rushed to the decorated table where a blue and white birthday cake sat. It was the size of a small pond, and it begged to be eaten. "That must be Taddy's cake, but I don't see him. He doesn't know I'm gone from Texarkana. Or that I'm in Jefferson. I need to be careful."

A brown pickup with a grumble-tick-burp sound parked beneath me. Hiding behind some branches, I peeked to see if the person driving was the person I suspected, since I knew the growl of the engine. It was the same truck that once honked at me behind my grandma's house. It must be Pastor Cody's truck. What is he doing here?

From the cab, Pastor Cody appeared, and on the other side, Slow Tom and Fast Tim jumped from the seat. They hurried like kids to the gathering crowd.

I mouthed. "Slow Tom and Fast Tim?" My heart jumped from my chest and flew into the air like a bullet. Struggling to stay put, to stay out of sight, I hung on.

A maroon car parked behind Pastor Cody's truck, and a woman stepped from the driver's side. She stuck her head inside the cab before shutting her door. "Priscilla, I'll be right there to help you."

I lost my grip when she said Priscilla. "Oh, my word! Taddy's mama is here?"

Priscilla graced the plantation in a yellow dress, and walked with small steps, an elegant move like a dance of hope. She held the arm of her friend, smiling and chatting with her. "Thank you for driving me here. I can't wait to show Taddy how I'm walking. How I'm out of the wheelchair. He can come home now, and we can be a family again. This is a miracle birthday present for him."

I clung to the tree like a monkey, unsure how to hide from Taddy and his mama. Or from Tom and Tim. Or Pastor Cody. I watched Mr. Marion and Carl join a group of people near the chairs and the cake, while I spied on the kids. I hoped to get a glance of Taddy, but the crowd blocked my view.

Ruff. Ruff. Ruff.

Bingo barked from the top of the front castle steps, pawing at the gate-like door. This is my chance to look for Mahlee, for clues to see if she's gone, or hiding, or if she's hit the rail again. I'll have to catch the tent rising another day. I shimmied down to the ground, ducking behind pickups and cars, and dodging and darting around the trees by the driveway. No one will mind if I do some 'vestigating of my own.

I vaulted up the stairs between the columns. "Bingo, what are you doing? The boys are by the elephants. You better get them. Go on now. Go." I shooed him off the porch, and he tucked his tail, running from me with his ears down. I whispered, "Sorry boy, I need to do this alone."

I latched my hand on the gold doorknob, unlocked it, and the swinging door allowed me inside. The path of the long hallway stretched to the back of the house, with doors on each side, leading to freedom or to traps.

Shuffling ahead, closing the door behind me, I cracked the door to my right, peeking inside. "Too many chairs for me. Dozens at a dining room table with a red carpet underneath. Must be for catching crumbs." Four chandeliers reflected the sunlight beaming through the windows. "This is a room for rich folks. A room to wear fancy dresses and suits."

I shifted back to the hallway to the room on the left, disappearing inside of a bedroom with more red. A red bedspread, shiny and slick. A red rug. A red lampshade. I ran my hand over the slick fabric on the mattress, and it felt like Crisco oil on cotton. "If I were to sleep in this bed, I'd slide right off."

Drifting toward the fireplace to the right of the bed, the logs burned low as if the fire from the night simmered with unwanted heat. The mirror on the mantle revealed the curtains behind me, gold and red spots. "Who likes all this red? It's ugly. Mr. Carl has poor taste."

A door half the size of those in the hallway led from the bedroom to another place. Muffled sounds of people coming from other rooms stopped me from inhaling or exhaling. Frozen by the talking, I took a breath, and put my ear against a door. From behind me, the chatter faded into another part of the red castle.

Whispering, I talked to the lamp beside me. "Let's see what's in this room." I swung the door wide, escaping from the red spots, only to land in a room of royal blue. Blue and white striped curtains. Another fireplace. Only no fire in this one. A nightstand next to a twin bed. And a dresser with photographs in frames.

I scooted to the display where, in one photo, Carl sat at a giant desk in a chair big enough for three people. I recognized the fireplace in the background. It matched the two I've seen in these rooms. Carl's hands were folded, and a pocket watch lay next to his fingers, with a chain draped over his wrist. He looked grouchy, like a principal from a school.

I squinted, looking closer at the photo. The cluster of pearls caught my attention. "Hmmm … I have a pearl. I wonder if … if Mr. Carl … lost a pearl recently." I shook my head. "No, I don't even know where my pearl came from."

Next to the photo was another photo. This one … this one had … I picked the frame up, stumbling backwards, falling on the blue blanket folded up at the bottom of the bed. I parked myself on the edge. "This is my Taddy." I touched his face. "You're with Mr. Carl. You look a couple of years younger, but I know you. Your grin is like you're studying someone or something. Like you just finished memorizing a part of the encyclopedia."

I spoke to Taddy's photo. "I never had a best friend, until we met. I will always remember you. You're gonna be so surprised to see your mama." Walking to one of the windows, I moved the curtains apart, and on the windowsill a row of acorns lined up the bottom of the window frame. "Taddy. Your acorns are no good. They don't keep the storms away." I shook my head, grabbing one of his acorns and sticking it inside my satchel.

I ripped into the photo frame, tearing the photo in half, dropping the part with Mr. Carl to the hardwood floor, stomping on it. I stuck the Taddy-half of the photo inside my satchel, headed to another door, cracked it open, and found myself at the other end of the breezeway.

The stairs leading to the first floor looked inviting, and more voices chatted in the rooms across from me. I padded down the steep stairs to a wooden floor not quite as finished as the hardwood floors upstairs. The air felt trapped like old dust. "I don't think Mr. Carl uses this part of the house."

A muttered and muffled cry like a ghost whimpering sent me running down the hallway, ready to dart through the lattice to the front yard. I felt like a circus clown caught in a maze under the Big Top. With my hand on the wall, I paused, unable to keep going, because the familiar weeping bounced in my soul.

I swept myself back down the hallway, ignoring the fear rising up in my veins. My ears ached like they were going to explode from the sobs seeping from the broken heart calling for help. The sour taste of spit stuck in my mouth while the wails grew louder. Charging to the last door, the one on the left, the one under Taddy's away-from-home room, I twisted the doorknob. It wouldn't budge. I pounded, "Who is in there? Mahlee?"

The ghost shouted, "Stay away. Don't come in here. Stop the hurting. Stop the pain. Stop!" The words of the ghost rushed from under the door like a mist, and the shouts crushed my eardrums with a crackling sound of horror.

I was caught in the hallway, stuck in despair and dread, while my Mahlee was locked inside. I had to save her before the color of death like red carpet and red spots swallowed her up.

When Doors Shut

I cupped the doorknob, shaking and twisting, but my fingers slipped off. "Mahlee? Mahlee?"

"Leave. Carl, get out of here."

"I'm not Carl. I'm family. It's me, Shoelace." I fell against the door, out of breath, blubbering, unable to rescue Mahlee from the storm. "Mahlee, I'm going for help. I'm getting Mr. Marion. Or someone."

Kaploweeee.

The boom on the other side of the door startled me, causing my legs to crumble. My satchel shot to the floor, unlatching, and my prized collection of memories tumbled to my feet. The bullets. One of Archie's handkerchiefs. The pearl.

"Who is there? This ain't no party. Go outside."

Gathering my jewels, I stuffed them inside the satchel, and pounded on the door. "Mahlee, it's me. Your … your … other daughter." I slammed both of my fists. "I'll be right back. I'm getting someone to open this up." I stomped away, shouting. "Someone save my Mahlee."

Creeeaaakkkk.

Spinning around, I goggled at the opened door, ran back, and a hand nabbed me by the neck, uprooting me from the hallway.

Mahlee screamed, "What are you doing here? How did you find me? Miss Ginny will plod down here to see what the commotion is."

I froze. I stared. I grappled to stand. One second, I'm pounding on the door; the next second Mahlee opens the door. I shrieked at her. "You made me stand out in the hall? You weren't locked in this room? You can leave if you want, so why didn't you open the door?"

Mahlee's calloused hand smothered my screams. She whispered inches from my ear. "Keep quiet. Miss Ginny will not put up with you being here. She'll report this to Mr. Carl. I'll pay for your foolishness."

Mahlee...who...is...Ginny? My lips wiggled under her hand, and my words backed up in my throat.

"She is Carl's private maid, and she won't take to you being here."

I bugged my eyes, afraid of the horror in Mahlee's on-looking glare.

Mahlee quizzed me, "If I move my hand, will you be quiet?"

I nodded.

"I mean it."

I crossed my heart, and silently hoped to die.

Mahlee released her fingers one by one. "Tell me. Why are you here?"

I whispered, "You first. Tell me why you're in this room. The police are looking for you. There's been two murders, and now the cops think you're missing." I rubbed my mouth with the back of my hand. "What about Taddy? Have you seen him? Does he know you're here?"

"I knew he arrived, but Carl's kept a tight leash on me. This house is big, plenty of rooms to keep me from seeing anyone. He's kept me down here when I'm not at work. No one comes to this floor. It's not used by high-falutin' folks." She folded her arms, rubbing them.

"Really? You're hiding in a room with the curtains closed. You're crying in the shadows in this mansion. Everyone's having a party and the circus is here. You can leave. No one would know. After all, your door wasn't locked!"

Mahlee backed away from me, shaking, her skirts hung loose. Her clothes seemed too big, and I could tell she was wearing several of them.

"Mahlee, are you sick?"

She moved strands of hair from her face. "I'm not sick. Just tired. I have to show you something. Then you'll know why you need to leave. Why I have to stay."

"What? Need to leave? I'm not leaving. I just found you. I'm keeping you this time."

"You don't understand. You have no clue."

"I do understand. I understand you are here. And we can go."

Mahlee charged at me, pulling me by the arm to the window. She swiped the curtains to the side, letting in sunlight. "Look at my arms. See the bruises? I took those for you. For you! Never forget how my face looks." She twisted to the window. "This mark on my temple came from Carl's hand. I know his past, and he's afraid of me. I'm a crushed spirit without hope."

My breath escaped like sorrow. I reached for her cheek. "For me? I don't understand. Why?"

"Carl is the man your daddy walloped with the metal bar in South Texas. Along with those other two men."

I squinted. "But he's Taddy's family."

"Carl might be his family, but he's also a bank robber and a crook. How do you think he bought this plantation?"

I stomped in a circle. "No, this is too mixed up for me. Taddy's here for his birthday. Mr. Carl is ugly, but he can't be … can't be a bad man."

Mahlee grabbed my arm. "Listen, and listen good. The two men who drove me this week were with Carl, after the bank robbery before I met you or your daddy. See, when your daddy saved me on the rail all them years back, I never figured I'd see Carl again. Even your daddy thought they were all dead after he walloped them with that pipe. But they lived. And now I've gone and shot two of them."

I backed up. "You shot them? The drivers? No way!"

"I told you, it's complicated. Right after lunch yesterday, Carl came up on me at your grandma's house, tossing me inside the trunk of his car. He kept me bound there all night, and had one of his other hired hands bring me here this morning. He socked me in the eye, and told me if I leave, I'm dead. And so are you!"

I screamed. "Carl knows about me? And now he's going to kill me?"

She put her hands to her ears. "Yes, it's my fault. Ginny told Mr. Carl. She sleeps in the room next to this one. We talked late one night, and I thought she was my friend. Not so! She ran to Carl and ratted me out. I had told her about you, and your daddy, and life in Texarkana."

I shook my head. "Did you tell her about your other little girl, Lizzy Beth?"

"No, I've gotten Lizzy Beth tucked so far into my memories, the only one leaking out has been you. On Monday night, Carl pinned me against the backseat of his car, threatening to get rid of you."

"How did he know I was in Jefferson?"

"He didn't right then, not until the next day. But he knew your name. This is a town with talkers who meet for coffee. Everyone is related or talking about someone."

I marched in a circle. "How did Carl find you in the first place?"

"I was hanging out your overalls on the clothesline at the manor. He stepped from a parked car on the road, and he was going to see Priscilla and Taddy. He asked me which apartment belonged to them. Next thing I know, I'm taking my nap and crying about Ernie. Then the phone rings, one of Carl's men shows up, and he forces me to leave."

"Did you go out the window?"

"No, he cut the curtain with a knife and left the window open. Said he wanted to make it look like someone broke in."

I took her hand. "How did Carl know you after all these years?

Mahlee squirmed, her hand going through her hair, her eyes looking to the ceiling.

I shouted at her. "Mahlee, come back. Don't disappear. We have to figure this out."

"It's my fault. Mine! I hollered at Carl from the clothesline, screaming and accusing him of coming to Texarkana to get me. I had no idea he was there for Taddy. I wish I'd kept my mouth shut. I called him words best left at the door of the church. Too ugly to repeat. Words I didn't even know I remembered."

I put my arm around her waist. "We should call the cops." I shuddered, my satchel tumbling from my shoulder.

"No, we can't call them."

"But I can get help. Taddy's mama came in for Taddy's birthday party, and Pastor Cody, and ..." I sighed, choking on my confusion.

Mahlee grabbed my shoulders. "Priscilla's here?"

"Yes, they all came for the birthday party."

Mahlee counted on her fingers. "It's our Taddy's birthday?"

"Well, not quite. It's in three days. Mr. Carl is having a circus for him. Everyone is here. Most of the town, I'd say."

Mahlee spoke her words fast. "You have to go. I let you know the truth so you'll leave. If you don't, Carl will have you killed."

"What about Lizzy Beth? He could kill her, too. He could find out your Lizzy Beth is the same Lizzy Beth who lives by the library."

Mahlee yanked me to my toes. "My Lizzy Beth? She's here? In Jefferson? It can't be."

I coughed, unraveling her fingers from my skin. "Gladys and Boyd Winston adopted her from Wheelock Academy. They live here. Gladys goes by Susan, and she runs the cafe."

"I'm this close? This close to my little girl?" Mahlee planted me into a sitting position on the bed. "What? Wait! Lizzy Beth was at Wheelock? Was she there when we were there? You mean, I was that close to my baby girl and you knew it? And you didn't tell me?"

I wrinkled my brow, wishing I'd told Mahlee some of this before today. "I wasn't sure at first. Then you left Wheelock early, and it never came up. Lizzy Beth is … Bright Eyes, the little Indian girl who didn't talk when we first got there."

Mahlee stammered, rolling her eyes. "Why would you keep this from me? Why?" She rubbed her hands into a ball. "Wait, Lizzy Beth isn't Indian."

I sighed, exhaling the sadness in the room. "But you said my daddy was her daddy, and he's part Choctaw. She got her looks from him. They said she came from the orphanage in Memphis. It has to be her."

Mahlee shook me like a rag doll. "You knew this, and you kept it from me." She shoved me away.

"I didn't know she was in this town, until I ran away. Don't act like you're better than me; you didn't even tell me she was my sister. You didn't tell me my daddy even liked you, like a wife. You kept secrets from me, too."

Mahlee tossed me to the mattress. "I could never take your real mama's place. I don't know how to be a regular person. I have blood on my hands now, and you know I gave up my Lizzy Beth. I would end up giving you away, too." Mahlee melted to the floor like a blob of sobs.

I climbed from the bed. "Mahlee, we have to find a way. I'm not leaving without you."

Mahlee's cocked head told me she was hiding in plain sight again. She cackled. "I'm not sure. I don't know what is going on, but I can't take the risk of you being caught here. I've killed two men in self-defense, but Mr. Carl has more men than we have answers."

"In self-defense? It doesn't add up. You didn't come for your gun until Tuesday, and the first man died on Monday night."

Mahlee slapped her face in taps of craziness. "I shot the first man with his own gun, when he tried to do unfriendly things. We had struggled by the river, and the gun fell from his belt and went off. I tossed the pistol into the river."

I corrected her like I was the mama. "You should have told someone."

Mahlee rocked on her heels. "I couldn't. Your life was in danger." She rose, stomping in her boots. "The second man was the one you saw driving me around. He was aiming to see if I'd taken care of you, because he didn't believe me. He didn't like you seeing him. He rammed his fist into my jaw when we got inside the house, and we argued about how he could help catch Carl for me, but he didn't like my idea. So I shot at him, and thought I'd missed, but it seems I killed him, too. I did it to save you, to save myself."

Screaming, I collapsed, this time making myself into a blob. "Mahlee! This can't be happening."

Tump-tump-tump.

Mahlee's hand landed over my mouth, and she turned the latch on the door, locking it tight. "Quiet."

Knock. Knock.

A voice called from the hallway. "Mahlee, are you feeling better?"

"No, Miss Ginny. I'm throwing up. The change in weather has gotten me down."

I wiggled, my breath soured, and I vomited right into Mahlee's fingers.

Yack-up-kerchup.

Mahlee gave me one of her I'm-never-gonna-let-you-forget-this glares.

Miss Ginny called again. "Are you sure? I can get you a warm cloth."

Jiggle. Jiggle.

The doorknob shook. "Miss Mahlee, let me in."

"Just a second." Mahlee motioned for me to slide under the bed.

I wiped my face with my sleeve, my tummy gurgled, and my ears burned. I reached for my satchel, and scooted across the floor, barely fitting beneath the mattress.

Creak. Squeak.

Mahlee announced, "The door's open."

Miss Ginny's shoes came into view, black and shiny, and the body standing in them complained. "Oh, what a mess. I'll get a mop. I'll be right back to clean this up."

Mahlee moaned. "I may not be finished. Don't worry about this. It's just a little vomit."

I giggled, a silent laughter at her saying she might not be finished.

Miss Ginny's shoes shuffled to the doorway. "Well, Mr. Carl loves a clean house. This won't do."

The door closed, and Mahlee knelt to the floor. "Hurry up. Get out. And get out now."

I rolled from beneath the bed, put my hands on my hips to scold Mahlee, but she tumbled to the floor, curling into a ball. I pulled on her skirt. "Don't go into your mumbling now. We have to leave."

She rocked on her side, kicked her feet, and beat the floor, wailing, "My girls will die because of me. Because of me."

I unfolded her, helping Mahlee stand. "You're coming with me. I'm getting Crush to help us, and I'm taking you to a place where music plays, lives change, and hearts sing."

I found her coat on the side of the dresser, and Mahlee slipped her arms into each sleeve. I straightened her collar. "Why is your coat so heavy?"

"It's just my gun. It's in my right pocket. I'm out of bullets though."

We held each other up, my one arm on her waist, my other holding my satchel. We tottered past the lattice, to the trees, over to Mr. Marion's truck, and into the shade.

Sitting Mahlee down, she whimpered, "I give up. I can't save you."

"Not to worry. I'm saving you."

The hooting and hollering coming from the crowd told me the circus top was rising into the sky. Mahlee was having one of her meltdown spells, the kind that sends her to a land where her arms fly.

"Mahlee, I'll be right back. I'm getting Crush. He can drive. He'll take us away from here. Don't move. Stay right here."

A redbird landed on a low branch in front of Mahlee, and he bent his head from side to side. Bingo darted up to Mahlee, and she hugged his neck. She wept, "My little girls. My little girls. My little redbirds. Fly away to safety. Fly away home."

Never Eat the Cake

I threw myself between bumpers of cars and the front of jalopies, jumping over a few patches of leftover snow. Breathing with gasps escaping like steam on a train, I barreled into the crowd, circling the tent arena, doing my best to set my eyes on Crush. Stomping between tall and short men, around kids pointing and laughing, and around mamas and girls in frilly dresses, I still couldn't find Crush.

A red-haired boy and a blonde-haired boy waved at me. "Tak? Timmons?"

Tak clasped my hand. "We were looking for you. Did you see the elephants? Did you see how the tent waved in the air like a thousand flat balloons?"

I squeezed his tiny fingers, and took a glance at the Big Top. "I see it. I do. I did." I sighed, glancing back over my shoulder in time to catch Miss Ginny in her white and black work dress sprinting across the lawn to Mr. Carl near the cake table. "Tak, where's Crush? You two were supposed to stay with him."

Timmons curled his arm around my waist. "We skipped away to find you."

Tak tugged on me, announcing, "We can have cake. I don't remember ever having cake at someone's party."

Timmons giggled, "We had a muffin just yesterday, but cake is sweeter."

Tak jumped in a circle around me. "Come. Let's get some cake."

I tilted his chin. "I need to find Crush. Where did you last see him?"

Timmons answered for his sweet-toothed brother. "Crush is talking to the man who washed the elephants. He's over there."

I spun in the direction where Timmons pointed. "I don't see him. And I need him. I've got to get to him, and now." My voice rose to a pitch, bordering on a shout.

Tak grimaced and took a step backwards.

"Sorry, Tak. I didn't mean for my words to bite. I'm … I'm in a bit of trouble."

Tak whined, "Trouble? Did I make you mad?"

I wrapped my arms around his yellow hair. "No, never. You are too sweet. I have some things to work out, and Crush can help me."

Timmons held Tak's hand. "Come on, Let's get some cake. Shoelace will come in a minute. She can meet us by the table."

I smiled. "I'll see you both before you can swallow two bites of cake."

Tak and Timmons dashed to the spot where the children gathered, and right near the cake table two men dressed in Sunday suits were nodding and listening to Mr. Carl. They kept glancing back at the plantation house, and Ginny swished her arms like a lost bird.

I whispered to no one in particular. "Oh no. Carl knows Mahlee's gone. Ginny's a rat fink." Running between elbows, and bouncing off of bodies, I barreled up to the trunk of an elephant.

Baraaag-ummmmpt! Baraaag-ummmmpt!

"Girl, move away from the elephant. Did you see the rope? We marked off the spot for you to watch from a safe distance. Don't move. Let me help you away. Don't panic. Don't be afraid."

The man stepped from behind the tail of the elephant.

"Archie? I'm not scared of this elephant. You sound more afraid than me."

Archie moved a swanky, smooth tiptoe dance. "This one is temperamental. Seems he gets spooked by short people."

Laughing, I inched away, until I found myself on the right side of the rope. "Sorry, I didn't see the rope."

Archie secured the chain around the elephant's back leg, walking up to me. Tapping my shoulder, he quizzed me. "Now, little bit. Aren't you surprised by the size of these elephants?"

I snarled. "I was kind of surprised to wake up and see you'd left me."

"Oh, sorry. I didn't know we were traveling together."

"We're not."

"So are you looking for work? I hear they could use some clowns."

I didn't smile, his smart funny talk, not too funny. "I don't have time to join the circus. I have plans. Something's come up."

Archie nodded. "Well, I'm leaving on the train in three days with the crew. They've hired me on. My search for the pearl ends now. I'm on to the next great adventure. It's been nice following you around."

I gulped, wondering if Archie was lost in life, or if he loved riding the rail. I reached into my satchel. "Hey, I've got something for you. It just might make you rich."

Archie knelt down to knock some of the mud from his boot. "For me? Now what would you have that I might want? I've got everything except the elusive pearls. Maybe someday I'll go to Uncertain and do some digging."

"I have a pearl. My friends say it's a pebble. I say…" I clasped the pearl in my palm, opening my hand flat. "I say … this is a pearl. And it's valuable."

Archie picked the pearl up with two fingers. "My sweet girl. This is yours. It is valuable, I'm sure. You keep it. Just knowing you is like having a pearl."

"Now, you're acting mushy. I don't do mushy." I put the pearl back into the pouch inside my satchel. "Oh, no! What am I doing? I have to help Mahlee. I have to go." My tears fell without warning. "I'm sorry. I have to go."

Archie pulled a handkerchief from his pocket. "Go, be a messenger of hope with your life."

I shook my head. "You don't know how hard this might be."

"I know what I see. I see hope written all over you."

I hugged Archie with a sideways squeeze. "Bye, Archie. See you at the circus someday." I dashed in and out, and under and back, through the maze of people. I found myself standing in front of a fancy royal blue car. Jumping onto the bumper, I stood on the hood, scanning heads and hair. "There's Crush. He's with Marion Kane."

I waved my arms, shouting like a crazy girl. "Crush. Crush." I hurled myself to the ground, and charged toward Crush. Once there, I pinched him on the leg.

"What the … heck. Who did that?"

I popped up. "It's me. Come with me. It's life or death."

Crush squeezed past the man, following me, and we moved behind the car, the one I'd left my footprints on. He yanked on my satchel. "What are you doing? They're about to sing 'Happy Birthday' to Thaddeus."

"You don't understand. I found Mahlee. She was being kept in chains in a dungeon." I stretched the truth by mentioning chains, in hope of convincing him. "She has bruises on her face, and she's a witness to a crime Mr. Carl was involved in, from years ago. Now he's found her, and is making her work for him, to keep her quiet. He even put her inside of his trunk all night. She was in the car when he nearly hit you by the synagogue."

Crush shook me. "Slow down. A dungeon?"

"Is that all you heard?"

"No, but this is a plantation. Have you noticed? It's not likely there's a dungeon."

I slugged his arm. "Stop it. I don't have time. I've rescued Mahlee, and need the truck keys. I need you to drive us somewhere."

"No way! I'm not your chauffeur. The day you saw me driving was only the second time Mr. Marion let me behind the wheel. He's not going to just hand me the keys."

"Show me where he is, and I'll distract him. You can pickpocket the keys."

"Do you think I'm going to risk stealing for you?"

I pulled his ear, and he slapped my arm away.

"Shoelace, you are not worth this."

I tumbled to my knees. "Mahlee's my almost mama. I have to save her."

Two men sprinted by us, and one shouted, "You were the one who didn't stay by Mahlee's room. I was in charge of watching the gate. You had door duty."

The other man argued, "No, you've got it backwards. Now she's gone, and Carl will not let this go without someone taking the heat. I'm not going down for this. It's your fault."

They sounded like two birds fighting for life. I grabbed Crush. "See, they were holding Mahlee against her will."

Crush folded his arms, shaking his head, and then nodding. "You better be telling the truth. Mr. Marion trusts me. I'm risking his faith in me, for you. Do you hear me?"

I felt a rush of life run through my veins. "Yes, I understand. The keys. We need the keys. I'll run up to Mr. Marion, rattle on about the Big Top, and how much I love cake. I'll get Tak and Timmons tangled up in the laughter, and you can work your magic."

"Magic? This is not good for me. I used to do plenty of pickpocketing before the flood. The day after I saved Timmons and Tak and the others. Well, that's the day I met Marion Kane. He was helping clear wood and brush, and searching for survivors in the bayou. I picked his pocket, took five dollars."

My heart raced. "You weren't too smart."

Crush winced, and held his gut. "Stop it. He caught me with the money, but Mr. Marion took me under his wing, and told me to keep the five. He's guided me. He's trusted me. He's let me work for him. He started feeding us. He even buys the boys shoes. I could lose everything. They could lose even more. They could lose each other."

I felt time ticking, and Mahlee's life becoming more important than ever. Seeing Crush act like a real boy caused me to think of him as a human, barely.

Crush reached into his pocket. "I carry this five-dollar bill so I don't forget how close I came to going down the wrong path."

I found my tears returning. "But this is why I'm here. You can do a great thing on your new path." I hugged Crush. "I'm drowning. I can't do this without you. Will you save me? Will you save my Mahlee?"

The Key to Safety

Crush halted his marching, and I ran into him. "Sorry."

He tilted his head, peering around a wide man wearing a coat. He peeked back over his shoulder at me. "There's Mr. Marion. He's with the triplets."

I stood on my toes. "I can't see, but when I do get near Mr. Marion, I'll talk fast and chat about nothings, and include a few somethings."

"You already do that."

I smiled. "You've got me figured out."

Crush pushed between backsides of slacks and dresses, with me on his heels. He scolded me. "Hurry up. We have to time this exact or we'll get caught. I will slip my hand in his pocket when you ask him to pick you up. Hug his neck and scramble to stay on his hip, and I'll snatch the keys."

Skipping, I tapped his shoulder. "Thank you. You won't regret this."

He twisted his head. "I hope you're right."

We moved into an open knoll of winter grass, soggy from melted snow. I called to the man who knows too much already. "Mr. Marion." Bolting to him, I hung to his side like a daughter would her papa.

Mr. Marion cuddled me close, his strong arms wrapped me up, holding me higher than high. Tak and Timmons danced in skips around us, and Trip and Thicke galloped like ponies set loose from their corral.

Timmons and Tak yelled at Trip and Thicke, "We're going with you" and they trailed off with the other boys.

I stared at the woman by the cake whose dress came from the same stencil as Ginny's dress. She transferred flame after flame on the eleven candles from the lit match.

Crush inched next to me. "Stop goggling. We have work to do."

Nodding, I swallowed hard, nudging Crush with a stiff arm. "I am. Give me a second."

Thor tugged on my hand. "Go with me. They're going to sing to the boy. We get cake. Did you hear? Every child is invited to the party today."

Twisting my fingers from his, I whispered. "You go first. I'll catch up."

Thor paused, glanced at me, and then gazed at the other kids. He pointed to Thomas and Theodore who joined Tripp and Thicke. "I'll be with them," and he rushed off.

"Mr. Marion, will you hold me higher? I can't see."

"I will hold you up to the sun so you can see. The view of life is one of beauty."

I held onto his neck, wrapping my legs around his waist, and Mr. Marion patted my back. He gave me a clear view of the people, squeezing my leg. "Can you see? It's party time."

Glancing over the heads, I tried not to watch as Crush slipped up behind us, his hand reaching, his hand searching for the right pocket.

A singsong of voices rose up like a river rising from a flood. "Happy birthday to you. Happy birthday to you. Happy birthday dear …"

I shifted in Mr. Marion's arms, and my eyes fell onto my Taddy. He was blowing out his candles. My Taddy! His hair whipped in the wind, and Priscilla clung to his side, her arm draped over his shoulder. His smile went beyond his eleven years to a future where mamas smile, where mamas walk, and where mamas love.

I disappeared into my memories. Of me and Taddy climbing trees. Of our riding the boxcar on his birthday last year. Of the suds in the fountain downtown in Texarkana. Of finding my first best friend. I whispered, "Happy birthday. I love you, Taddy."

Crush tugged on my leg, calling to me above the singing. "Come see the elephants with me."

I wiggled from Mr. Marion's arms. "I'm going with Crush. We're checking out the animals."

He grinned, patting me on the head. "Don't get into any trouble."

"We won't."

Crush and me bolted through legs like balls bouncing off of lanes in a bowling alley. I made a dash to the right. "This way. Mahlee's over here." Crush darted to the left past the bumpers of a bunch of cars. "Over here, this way."

**

Sklamp!

Falling to the ground, I bounced off the small boy whose grin sliced through my heart like a friendship arrow. Rubbing my head, I squealed. "Taddy? My Taddy? Why are you running between cars? Why aren't you with your cake? You were just there. I saw you."

Taddy dusted his knees. "What in the heck are you doing here?" He hugged me. "I knew it! I knew it! Pastor Cody brought you, didn't he? That's the best birthday surprise. Almost better than riding boxcars eating cupcakes."

Together we jumped to our feet, dancing around each other like little elephants in a circus. I rubbed my chin.

"Umm… yes, it was Pastor Cody. He didn't want me to miss your party. I … I am so thrilled your mama made it here, too." I covered up my real story with a not-so-real story to keep Taddy from knowing anything about the ghosts of the week, or from letting on that my visit had nothing to do with Pastor Cody.

Taddy let go of my hands. "I'm after my mama's sweater. She's cold and left it in the car." He gazed at the maze of parked vehicles. "There it is. She said it was in the one next to Pastor Cody's truck."

I slugged his arm.

"Why did you do that?"

"It's for being the best friend ever."

Taddy winced. "You have a weird way of showing me."

I leaned in, my lips puckering for the first time since I could remember. *Smack!*

"What in the world? You just kissed me. Why? Why would you do that?"

"I have no idea." I spit on my fingers and scrubbed his cheek. "Wipe the kiss off. What was I thinking?"

Taddy moved my hand, clutching my fingers. He held onto my hand like a boy who likes kissing, and smiled. "So you do like me?"

I backed up. "I do not. Not like that."

"You do. Or you wouldn't have kissed me." Taddy squeezed my hand, letting go. "I'm getting Mama's wrap. Hurry and meet me at the table by the cake. I'll save a chair just for you. I can't believe you kissed me."

"It was an accident. I'll be there in a second." I knew I'd never sit in the chair next to Taddy. I had to find Crush, find Mahlee, and get off this plantation.

Taddy hurried between some cars.

I called to him. "I'll be right there. I'll be right there."

**

I blew across the grounds like the wind, moving away from Taddy, circling near a patch of trees by the driveway. Stopping behind a bush, touching my lips, I whispered. "I kissed Taddy. I kissed Taddy."

Commotion called to me from the front porch of the main house, confirming the gathering of Mr. Carl's men. "We have to find her," one of the six suits yelled. The mob charged down the steps, climbing into the back of a pickup. The driver sped off behind the mansion toward a dirt road leading into the woods. Two more men jogged inside, while another positioned himself at the foot of the stairs.

I ran to Crush whose head bobbed up and down across the way. "We've got to hurry. We don't have much time."

Crush snarled, "Where did you go?"

"I was right here. You're the one who left me." I motioned. "Mahlee's by the driveway in the shade over there." I zoomed around Mr. Marion's pickup, and Crush bumped into me. I shook my head. "What? Where is she? Where did Mahlee go?"

Crush pushed me hard, knocking me to the ground. "You are mixed up in something that's not good. Where is she? What is going on?"

I dove at Crush, slugging his chest. "Don't ever push me down again, or I'll beat the tar out of you. No one gets to hit me for nothing."

Crush threw me to the ground. "You need to stop acting like a spoiled brat. I can take you out any time. I'm tired of you and all your bossing. Look, your Mahlee isn't even here. Where do you think she went? Was she ever here?"

I jumped to my feet. "Yes, she's wandered off. Her spirit was breaking from being kept in the trunk and from Mr. Carl's beatings."

"Well, where would she go? I'm not sure you're telling me the truth. Truth hasn't followed you much these last few days."

I socked him, and we rolled on the ground again, and I released my anger. Anger at this terrible week. Anger that Crush was being such a bothersome boy.

Someone yanked on my collar, but yelled at Crush. "You're a boy. Hitting a girl isn't *ever* all right."

I squinted, unrolling myself, and standing up. "Toby? Where did you come from? Better yet, where have you been?"

"I met Pastor Cody from Texarkana. He holds Creek Church. It's called Swampoodle Creek. Isn't that exciting? I might replace him someday if ..."

I finished his sentence. "... if you don't make it in Hollywood. He's my pastor. I'm not sure anyone can replace him."

Toby nodded. "So why are you fighting with Crush?"

Crush dusted his shirt off. "She's gotten me mixed up in her con game. She talked me into pickpocketing Mr. Marion's keys to save her Mahlee friend, but there's no Mahlee to be found. I think she's lying to me, so she can steal the truck."

I zoomed at Crush, only for Toby to pull me back by my overall strap, causing my satchel to swing like a rocket, slamming into his face.

"Ouch, my eye. My eye. I can't see." Toby rubbed his face, whimpering on the ground.

I hurried to his side. "I'm sorry. I didn't mean for you to get hit."

Crush moved me aside. "Toby, let me see your eye." He peeled Toby's fingers from his cheek. "Red. Gonna have a bruise." He shook his head, giving me a not-so-happy glance. "This is your fault."

I yelled, "And yours. You were fighting with me."

**

I was scared to think where Mahlee walked off to, and worried she became afraid and disappeared back into the mansion to keep from dealing with Mr. Carl's wrath.

Leaning on the side panel of the truck, a hand grabbed my hair, and Mahlee screamed. "Where did you go? Carl's men were coming this way. Remind me to never leave you in charge if we're in a hurry." Mahlee jumped up and down in the bed of the truck. "I hid in here so they wouldn't see me. So what's your plan?"

"Mahlee, you're making too much noise. Stop it. And sit down."

Crush climbed into the truck. "Miss Mahlee? It's me, Crush. I'm here to take you to a safe place." He grinned at her with a calming smile, not the one I'm used to seeing. But it's the voice he uses with the boys.

Mahlee plopped into a kneeling position, and slid to one side on her hip. "Are we going away? Will we be safe? Is it possible?"

Toby asked, "What is going on here?"

I took Toby aside. "Just trust me. Remember the shooting at the Soda Street house? Remember the man by the river?"

"Yes, but … how is she connected?"

I glanced at the worn and tired face in the back of the truck. "Mahlee killed them both." I felt air suck from my lungs. "I think it was in self defense."

Crush lunged from the truck, leaving Mahlee rocking. "What? She's murdered two men, and we're helping her get away?"

I screamed louder than planned. "She did it to save her own life. She's not a killer. She's my mama."

Toby put a hand on my shoulder, and one on Crush. "Look at her. She's having a breakdown of emotions. Something tragic has happened to her. We have to find a way to help her."

Crush clutched the keys. "Shoelace, lay down with her in the back. Toby, hop in the cab with me. We're taking her ..." He stopped in his tracks. "Where are we taking her?"

Toby inhaled the rest of the air in the county. "We have to take her to the secret room."

Crush turned to me. "The secret room?"

"Yes, at my grandma's house."

Crush bounded to the driver's side, swinging the heavy door. He glanced at me, a glare of un-trust. I was glad Toby had faith in me.

I hopped into the bed of the truck, curling up next to Mahlee, holding her. Toby shuffled to the passenger side, twisting the handle and getting in.

Kaplunk-swish!

Bingo trapezed into the truck, ready for a ride to anywhere. He snuggled next to me, licking my face. "Good boy. Be still. We're having a rescue. And you're going with us."

Fear landed in my throat with each bump, as the gears grinded in the engine. I almost wished for another driver as we skidded from the driveway of the mansion. The squeal of the tires on soggy spots left a spray of mud flying from behind the truck. Each time we passed other cars, I pulled Mahlee down,

234

ducking with her. It was a ride of despair soaking my heart with anxious worry. "Mahlee, it's you and me. We can be together forever."

She hummed a tune from somewhere in her soul, a squeaky broken song, while petting Bingo on his ear.

I touched her tangled hair. "Mahlee, are you fading from me?"

She shook her head, her words slurred. "My days are gone. My life is spent. I can't go on. I've done much wrong."

I held her. "You can go on. We both can."

She repeated. "I'm here. There. Somewhere."

I prayed a prayer. "God, my Mahlee's broken. Help her. Please?"

Tub-a-blup. Tub-a-blup.

The rear tire hit a pothole on the slushy road, and sent us bouncing. Mahlee popped up. "No more guns. No more shooting. No more!"

"It's just a hole in the road." I cradled Mahlee in my arms, unsure what to do next. "Hold on, Mahlee. Hold on."

She slammed me against the side of the truck. "Get away from me."

"Mahlee, you can't toss me around. You need to act right."

Mahlee snatched me to her chest. "Mahlee is sorry. Mahlee is sorry."

Grrr! Grrr!

Bingo raised his head, and let Mahlee see his teeth.

I rubbed his head. "Mahlee is our friend."

He placed his snout on my leg, his nose bouncing from my shivers, and I'm afraid my saving Mahlee might not save me. I hope I'm wrong.

Secret Doors

Clunk-screech.

Bingo stretched his torso, leaping from the bed of the pickup.

Mahlee grabbed her ears. "My face is burning. The cold air whipped at me like a fly swatter." She sat up, craning her neck. "Do Crush and this Toby know what they're doing? Can we trust them?"

I climbed over the tailgate. "They're friends. They're making a way for us. This is Toby's grandpa's ... house. What are we doing here?" I scanned the yard, seeing the back porch where I borrowed milk the other morning. "Mr. Marion's driveway circles to the back of his house. Crush must be hiding the truck."

Mahlee mumbled. "Where are we going?"

"Next door. Just a second."

Crush and Toby emerged from the cab, both of them talking to each other, not listening, but explaining. Crush rushed around the front of the truck, his arms following every vowel of Toby's chatter. Crush shook his head. "I don't agree with you. This isn't the best idea you've ever had. You should stick to preaching."

Toby cleared his throat. "Crush, this is perfect. If she stays in the secret room, they'll find her."

I nodded, not sure why. "Wait? What's perfect?"

Crush folded his arms, clutching the keys with his right hand. "Toby figures Carl or his men will find Mahlee next door. He thinks hiding her here at his grandpa's house is better."

I tossed in my thoughts. "But we have a secret room."

Crush echoed, "Yea, a secret room. Or so you both keep saying."

Together, Toby and me answered, "We do."

Mahlee lunged like a whale falling from the truck. "Stop it. You have no idea what you've put yourself in the middle of." She turned to me. "I left with you only because I needed to get you off the plantation. I'm not staying here. I'm catching the next train out of Jefferson. I know them tracks is right across the road."

Shaking my head, I stuttered. "No, this … is not … happening. I have you now, and I'm keeping you." I shook my fist at Crush, then Toby. "I have the plan. I saved her. We do it my way."

Mahlee swung me around, like she was looking for a fast escape. "I have to leave. Carl will come searching for me. I can't let him hurt you."

Crush jingled the keys. "I had a major part in the saving."

I frowned at Crush. "But, I had the plan. The secret room is … a secret. No one will find her there."

Toby argued, flaring his nostrils. "They might find her. Since one man died there, they'll search your grandma's house for sure. This is why I came up with a new plan. This one will guarantee her safety."

Crush laughed like a frog. "Toby, nothing is guaranteed in this life. If we had guarantees, me and the boys would have our parents."

My gut rumbled with pain at those words, knowing the deep pit of sorrow he felt was the same pain I faced. "Crush, you're right. No guarantees. So my idea is as good as any."

Toby put his hands inside his pants pockets, kicking a leftover mound of snow. "We can't use the secret room. There's a reason we can't."

I shouted. "Why? Tell us."

Crush joined me. "Tell us, what you're not telling us."

"The secret room has more than one entrance."

I galumphed in a circle, thinking hard on what I remembered seeing in the secret room. A window with a cloth. A rising door entrance in the staircase. A piano bench. A piano up against the wall with a painting above it. A painting of a door. I rubbed my chin, and shrieked. "A painting of a door? Or was it a real door? No way. No way. There's a door behind the piano?"

Toby nodded, sighing. "Yes, there's another way into the secret room through the closet next to the blankets. It's a hidden door. And there's a mat with a key under it. They'll find it, and get inside."

I blinked long and hard. "Nice, a secret door to a secret room. You knew about this door and didn't tell me?"

"Wasn't the rising of the staircase more exciting?"

"Well, of course. But ..."

"It was grand. Anyone can walk through a regular door, but you made a grand entrance to the music room where lives are changed."

I needled Toby. "So does anyone else know about the secret room?"

"Not that I know of."

Crush stepped closer to us. "I know about it. Maybe someone will take me there someday."

Toby folded his hands. "Lord, we have to make a decision. Show me what to do."

I snarled. "Let Him show all of us what to do, not just you."

Toby continued with his reasons. "If Carl comes, or any of his people, then they'll search every part of the house. It's too risky."

Crush made a snowball from the slush. "Toby's right. I hate to admit it, but he's making sense."

Mahlee stomped in her boots, her twitching hands going to her neck. "Shoelace, you have no say in this matter. No one has to put me anywhere. I'm leaving."

I mocked her. "This is more than *this matter*, it's our life. We're family. And you can't leave now, not after all of this."

"Carl is not letting me get off. He's sure I'm involved in the other two murders, and he's right. He'll see me dead or not at all."

Crush whispered, "So you did shoot the other two men?"

Mahlee stormed at Crush, stopping a few inches from his nose. "It was self defense. Me or them. I chose them."

I parted them like peeling icing off the top of a cake, growling at Crush. "They held Mahlee against her will. Like Mahlee said, it was self defense."

Crush grimaced. "I hope you're right."

I got back to Mahlee who was mouthing under her breath. "Mahlee, I did this for you, so we can be together."

Mahlee snorted, wrapping her coat tight around her. "I did this for you. I rode with you to get you away from Carl."

Toby inched between me and Mahlee, and he interrupted us. He sounded like a pastor who loved people. His way of gazing at us reminded me of Pastor Cody and how he makes me feel.

Mahlee burst into song, chiming lost notes from the rail, from our past. Her words were off key, but a rainbow of hope resounded through parts of the lyrics. She whispered low and sweet, something I rarely hear. "Someday I'll wish upon a star, and wake up where the clouds are far … behind me, where troubles melt like lemon drops."

I smashed the snow close to the house with my tennis shoes, pretending lemon drops were melting on the ground, taken in by the call of hope coming from my Mahlee.

She paused in her singing, her hands covering her mouth as if she was a child too embarrassed to sing.

Toby clasped Mahlee's hand. "Now, let's go inside my house, and talk this over."

Mahlee yanked her hand away. "I have to leave. I am putting you all in danger."

I rolled my eyes. "Toby, she's not going with you. When she gets nervous or upset, she goes to a deep-land of rocking, and well, acting worse than me. She'll scream, and even hit."

Swa-lap.

Ouch! I rubbed my face. "Mahlee! Stop acting crazy in front of them. Don't hit me, either."

Mahlee hugged me, apologizing. "You are my wish-upon-a-star girl. You and Lizzy Beth. If I can make you mad enough, you'll not want me. I want you to live. If you stay with me, they'll get you."

Tears ran down my face. "Mahlee, I'm never letting you go."

Toby slipped his fingers into Mahlee's palm, trying to persuade her once more. He offered her mercy. "Mahlee, the sadness you hold tends to show up in anger and fear. Come inside. You'll be safe in my house. Remember, your help comes from God."

Mahlee closed her eyes, and she pulled Toby's hand to her cheek. "You speak life when you talk. You have hope inside you." She opened her eyes, and kissed his forehead. "I'll go with you and listen to your plan. The longer we stay here in the backyard, the better chance Carl's men will drive up next door."

Crush pursed his lips and gave me a gaze, and I puckered my lips, ready to spout off. Mahlee and Toby sauntered to the back porch where Toby escorted Mahlee inside. Crush and me shadowed them, me first, then Crush, and Bingo slipped in with us.

The kitchen danced with yellow and white colors, bright like a new day, clean like I've never seen before. Toby motioned to me, grinning at how I ran my hand over the white countertop with the yellow canisters. Across the room next to the breakfast table, an armoire with glass doors held dozens of jars of syrup. I whispered. "Your grandpa has syrup everywhere, doesn't he?"

Mahlee called from somewhere down the hallway. "Where am I going? Toby?"

"Coming. We're right behind you. There are only two bedrooms. Mine is the second one."

Crush answered my forgotten question. "Mr. Marion loves sweet syrup on grilled cheese sandwiches and on cheese toast. He's the kindest man I've ever known." I watched as Crush ran his fingers across the front of the syrup cabinet.

Shuffling into a bedroom painted in blue with clouds on the ceiling, and a rainbow in the corner by the window, Mahlee plopped onto the bed, right onto her back. She started singing in a girly voice, one I had no idea existed. Her lips sent lyrics to the ceiling. "Somewhere over the rainbow, way up high, and the dreams that you dreamed of, once in a lullaby."

Crush leaned against the dresser next to a stack of Bibles. "Is she normal? Does she drink?"

Mahlee grinned. "Don't talk about me like I'm not here. I don't drink anymore. Used too, long time back."

241

He chuckled. "Sorry, you just … seem to … flip back and forth. You act a lot like …" He paused, biting his bottom lip.

Mahlee finished his sentence. "I act like a little girl who wears red PF Flyers and overalls, who's in this room."

I stomped, wishing I'd not reacted with a fit. "I don't have a flip-flopper attitude."

Toby smiled, and patted my arm. "You might flop some."

Mahlee waved at one of the clouds. "Shoelace is a wanderer who is looking for her a family. She thinks it includes me. I wanted it too, but now Carl's after me. It just won't work. Poor thing, she's spent way too much time with me in boxcars and at missions these past few years. She's acting like me more and more!"

I announced, "I don't mind. I love you, Mahlee! It will work!"

For a few moments, our time in the blue room with clouds seemed as if we were in a meadow by the river after a spring rain. Perfect. Calm. And quiet. We all listened to Mahlee hum, and I sighed with relief at getting away from the plantation.

Toby brought us back to our purpose. "Mahlee, you and Shoelace need to stay here in my room. My grandpa doesn't ever come in here without knocking. He respects my studying my verses, so he whistles when he's coming down the hall. This way I know he's about to knock."

I planted myself on the bed right next to Mahlee, and I gazed at the clouds on the ceiling. "Toby? That's your plan? To keep us in this room?"

"For now. I have to think. We'll come up with more later. At least this way, you're not in Carl's sights."

Crush clapped his hands, clanking the keys together. "Has anyone thought about the time? I need to get the pickup back to the plantation before Mr. Marion misses his keys. Toby, come on. You'll have to ride with me. He'll expect you to be there."

Toby agreed, his head bobbing up and down, a sideways bob, since my head was flat on the mattress. I wiggled close to Mahlee, turning my head toward Toby. "Hey, will you lock us inside the house? We are safe, right?"

Crush left the room, while Toby gave his final orders. "Stay in here. This is now your secret room."

I mimicked Mahlee's singing. "Somewhere over the rainbow is … our new life."

Toby shut the door, and I jumped to peek from the window on the side, catching a glimpse of Crush driving the pickup away. "Mahlee, they're gone. We can rest for now. I can't believe you're here with me. I can't believe this week is over. I can't believe …" I put the shade down and twisted to get a glimpse of my new mama, who was fast asleep on the royal blue bedspread, who clutched a pillow like a small girl dreaming about real rainbows.

I found new tears streaming down my face, dropped my satchel, crossed my legs, and sat on the wooden floor next to the bed, listening to Mahlee breathe. I noticed her broad nose and strong cheeks, and her calloused hands. She almost smiled in her sleep, and she gave me a brand new memory to save. I'll tuck it away in a secret pocket of my heart.

I placed my head on the edge of the bed. Bingo snuggled up against my feet, and my heart ticked slower than it had in the past few hours. Tired from fleeing, worn from worry, and relaxed to be with Mahlee, my eyes closed, and sleep was sending me to my own dreams.

**

"This is not acceptable behavior. Crush, I'm shocked. After all we've been through together. And you, Toby, the preacher. How do you think God feels about two boys who steal a truck?"

I jumped to my feet, putting my ear to the door. The shouting from the front room belonged to Mr. Marion. I listened, kneeled, and waited.

"So when you drove back to the plantation, how did you plan on returning my keys? Who took them? Crush, did you? Or was it you, Toby?"

"Me, sir." Crush answered with a sorrowful whine. "Sir, there's more to this than we can say. But it's not what it seems."

"That's right. We have a secret and if we tell anyone, someone will die." Toby added his part, the part I wished he'd kept to himself.

"Secrets? We don't keep secrets from each other."

Toby finished his explanation. "No, sir. Not usually. But this is different. I've given my word. You want me to stay true to my word, don't you?"

"Son, you never lie to me, but tonight, you've disappointed me. Crush, I'll run you home. Thomas and Theodore are getting the boys down for the night. We'll talk more later, but for the next few days, I won't need your help at the syrup factory."

"Sir, I will work for nothing. I won't take your keys again. It's the girl. She made me. She talked me into it. She's nothing but trouble. She convinced me to take her … to take her away."

Toby countered Crush. "That's not entirely true. It's my fault. I wanted to help her. She caught the train out of town, and hopped a boxcar. She was ready to go home. Said she was tired of running."

I realized Toby was making up stories to cover for me, to cover for Crush, and to keep Mahlee and me a secret.

Scraaaatch. Ruff! Ruff!

"Who's in your bedroom? Shoelace isn't in there, is she?" Mr. Marion didn't whistle, but somehow I knew it was his shoes clunking down the hallway, getting louder and louder. Bingo was ready to invite Mr. Marion into the room. My heart throbbed, and I swiveled around, ready to wake up Mahlee. But she was gone!

Pam Kumpe

Ghost and Memories

The doorknob tweaked, and Bingo pawed the floor, growling a whine with his snout near the crack under the door. I dove into the closet at the end of the bed. The empty, Mahlee-is-missing bed!

Hiding behind Toby's hanging shirts and facing outwards, I hovered next to his dangling pants on hangers. What a precise, organized fashion of putting clothes on hangers. I glanced at my tennis shoes, dirty and stained, and in need of laundering again, and they stood out next to Toby's polished loafers.

"Grandpa, it's not what it appears." Toby's response to his grandpa left me wiggling deeper into the closet.

"What have we got here?" Mr. Marion's question bounced off Toby's clouds in the bedroom. "Bingo, you've gotten my floors tracked up with mud. Come on, boy. Outside. It's the back porch for you. Or you can ride with me to run Crush home. Toby, I'll talk to you more when I get back."

Sla-amb.

**

"Are you in here? Shoelace? Mahlee?"

Watching Toby from the opened closet, I knew my shoes were poking out at the bottom. I whispered from the shadow of preacher clothes. "Toby, are you alone?"

Toby spun like a top. "Is that your nose between the hangers?"

"Yes, can I come out?"

246

"Sure, tell Mahlee it's safe now."

I parted the creases in the starched pants. "Mahlee's gone. She's not here, and I have no idea what to do." I hugged my arms, plopping onto the bed, slapping the mattress, and rocking. "We were here. Together. We fell asleep, or she did first. Then I watched her, and fell asleep myself. She can't be gone. She was here. Why did she leave?" I picked up my satchel from the floor, the flap open, and latched it, tossing it on the bed.

Toby sat next to me. "She is afraid. People act unusual when scared, and she thinks you're in danger. She may have gone for the police."

I pushed Toby to the floor. "For the cops? She's not going to do that. She's run off again, and left me here. I'm tired of chasing her, tired of fighting to keep her." I hollered. "No, I have to go for her. She makes my head feel like dreams never come true." I hugged my tummy, the rumbling sour taste rolling up my throat, ready to spew.

Toby tilted his head, standing at attention. "Are you about to throw up?"

I pursed my lips. "Yes, where's your bathroom?"

"Down the hall to the left. First door."

Charging out of the bedroom, I scooted to the bathroom, slamming the door behind me, and hovering over the toilet, hurling the hurts Mahlee left behind in my soul.

Acck-splurk! Acck-splurk!

I tumbled to my knees, hugging the toilet lid. "Mahlee, I love you. I can't believe I found you, got you here, and now you've deserted me. I am so mad at you. I hope I never see you again. Ever!" Saliva and tummy acids crept into my throat, and vomit dripped like pain into the water.

Knock. Knock.

"Are you feeling better? My grandpa will return in a minute. We'll need to tell him the truth. The truth will set us free." Toby reasoned with himself, using his reasoning on me.

I grappled for one of the three towels on the rack above the toilet. Two blue, the middle one yellow. I snatched the yellow towel, wiping my face and smearing tears from my eyes. My ears burned, my throat stung, and I glared at my bloodshot eyes in the mirror. I shook my fists. "Mahlee, why can't we be a regular family?"

Swinging the towel, I slapped the cloth against the ghost image taunting me in my memory. I swung. I screamed. I battled the shadow, which favored, favored my Mahlee. The ghost was the shape of her, and even wore the same brown skirt and tan top, and the long coat that hung over her clunky boots. It seemed ... seemed ... real, just like Mahlee. I swallowed my spit. "Mahlee?" I shoved the not-ghost memory and she toppled backwards into the claw-foot tub.

Cla-plud-kunk.

"Mahlee? What in ... what are you doing in the tub?"

"Shoelace, stop hitting me, and help me out of this bathtub."

"What? You're not a ghost? You're not a memory? My ... my Mahlee is still here?"

"I am. I'm as real as you are."

"But you left. You were gone."

Mahlee swung her legs over the tub, bracing herself on the edge. "I woke up and simply went to the bathroom."

"What? You were in here the whole time?" I didn't wait for an answer, and studied the bathroom, looking at the tub, the white sink, and the toilet. No closet. No place to hide. I accused Mahlee. "You came in through the door. You weren't in here. There's no place to hide."

"I was curled up in the tub, balled up and out of sight. I hid from all the talking in the other room. I didn't know you were coming in here. I heard the puking, and the crying. You've splashed the floor, made a mess, and even gotten vomit on the wall."

"Well, you made me sick." I wrapped my hands in the towel. "So you weren't leaving? You just came to the bathroom?"

"I told you. I woke up. Most people go the bathroom when they get up." She used her firm, in-control tone. "How did I make you sick? I'm not capable of churning your stomach up like that."

"You did. All the hellos and goodbyes make my stomach ache."

Mahlee balanced herself on the edge of the tub. "Toby's grandpa yelled and made me nervous. I'm not sure he's on my side. Where … where is he now?"

"He took Crush home. Toby's in the hallway. It's time to tell Marion Kane that you're here. We need to figure out how to save you, and me, and even Lizzy Beth."

Bam. Bam. Bam.

Toby called to me through the door. "Shoelace, do I need to help you?" His muffled words dropped like a mist.

I shook my foot of vomit. "No, I'm better. I have to tell you something, so don't freak out." I swung the door open. "I've made a mess in here."

Toby's faced drained of any color, and his hand went to his face. "My goodness. What have you done in here?"

"I was sick, but look who I found. Mahlee's here. She never left."

Toby grabbed towels from the linen closet and wiped the floor, the toilet, and the sink. "My grandpa can't stand a dirty house. Gosh, Shoelace, this is flat out nasty."

I watched from the hall, and Mahlee shook her head, standing next to me. After Toby cleaned my stink up, we moved from the bathroom, down the hall to his bedroom.

Toby tossed questions at me as if he was cleaning up my story. "So, Mahlee never ran off? She's not running away?"

I giggled. "She never left. She was in the bathroom." I twisted my mouth to Toby's ear, whispering. "I think she was getting ready to run when Mr. Marion brought you and Crush back. She hid in the bathroom because she didn't escape fast enough."

Mahlee twirled around with a clunk. "I can hear every word. I started to leave. I wanted to keep you out of this. I'm confused about so much of it, and clear on parts. Don't talk behind my back. If you have something to say to me, be brave enough to speak your mind."

I plodded up to next to her. "Since when does that work? I've begged you to be my mama, and I know Carl and his men hurt you, but you run from family more than anyone I know."

She mouthed. "Not more than you."

"That's not true. I want a family. I just have trouble being in one place sometimes."

"Me, too. Staying put is hard after riding the rail all these years. With Ernie dumping me, then Carl seeing me, I lost my way."

Toby asked, "So who's Ernie?"

I uttered, "Mahlee's old boyfriend. He broke up with her."

Mahlee shook her head. "He broke my heart, but I kept the ring. I'm not so sure about Ernie. He disappeared so much without me knowing why when we were dating, like during all those murders in '46. He kept all the newspaper stories he wrote about the Phantom Killer. He would read them at night and touch the photos in the paper. I'm sort of scared of him in some ways. Now he's taking that new job. He's stranger than us."

I reminded her. "No, you didn't keep the engagement ring. You left it at the manor with your blue ring."

Toby followed us into the bedroom. "Blue ring? Who is the Phantom Killer?"

I sighed. "He's a masked killer in Texarkana who attacked people. He killed five, and hurt three others."

Mahlee sat down, explaining her rings. "The blue ring has my initials. Taddy's mama, Priscilla, gave it to me for Christmas. My engagement ring is prettier than anything."

Toby rubbed his ear. "Is Taddy the same boy at Carl's house? He's the same one, isn't he?" He squinted his eyes, like he was putting puzzle pieces together. "It's odd that God would bring Taddy here to Jefferson, and the both of you, too. I wonder what God's up to?"

I slugged his arm. "He didn't bring me here. I followed the rail."

Mahlee agreed. "I was brought here by Carl and his men."

Toby shook his head. "I believe God brings good from things even when we don't understand. I think He's up to something big."

Mahlee stomped her feet. "He needs to let us know. I'm not too fond of living in the dark or being held hostage."

I hugged Mahlee on the waist. "I want to see what He's doing. Maybe God did this so we could find each other, and never let go."

Toby smiled. "Yes, that's a good start. Never let go."

"I put your rings inside my satchel." I reached into my satchel at the end of the bed. "Here they are. They're pretty, huh?" I unfolded my hand, holding them out.

"Why did you take them?"

"Why not?" I clasped them in my palm, and stuck them back in the satchel.

"Because of the memories. Memories remind me of what could have been. I don't want no memories."

"Fine, then keep me. I don't want to be a memory."

Tak-a-tump.

Toby shut his bedroom door. "That's my grandpa in the kitchen. He's just come in the house, and we need to tell him what's going on. Be ready. He's going to shout, and his eyes will bug out, too."

Mahlee paced, picking up one of Toby's Bibles from the dresser. "This is heavy. I've never seen this many giant Bibles in one place."

Toby retrieved his Bible. "Thank you, but this is my pa's Bible. He has notes written on the pages, and scribbles. No one touches this one." Toby placed the Bible right where it had sat, exactly in the spot designed for this Bible.

Mahlee apologized. "Sorry, no disrespect. I was going to suggest we pray."

Toby's face lit up. "We better whisper silent ones, because the time has come to talk to my grandpa. Are you both ready? I'm opening the door."

Marion Kane called from the front part of the house. "Toby, we aren't finished with our talk. Join me in here, please."

Toby cracked the door. "Yes, sir. I'll be right there. I'm ready to tell you everything." He turned back to us. "Are you ready?"

Mahlee nodded, and I did, too.

Toby marched ahead, and I followed him part way down the hallway, and then he made a right to the front room.

Clunk. Clunk. Clunk.

The pounding of Mahlee's shoes kept going down the hall. I called to her. "Mahlee, this way. Not that way. That's the kitchen. That's the KITCHEN!"

Mahlee charged to the back of the house, and I ran after her. "Wait, you can't leave."

I barreled out the screen door and onto the porch, and Bingo danced up next to me. Mahlee scooted to a stop in the yard and charged me. She dug in her coat pocket, and flicked open a straight razor, waving it at me. "Stay here. You can't go with me."

"No!! And where did you get that?" I screamed at her like a daughter whose heart was sliced in half.

"I found it in the bathroom." She pointed the razor at my face. "Stay. I mean it. Don't follow me."

I held my breath, and Mahlee disappeared into the shadows of the sunset. She darted between Mr. Marion's house and my grandma's house, heading toward the street.

Bingo sprang like a gazelle, and I felt my skin crawl with bumps of anger shooting through my veins. I screamed, "I knew you were leaving. You only went to the bathroom because Marion Kane almost caught you. I never want to see you again. And I mean it."

Toby shadowed me. "She left? Why now?"

Marion Kane joined us, and I stomped my shoes. I yelled into the darkness, the shadows of the night loomed over us like death. "Mahlee, I don't mean it. Mahlee, I want you more than anything. Come back."

Suitcases of Our Past Hide Secrets

Mr. Marion spun around and headed to the kitchen door. "That's it, I'm making the phone call. I should have gotten the sheriff involved when my truck came up missing. Something bigger than a hobo girl running into my truck is underway here." Marion Kane stormed inside, leaving me and Toby staring at each other on the porch.

I jumped to the ground. "I'm going after her." I tramped in Mahlee's footsteps, and rounded the back of Mr. Marion's house. I rushed between the single-story house where Toby lived, the place where calm embraced the ordinary, where home felt safe and in this case, clean. I came to the corner of the lonely house belonging to Mahlee. An empty home of Grandma's past, the empty place of my future.

Ruff. Ruff. Ruff.

At the corner, I peeked around a bush, trying to figure out what Bingo barked at. Headlights by the mailbox meant a car had driven up. The commotion near the front porch sent me behind the shrubs, watching. Mahlee was on the first step, stopped in her tracks because a small shadow had latched onto her leg. "Miss Mahlee, I remember you. You were in the hall at Wheelock. I sat on your lap."

Mahlee clicked her razor closed, slipping it into her pocket, and her fingers ran through Lizzy Beth's black hair. "Hey, my precious little daugh ... ter. I mean, friend. What are you doing here?"

Susan walked around from the back of the sky-blue car, carrying suitcases in each hand. "There, that's all of them. I've gotten the basement at the synagogue cleared out. Oh my ...

hello there." She dropped the suitcases next to the others on the porch.

I barged from the bushes, waving my arms like I was attending a party in the night. The past of Mahlee's life collided with mine, and derailed with Lizzy Beth. "Susan, it's me, Shoelace. What are you and Lizzy Beth doing here?"

Susan rubbed her hands together, and pulled Lizzy Beth close to her skirt. "I've gotten my cleaning finished up at the synagogue, and these suitcases belong to Toby and the Crush boys. I know they come here for secret meetings, too. I brought them here, but I can't get that blasted door open. It's jammed."

Mahlee held out her right hand. "Hello, I'm Mahlee Shaw. I met Lizzy Beth in Oklahoma last month, right before you and your husband adopted her, I believe."

Lizzy Beth acted like a grown up, grasping Mahlee's twitching fingers. "Hi, Mahlee. I'm your friend. Will you be my friend? Shoelace is my friend, but she keeps hiding and leaving. I want her to stay."

"I'm back for now." Hugging her, I bent down, getting eye to eye. "Did you see the elephants today?"

"No, my mama is taking me tomorrow. We had cleaning work to finish."

"You will love them. They have lions, too. And clowns who act silly, who chase each other. It's just like we saw at the cafe this morning."

Mahlee coughed, kicking her boot on a loose piece of wood, her glare constantly on Susan.

Susan shook the handle on the front door. "Can anyone get this opened? It's stuck. I had trouble with it the other day, too."

Toby came into view from the side yard, and he frowned at me. "Hi, everyone. What are we having here? A suitcase party?"

I chimed in. "Susan brought your ghost tour suitcases back. She's wanting to put them inside so you can give them to Crush, but as usual, the door is hung."

Toby greeted Lizzy Beth. "Hey there. I haven't seen you in a while. You're getting so big."

Mahlee sighed and gave a snort. "She's not so big. She's petite like I used to be when I was nearly four."

I tugged on her coat sleeve. "You probably don't remember being four."

Mahlee slapped my hand free. "I do. I remember staying in the old house by the creek, and my mama and papa kept me close by. They thought I would never grow, and then when I turned ten, I grew two feet. I turned into a monster beside the other kids in the hills near Washington, in Arkansas." Mahlee rubbed her ears, both of them. "Them spring tornadoes came one after another. On the year I turned thirteen … and the funnel clouds wiped out our home, and knocked over the trees. Our one cow was gone. The barn in splinters. My pa under the barn. My ma never was found. I was alone in a collapsed room layered in splintered wood. By myself. Sitting in the rubble."

Toby touched Mahlee's arm. "I'm so sorry. How sad."

Mahlee swiped his fingers from her sleeve. "A couple of the boys up the road got left behind too, and they hit the rail, and so did I."

I got lost in Mahlee's reminiscing, and Susan shoved her shoulder on the door, with no luck. Her mission to drop off the suitcases became more important than listening to Mahlee unpack her past.

Toby offered to help Susan. "Let me see if I can get the door open. The frame swells when the weather's damp and cold."

Lizzy Beth latched her hand with Mahlee's again. "I like you. You is tall. You is big. You has a nice smile."

Mahlee grinned, the first one I've seen since I don't know when.

Susan twisted around, and swiped her hand between Lizzy Beth and Mahlee, causing them to let go of each other's hands. Mahlee grunted, losing her smile.

Susan ushered Lizzy Beth to the curb. "Why don't you sit in the car? The air's chilly, you'll catch a cold. You've had your bath already, too. No need for dirt to find a way to cling to you."

Lizzy Beth shook her head, blinking her eyes. "But we have company, and I like company."

Susan argued, "Company is when they're at your house."

"Then can they come over?"

"Not tonight, my dear. We have much to do."

I inched near Lizzy Beth. "Maybe I can see you before I leave for home. Me and Mahlee are headed home. Right, Mahlee?"

Mahlee nodded, but her dogmatic stare told me *no*.

Toby threw his arms up. "I can't get this door open for nothing."

From the side of the yard, Mr. Marion appeared, his stomping in the slushy winter grass purposed and steady. "What is going on here? We're standing in the yard freezing, I see. All of you come on. Let's go in my house where there's a fire, and lights. The darkness has settled in on our town tonight." He touched Mahlee on the shoulder. "And you my friend, why don't you show them the way to the kitchen?"

Mahlee snarled at Marion, his intent words caused her to flare her nostrils. "I'm not the one to lead them in. It's your house."

Susan countered his offer. "No, thank you, Marion. Just making a stop to get rid of these suitcases."

Mr. Marion shuffled to them, running his hand over the handles of the suitcases. "These are special ones. I expect the secrets inside have not been discovered yet."

Toby followed his grandpa's steps. "What are you talking about?"

"Oh nothing, Son. But the message inside of them might be the answer to having life and family."

Toby hugged his grandpa. "You talk in riddles like my pa. It makes me miss him so when you do."

I spoke up. "I have a friend at Wheelock who loves riddles. She smokes cigarettes."

Everyone glared at me as if I'd said a cuss word. "What? What did I say? It's not like I said I smoked, although I have burned some cigarettes in an ashtray to remind myself of my pa."

Mr. Marion motioned. "Come on. We're having a walk down memory lane, and the temperature is dropping." He no sooner got his words out than two cars approached, one from the left, the other from the right. They rolled up, headlight to headlight, in front of the house. One was a Cadillac. The other was a police car.

I stepped to Mahlee, and she and I inched backwards, then sideways, moving closer to the edge of the yard between the houses. I whispered to her. "Don't you run off and leave me. I know where we can hide."

Toby must have read my mind, and moved to us. "Walk to the back of the house. No one is watching us. Mr. Marion and Susan are checking with our guests."

I swallowed hard. "I'm not so sure they're guests."

Mahlee yanked on my sleeve. "Stop your squawking."

Toby agreed, "Hurry up. Let's go to the secret room and … beyond."

The three of us charged to the backyard of my grandma's house, flying into the kitchen where a lone syrup jar sat on the dusty counter.

Toby hollered in a whispered command. "To the quilt closet. I'll get the key. We'll grab some blankets and slide into the secret room. We'll stay there until they leave. That had to be Carl in the Cadillac."

Mahlee's voiced rang out in the musty air. "I hope you know what you're doing. If I hadn't run into Lizzy Beth and Susan, I'd be gone."

Toby answered, "I see that God's up to something again. He kept you here."

Mahlee rebutted, "He did not. They just got in my way."

I could hear talking through the broken windows in the house, where the chill rushed in, where words rang out. Those of Marion's, and the other men, who had a gruff crack in their tone.

Toby climbed into the closet over the quilts and shoved his body into the door in the back. "The piano's in front of the door. I'll get it. Just a second. Here we go. It's budging now."

I pushed him. "Hurry. They'll find us if you don't open the door."

Mahlee squeezed past me, shoving Toby aside. "Let me do it." She body-slammed the door, and the wooden entrance opened wide enough for us to slip into the room.

Mahlee tumbled in first, and I tossed her a stack of blankets. I caught my satchel on the door handle, untangled it, and fell inside. I turned back to check on Toby, but he was facing the hallway, next to the stairs.

A shadow asked Toby a question. "Hi, Toby. What are you doing? Are you playing hide 'n seek?"

Toby put his hands on his knees. "Lizzy Beth, what are you doing here?"

"I followed you. You left. Everyone keeps leaving."

"You need to go back to your mama. This is a secret spot. Promise you won't tell."

"You have a secret?"

"Yes, Mahlee and me, and Shoelace."

I stuck my head around Toby. "Please don't tell anyone we're here."

Lizzy Beth ignored my comment and gave me her toddler thoughts. "I have a secret. Want to know what it is?"

I could feel Mahlee hovering behind me, like she was ready to dart from the house. I moved to the side, making sure Toby and me were blocking her exit. I patted Lizzy Beth's shoulder. "Sure, tell me your secret."

Lizzy Beth hiccupped. "I have a big secret. It makes me special."

Toby asked, "We know you're special, but you need to be going."

Mahlee pushed me out of the way. "Let her talk, Toby. So what's your secret, Lizzy Beth?"

She gulped, her hiccups caught in her throat. "Mama Susan told me that when she and Mr. Boyd gave me a forever home, that I now had two mamas. Mama Susan said she loves my first mama, cause she made it so I could live with her. That makes me special."

Mahlee's sobs rang out in the dark of the closet. "Bless your heart, child. You are more special than you know." Mahlee embraced Lizzy Beth. "Remember this hug, it's the one that confirms how special you are to me."

Lizzy Beth touched Mahlee's hair. "I will keep your secret, if you'll keep mine."

We all answered yes, and I jumped inside the secret room. Mahlee gave Lizzy Beth a peck on the forehead. "Bye, sweet girl."

Lizzy Beth waved. "Bye." She shuffled into the dark hallway. "I don't remember which way."

Toby handed me the key. "Lock yourself in the room with Mahlee. No matter what, don't come out tonight. I'll take Lizzy Beth to her mama. My grandpa will be looking for me, anyway. I'll come over in the morning before school."

"I'll see you then." I shoved the door closed, locking it behind me, putting the key on top of the piano.

Mahlee leaned against the piano. "Help me push this against the door, just to make sure it's secure."

In three shoves, we were bound up in the secret room, me and Mahlee without an escape. Although, I did know how to open the staircase entrance with the button, but I'm not showing Mahlee—she'll run off again.

Mahlee paced, muttered, and circled the room. "Lizzy Beth knows her real mama is not a bad mama. Susan will take good care of her."

I tried to hug Mahlee, but she mumbled words and circled by me, lost in her own secrets, those of her past, those of tornadoes, those that took her parents, those that sent her to the rail. Seeing Lizzy Beth tonight has sent her mind into confusion, and she muttered her daughter's name over and over.

"Mahlee, promise you won't leave me."

She stomped by me, not answering, but she whispered, "Lizzy Beth. Lizzy Beth."

"Mahlee, promise you'll take me with you."

She paced to the corner, her hands flying up, her words filled with letters and vowels, but no sentences that I could understand—except Lizzy Beth.

I unfolded a blanket and wrapped up in it, shaking, moving to Mahlee who now slumped to the floor in a corner. I covered her with my blanket, and rushed to get the rest of the pile.

I layered our bodies with the fuzzy blankets and quilts, and the only light sneaking in the room came from the lone window across from the piano. I sat next to Mahlee and placed my head on her shoulder.

She ran her fingers through my tangled hair, and I let my satchel fall to the floor by my feet. Mahlee whispered, "Lizzy Beth, I'm sorry I gave you away. My heart is dead, I'm empty. How I wish I could go back, and keep you."

I wanted to remind Mahlee of my name, but somehow just sitting next to her in the dark allowed the music of tomorrow to slip in, and it gave me hope. I pray we'll always be together, but her mumbles aren't including me. I just hope when the sun comes up, my name rolls from her lips.

Knife to my Heart

Tangled in the quilt, the biting chill from the hardwood floor zapped my right arm that was tucked under my body. My left arm hung over my head, and I sat up. "My goodness. My hand and most of my arm are asleep." I roused; squirming, and my skin tingled, the prickled-itch running up and down my arm. "Mahlee, the sun's up. Mahlee?"

Grappling with the folds in my quilt, I jumped to my feet, with my sound-asleep arm wobbling in the air. "Mahlee?"

I darted to the window, shoving the dangling pillowcase to the side, staring at a row of man-size trees with no leaves. I whirled around, tumbling over a stack of quilts, and my satchel lay opened again. "The snap on my satchel must be loose." I picked it up, closing the bag, and tossed it to the pile of bedding.

Footprints littered the dusty floor, that of Mahlee's boots, and mine. The others must be Toby's. "Why does she keep leaving? Is she that scared for me? We're free now. Free." Bolting to the now-twisted-sideways piano, my heart lost all of its joy in one swoop, in one sunrise, in one moment when all went numb. So much for being free.

I could go any direction searching for Mahlee, and miss her by one house or one block. Or even by one town. The pain of the week cut deep, and my weathered heart pumped tired blood into my veins. Chasing a mama who doesn't want me is worse than losing a daddy in a river from an accident.

A glittered speck caught my attention from the top of the piano. "What's that? Mahlee's razor knife?" I reached for the blade, clutching it, clicking it open, and flicking the knife closed. "Why didn't she take this? Why? I don't understand her. I don't know what makes her stay and run, or hide and go." I flipped the knife open, slashing the air into pieces.

Screaming, I yelled at Mahlee again, and sliced the oxygen into more fragments. Catching my shoe on a quilt, I attacked the fabric with the knife as I fell, jabbing and tearing, slicing and ripping. "Life's not fair! No one wants me!!" I rubbed my forehead, the prickly stitches itching. I wasn't even sure when the stupid bandage fell off.

I stabbed the quilt again, the point of the knife going through the cloth and sticking into the wood. "Darn. Darn. Darn." I yanked on the knife with bold hands, tumbling onto my backside holding the blade.

Wielding the knife and pretending to fight off the ghosts speaking to me in the dusty air, I stabbed the invisible hauntings. I fought for some fun memories with Mahlee, but the final one is always the same—I end up alone. "I don't belong to anyone. No one wants me. Not anyone."

The ghost reminded me how Toby and Crush locked me in the synagogue, how Susan let me go to her house, and how Lizzy Beth's bed felt soft like feathers, and the ghost confused me with memories of truth about myself, of my being bossy, mouthy, and rude. I lunged at the ghost I could not see. "Stop bothering me. I will never have a home like Lizzy Beth. Or like Toby's. Never."

I melted to the floor, dropping the knife, the clinking an echo of my hollow heart. Sobbing, my pulse thumped in my neck, a pit-pat gush of sadness. "Why, God? Why am I alone?"

In one second, one flash, and one tick of my heart, I heard my grandma's words. *I love you. You are not alone.*

I popped up, wiping snot from my nose with the back of my hand. "Grandma? Are you here?"

Nothing. I glanced around the room, a barren empty place without music. Without singing. Only sobbing. Mine.

Sniffling, I tasted the salty tears on my lips, and scolded myself. "You should have stayed awake. You knew she'd make a break for it, but you couldn't keep your eyes open. Could you?"

I stomped my feet, shouting at the suffocation of not having answers. "I hoped she'd stay. I prayed she would, but God doesn't hear me."

A voice in my head spoke to my heart. "God hears you. His heart is for you. He's the hope you have. He's the song for you."

I put my hands to my ears. "Whoever you are, stop speaking to me. Don't ever tell me God hears me. If He did, He'd give me a message that I can hang onto, not just thoughts and pretend ghosts, or voices in my head. I need a God who loves me. I need to know it. I don't need a message written in sand that blows away. I need something I can count on. That's just for me."

I kicked the knife across the floor and paced in circles, going over what to do, what not to do, where to go, and where not to go. "I have nowhere to go. I have nowhere to stay. I will need to hop a train. Mahlee's left me for good. I can't stay here. Carl's men will find me, or he will. I have to go. I have to go."

I fretted, and peeked out the window, the sun higher in the sky, the roads empty. Toby would be at school by now. I wonder why he didn't check on me. Mr. Marion would be at work. Susan would be at the cafe, and Lizzy Beth would be with her. Crush and the boys would be at their house on the river. Archie would be working with the elephants. Taddy and his mama were probably going home. Pastor Cody, along with Slow Tom and Fast Tim, well, they might have left yesterday. But me? I don't have any place to be. I whimpered. "I am a ghost. No one sees me. No one needs me."

I tiptoed, realizing I needed to use the bathroom, and slung my satchel over my shoulder. I bent down for the razor knife, making sure it was clicked closed, tucking it inside my satchel. My tantrum left a trail behind, and I kicked the strips of cloth over to a pile, not sure why, unless Mr. Marion's cleaning traits were sticking with me. I smiled, thinking of his spotless kitchen, and those perfect clothes on perfect hangers in Toby's closet.

My gagging and puking were a reminder of another trail I'd left behind last night. "Sorry, Toby. I didn't mean to get sick."

At the piano, I hit some keys.

Dong. Ding. Dong. DONG!

"Nope, not music. Just noise."

A sparkle at the end of the piano keys glowed with flickers. "There's the key to my freedom. Or I could just push the secret button on the wall." Holding the key by the loop on the end, I knew it was time to make my way out of town for good.

I squeezed behind the end of the piano, bracing myself by grabbing the top. "Ouch! A splinter?" I stuck my finger into my mouth, using my front teeth to bite on the sliver. "Whew, that's better."

I stood on my tiptoes to take a look at what seemed like words etched in the wood, moving to the front of the piano. My satchel swung around my hip, dinging and donging on the keys. I read the letters to myself, stepping away and blinking hard, wondering if I was dreaming. I pinched my arm. "Ouch. That hurts."

I shook my head, and tears flowed without permission, while my heart beat with love notes from somewhere deep. A somewhere I'd never expected. "No way. This is not possible. It's not written in sand. The words are written in the wood."

I careened my neck like a stork, making out the words. Shuffling closer, my hands sweated, and my tears dripped like a leaky faucet. My chest tightened like four hundred balloons ready to burst. Rubbing my hand over each letter, I counted them. "One. Two. Three … Twenty-nine. Thirty. Forty-four. Forty-five." I lost count, but no matter how many letters, they were the most bestest letters I'd ever touched in my life.

I rattled them aloud, making words into sentences, making sentences into a chorus of hope. They read: Mahlee was here. She has two daughters and she loves them.

I tumbled to my knees, hugging my chest with both arms. "Mahlee loves me. She does. I have it in writing." I rocked on my knees, letting the anger go, letting the sadness flow, and hearing real music in the secret room for the first time. "God, thank you for sending me this note. If I never see my Mahlee again, I know she loves me."

Creeaaaak.

The door pushed open, and a voice yelled at me from behind the piano. "Who's in there? I have a gun. You better come out."

Runaway Notes Etched on Hearts

Pad-atak. Pad-atak.

A four-legged force skated into the room.

"Bingo? Bingo."

His legs danced four different ways, and he plowed into me, wiping me across the floor like a dust mop, my hands gathering up pieces of fabric. A puffy pile of scraps floated onto Bingo's ears.

Crush stuck his head into the room. "Shoelace? Is that you?"

I jumped in the air, not because it was Crush but because I needed a bathroom, and quick. I shouted at him. "How did you find this room? The door wasn't locked?"

"No, it swung right open, and I followed the noise. Took me a few minutes to figure out where to look."

I waved an arm. "This is the secret room Toby and me told you about." I pressed my legs closer, dancing. "I'll be right back. I have to go to the bathroom."

Crush blocked the door. "What? You're just running off. I'm not letting you get off that easy."

My tennis shoes tapped together. "No, I promise. I'll tell you about last night. Toby's the one who put me and Mahlee in here. We hid out from Susan and Lizzy Beth, and the cops, and Mr. Carl, even Mr. Marion."

"Really? Then where is Mahlee? Seems she didn't get the message to stay put."

I inched toward the door. "She ... she sort of left me."

Crush put his hands on his hips. "What did you do to our quilts? They're shredded."

I wiggled, sure I was going to have an accident on the floor. "I gave God a piece of my mind, and the quilts took the blows."

Crush interrupted me. "Go on. Use the old outhouse out back. It's behind the gazebo."

"I've been using the bathroom upstairs."

"No wonder it stinks in this house. There's no running water. Hasn't been for as far back as I know."

"There is, too. It's on. I have flushed the toilet every time. Check the faucets. The water is running. It doesn't smell in here either, unless it's the smell of your attitude towards me." I shuffled past him, shot into the hallway, and rounded to the staircase, dashing up the stairs.

**

I saw Crush tossing a log onto the fire. My frozen nose and ears, along with the tingle in my toes hadn't hurt from the chill, or from the freezing air. I sighed, thinking how my temper had kept me warm most of the morning.

In the middle of the room, suitcases were lined up in a row like they were waiting for passengers at a train station who forgot their luggage. I moved to the double-door opening, ready to finish my talk with Crush, ready to flee at the first chance I could.

Giggles rose up in the room next to the wall, and I peeked inside.

"Surprise! We thought we'd never see you again."

I tumbled to the floor, holding my chest.

The boys shouted. "We thought you were gone. We heard you left town." The voices of Tak and Timmons, along with the triplets, and Thomas and Theodore bellowed at me. They rattled on, talking together, repeating, and laughing. They all hugged me in one big swirl of happiness, rolling me around on the floor.

Crush folded his arms. "You spend a lot of time on the floor."

I pounced to my feet. "You spend too much time looking down on others."

He stepped to me. "You spend too much time giving others a piece of your mind. And you spend too much time screaming in empty rooms at empty air."

I pushed Crush with my finger. "You're too bossy."

Before Crush answered with more insults, Thomas pushed his glasses up, stepping between us. "Crush, you are bossy."

Theodore piped in, sitting on a suitcase with his legs crossed. "Bossy might be too stiff. He's more like a private investigator. He doesn't trust too many folks."

Crush knocked Theodore's foot to the floor. "I watch out for you boys. I make sure no one bothers us. It's my job. I ... care what happens to you."

I came to his defense, not sure why. "I love to 'vestigate things, that's why I get in trouble sometimes. I'm not good at living quiet, or without my nose checking into stuff, either."

Crush wrinkled his nose. "You're on my side?"

"I might be, but I'm not sure how I got there."

Tak hugged my leg, and Timmons wrapped his fingers in my hand, my heart swelling big like a watermelon in summer, ready to burst.

"So what are you boys doing here? This is not your house, you know."

Crush sat on a suitcase. "Toby came down our trail this morning before he went to school, letting me know Susan brought our suitcases. Seems our ghost tours are over for now. No more basement to use at the synagogue."

"Synagogue?" I rubbed my ear, scratching my head. "I've been wondering something. The other night when you and Toby put me in the basement to be a ghost, to hide out, the chain got locked. Locked! Did you hear me?"

Tak whined, "Someone locked you in our ghost room?"

Timmons joined in. "Who would do that?"

I tilted my head, pursing my lips. "Yes, Crush. Who would do that?"

"It wasn't me. Toby thought you'd run away, and I told him it might be the best thing. He locked the chain, so we could get Marion Kane, but then, back here, the police were here, and the dead man, and all kinds of commotion. We didn't get to go back until late to check on you, but you were gone."

I smarted off. "Thanks to Susan. She saved me. But her husband, Mr. Boyd, he didn't take a liking to me. So I had to leave."

Crush shook his head. "You leave places more than you stay. You're not good at staying put, either."

"No, riding the rail gets in your blood." I thought about Mahlee and how the rail was her life, how running was what she does, how I was so much like her that it scared me. I touched the handle on a suitcase. "What are you going to do with these?"

Crush ran his fingers over one of the suitcases. "We have thirteen. Empty. All of them. I don't know who leaves them, or why. I don't know why anything happens. All I know is you've been in our way."

Bingo padded into the front room with my satchel in tow. "Hey boy, thank you for bringing my bag." Wiping a tear on my face, I plopped to the floor near the fire, afraid to leave, afraid to stay.

Tak kissed my nose. "Are you crying? Why do you cry? Crush hugs us until we stop crying." He turned to Crush. "Hug her. She needs a hug."

Timmons didn't wait for Crush to respond, and wrapped his tiny arms around my neck, whispering, "Crush loves us. He just acts tough. No one knows he cries late at night when we're supposed to be asleep."

I wiped my nose. "Timmons, thank you for the hug." I gazed up, and Crush held a handkerchief for me. I giggled. "Is it clean?"

Crush sighed, "Yes, it's clean. Archie gave it to me at the birthday party yesterday. Well, before the birthday. Actually, it was when he let me touch the elephant's trunk, before you talked me into losing Mr. Marion's trust."

I grabbed it. "Thanks."

"Archie mentioned your knack for needing them, and he hoped I'd get the chance to hand it to you with his message."

I cradled the soft handkerchief in my hand. "What message?"

"He said that if I ever see you crying ..." Crush coughed into his hand. "He said ... goodness, this is weird."

"Tell me."

The boys hollered in unison. "Tell her."

"He said to tell you that you have special tears, and for every tear you catch in a handkerchief, it's as if God catches them for you. He said God holds your tears."

Blaahh!

I blew my nose, not sure how to respond to the message, and hoped a squeal from my nostrils might lighten things up. "When I blow my nose, what does that mean to God?"

Thomas stepped to me, pushing his glasses in place. "It means God catches your snot."

Tak and Timmons held their tummies, giggling, and my shoulders rose up and down. "Thomas, you're too funny."

"No, I'm logical. It only makes sense."

Crush placed a hand on Thomas' shoulder. "That's a good one. I'm going to remember it."

Thomas rolled his eyes. "I'm not sure what you mean, but it does beg the question. What are we going to do with our suitcases? Shall we carry them to our house? It's only a few blocks. Some of us can carry two."

Tak tugged on a brown suitcase. "I can carry two. I'm big." He spun toward Thomas, only to drop the suitcase, causing it to open wide, like it was ready for packing.

I stood, inspecting the flaps in the suitcase. "It's strange that someone leaves you these. Are you sure they're empty?"

Crush mocked me, using a high girly sound. "Are you sure they're empty?" He pointed. "It looks empty to me."

I stuck my hand inside the pocket of the lid, my fingers touching something flimsy. "What's this?" I pulled out a folded piece of paper from the pocket, yellow like the sun. I opened the paper. "Look, someone left a note in here. It's addressed to …"

Before I could finish, the Crush boys unlatched and unclicked the rest of the suitcases, opening the remaining ones. Arms waved and each of them held the same stationery. Thomas shouted, "This suitcase has a note. This one, too."

Thor had two notes, and so did Crush. The rest of the Crush boys held transforming, life-changing words, which had been hidden away for too long.

We each read them silently to ourselves, at first. Well, not Tak, he just stared at his note. I snatched his from him. It said the same thing. With puzzled faces, we exchanged papers, and we all kept reading the stationery as if we thought the words would change.

Tak asked again and again. "What do they say? What?"

Crush broke the silence, stomping in a circle. "This can't be happening. All this time, we've been getting the same note in every suitcase? And for months? And they're all from … the same person."

Theodore finished the sentence for Crush. "They're all from Marion Kane Raike. He wants to adopt all of us. Did you hear that? All of us?"

The triplets hugged each other, and Thor asked Crush. "Are these for real?" He rattled the paper in the air.

Thomas countered, "Yeah! How do we know he sent them?"

Tak closed the brown suitcase and jumped onto it like a circus trainer. "We can ask him. If he wants us, we will get another brother. Toby will be our brother. He can preach to us anytime he wants, too."

Theodore mouthed, "He already does."

Crush laughed, pulling Tak from the suitcase. "Slow down. We need to figure out how to handle this. After all, why didn't Mr. Marion just ask us himself? He doesn't have to hide notes."

The boys argued, discussed, and decided to wait until the right time to ask Mr. Marion if the notes were real. I tossed in my thoughts. "Toby would say God might be up to something good."

Crush waved his arm. "Or this could be some horrible joke."

Timmons held onto Crush. "You are a good daddy, but we could use a daddy who tucks us in bed, and who has more food."

Crush swallowed Timmons up, hiding his own tears.

The boys gathered around Crush, and Bingo lay by the fire. I sneaked off to the side, ready to skip out, to figure out my next move, to deal with the fact that no one left a note for me inside of a suitcase.

I stuffed the handkerchief inside my satchel, tossed the bag on my shoulder, and made my way to the foyer, to the next room, to the kitchen, and to the porch.

With the house being on the corner, I could slip off to the street, to the thicket, and to the tracks. A train would leave the depot soon, and I'd make a dash for it, and ride for a while, to write my own note, one that didn't include adoption, or a mama, or even a papa.

I darted out the door, to the street by the man-size trees, and a black car with a dent in the bumper rolled toward me. "No! It's Carl. No!"

Pam Kumpe

When Pearls Crash and Burn

I pressed my satchel against my side, my legs racing to the front of the house. Slipping behind the thicket of branches and bushes, the ones White Beard hiked through the other night, I ducked out of sight.

Ah! Uh! Ah! Uh!

My panting grew heavier with each stomp, the soggy ground leaving mud prints behind me. Most of this part of the woods remained hidden from the sunshine, and the sloshy snow waited for tomorrow's sun. "I've got to get to the tracks. I'll get away from Carl then, because his car can't drive where trains go."

I pushed the droopy branches, parting the way to the slope leading to the rail. Charging into the open, I bent over and cupped my knees with my hands, my chest heaving in and out like my breath was gone but returning. The warmth of the sun brought heat to my back. "What am I going to do? Where should I go? I can't let Carl catch me."

I spent the next few minutes spinning in a circle, taking a step, backing up, and twisting my body as if the wringer on a washer was squeezing me dry. I sat down on the rail, hugging my knees.

"Dear God, it's me. I'm getting in the practice of talking to you, but somehow I'm not sure you want to hear from me this often."

A flutter of birds at the top of one of the spindly trees laced the barren limbs with red. "Hey, it's more cardinals. I wonder if they're here for the funeral for the bird White Beard killed?"

They sang together a song of sorrow, a chirping of a song gone wrong.

Woo-cheer. Woo-cheer. Woo-cheer. Woo-woo-woo.

I swallowed hard, missing my kitty, wishing to hold his furry body close, wishing to feel his sandpaper tongue on my face. I called to the birds. "I'm sorry. I didn't know my cat would hurt your family. He … he's a wild cat. Well, he was …" I sniffled, putting my hands to my mouth, remembering my loud voice carried more than I wish it would.

The woodsy area between the road and me might be keeping me safe from Carl, but I'm going to have to leave. I slung my hair off my shoulders, sucked in courage from somewhere deep inside, somewhere around my toes, and stood up. One of the redbirds fluttered above my head, circling my hair, and he lighted on the rail to my right, twitching his beak, bobbing his head.

"Should I go that way?" Speaking to a bird that didn't understand me felt like talking to God.

The bird whistled the same trill notes, *woo-cheer*, only this time the whistle sounded sweet like syrup, like he gave me permission to go down the tracks. Or I hoped this might be his message.

I jumped from railroad tie to railroad tie, leaping with steps and keeping my eyes ahead, but checking behind me, too. "Bye, little bird. I'm sorry you lost your brother, or uncle, or dad. I know how you feel."

A nasty chicken hawk floated near me, too close. "Shoo! Don't bother me." The hawk spread his wings and landed on top of a dead tree.

Cheer-reek. Cheer-reek.

His squawks were bothersome. They reminded me of another bird that tried to kill my cat last year. "Get out of here!" I swung my satchel in the air, and erupted with more yells. "You're not wanted here. Go on. Get now."

The wind sent a gust of air and another group of birds soared into the sky toward Soda Street, to a place I would miss, to a place where Mahlee wrote me a love letter. I'd give anything to take the top off that piano and carry the wood with me forever.

Up ahead, the railroad sign acted like a warning for cars, which meant the road cut through and over the tracks leading to the highway. Or to a farm. Or to another town. The chugging sound of a car's engine echoed to my left through the thicket.

I froze in place, and the front of a bumper came into view on the road that led over the tracks. The chug-a-lug pickup bounced by, and headed to my right going on down the road.

I held my breath. "Phew! I'm glad that wasn't Carl."

"Shoelace. Shoelace. Wait up. I wanted to show you something." A squeaky voice called my name. "Shoelace, it's me, Tak. Wait up."

I reeled around, squinting my eyes from the glare of the sun, and the shadow of Tak waving his arms came at me like a small train without wheels. "What are you doing? You aren't allowed to be here."

Tak held his throat, breathing hard. "I can, too. You left without saying goodbye. You keep leaving. You have to stop that. I want to keep you."

Hugging Tak, I turned his body around. "Go on. Crush will get onto you. The trains barrel down these tracks. You could get hurt."

"I'm not getting hurt. I'm getting you." Tak spoke to the direction he came, but spun like a top, facing me. "I have something. I found it by the river by our house. I want to show it to you."

I knelt down, pushing the yellow hair from his eyes. "Show me. Show me what you found."

"I have it. I do." Tak dug in his back pocket, in the other back pocket. "Wait, it's in my front pocket in my jeans. I know it. I have it." He planted both hands inside his front pockets, and his right hand shot into the air, making a fist with his fingers. "Here, I've got it."

"What? What do you have?"

He held his hand out in front of me. "It's a pearl. Timmons said it's just a rock but I say it's a pearl."

I ran my finger over the shiny pearl, and dropped my satchel to the ground, unlatching the flap. "Wait a minute, I have one, too. We have matching pearls." I dug inside my satchel, retrieving the pearl, and placed mine next to Tak's. "See, they are the same."

"They do match. They might be brothers."

"They might be."

Choo-choo. Chugga-chugga. Choo-choo. Chugga-chugga.

A faint sound of a train somewhere in the distance rattled birds from the trees, and the echo of a steam engine bounced in the wind. "Tak, go home. Go now, and get off the tracks. Cut through the road over there, and stay off this rail. A train's coming, and I'm not sure from where." I grabbed his shoulders, shaking Tak. "Do you understand?"

"Look what you did. You made me drop the pearls."

"No time for pearls. Get off the tracks, and now."

"No, I have to have my pearl. Don't you want yours?"

"I do." I paused and listened, but no train whistle, no chugs. I put my hand on one of the rails, and felt no trembles. "Tak, get your pearl. I'm sorry. I don't want you to get hit by a train."

He reached for his pearl by one of the brown nails sticking up on a tie. "I found mine."

I ruffled his hair, and picked up my pearl from the dirt. "Now get going, I'll see you after a while."

Tak kicked the loose gravel, and stuck his pearl inside his pocket. "You promise to come back?"

I stuck my pearl into my satchel. "I promise."

Tak pursed his lips, as if he caught the tone in my voice, but he ran down the tracks from where he'd come. I watched him like a mother might, and kept waiting for him to leave the tracks. I hollered, "Tak, the train's coming. Turn. Turn now."

He shook his head, his words lost in the wind because he was too far away. Tak changed his stance, put his hands on his hips, and ran back to me.

I met him halfway. "What it is? Why are you not leaving?"

He whined, "I don't want to say bye to you. I don't think you meant your promise. You won't be back, will you?"

"Oh, Tak. You don't understand. It's too hard to explain."

"I am smart. I am. I can't read so good, but my heart knows things."

I hugged him close. "What does your heart know?"

"It knows you need me."

I broke down, sobbing for the umpteenth time this week. "Oh, Tak, you are so right. But if I stay, things will get too mixed up."

My shaking and jerking shoulders went in rhythm with Tak's shoulders, and we wept on the tracks. I knew I was saying goodbye for real, and for good. "Crush will be looking for you. Hurry on."

"I love you, Shoelace."

"I love you, too, sweet boy."

He gave me a grin, and for the first time, I noticed his snaggled smile. "Bye. I will go, but I won't forget." He held his hands over his heart. "It feels broken."

I put my hand to my chest. "Mine, too. But you have to go, and don't tell Crush you saw me, either."

Carl Says Goodbye

Tak headed home, and my shuffled steps were packed in loneliness. My thoughts were caught in the what ifs of staying in Jefferson, and the what ifs of having the boys for my brothers. Too many what ifs, with no good answers. I disappeared into the possibility, but all I could hear was Crush honking at me on the days when he'd drive Mr. Marion's truck. He would be like a mean big brother who would boss and order me around.

Honk. Honk. Honk.

"Wait." I shook my head. "Carl?" The honking was real, and not in my head. The Cadillac idled and sat straddled on the tracks in the road with the passenger door opened. Carl motioned for me to join him.

I backed up, not answering, but Carl bent his head to the side, and clutched the steering wheel with his left hand. He dug inside his suit jacket, revealing a pistol, and pointed the barrel at me. He yelled, "Get in the car. Don't make me use this."

I stepped a few feet closer. "I'm not going with you. If I get in, you'll shoot me. If I don't get in, you'll shoot me." I folded my arms.

Carl smiled, a sly crooked grin. "Seems your little friend is running to you. He might be a good enough reason to get in the car."

I glanced over my shoulder, and turned back to Carl. "Hey, don't get him involved. He's just a little kid." I smarted off, hoping someone would drive up. "What do you want with me? I'm no good to you. You don't even know me."

Carl coughed, "You know where Mahlee is."

"I do not. She's gone."

"Sure she is." Carl put the car in gear and moved up a few inches, then locked it into park. He pointed the gun right at Tak, who was running down the tracks toward me.

Screaming, I yelled at Tak. "Go away. Get. I don't want you here."

Tak stopped on the rail, whining and wailing at me, but I couldn't hear what he was saying. The *chugga-choo-choo* shouted from around the bend of the tracks, growing louder, but I still couldn't see the train. "Tak, get off the tracks!"

Tak didn't move, and I swirled around, facing Carl. He waved his pistol from inside the front seat of his dented car, right at my face.

Waving my arms, I put myself right between Tak and Carl, and hoped Tak didn't see the gun. I leaned inside the passenger door, shouting, offering my deal. "Mr. Carl, don't shoot Tak. He's not much younger than your Taddy. He's my friend. I'll get in, but you have to promise that you'll let Tak go. I have to watch out for him, there's a train coming. So I'm keeping my hand on this handle, in case I have to get him."

Carl patted the seat. "Hop in then, we need to talk. You can make this happen fast or slow. You decide."

I waved off Tak, hoping he'd get off the tracks, but he stood still like a pretend little boy without the will or ability to move. He rolled his pearl in his fingers. "Tak, put your pearl up, and go home!"

He didn't respond or move.

I turned to Carl, my throat dropping to my stomach. Choking, I sucked in fear. "You don't have to do this. Your Taddy thinks you're a kind and good person. I'm Taddy's best friend, and he would die if he knew you had a gun on me." I reasoned with Carl, while listening for the train, and at the same time, I kept looking back at Tak, who hadn't moved.

Carl patted the seat again. "It's up to you on how this turns out."

I climbed into the car, pulling the door closed. "It's not up to me. You have the gun in your hand. I'm just a girl trying to go home."

Carl argued his case. "Your Mahlee should have never shouted at me in Texarkana. I'd long forgotten her. I couldn't take the chance she'd tell someone about ... about the bank robbery and well, the other stuff."

"Mahlee can be mouthy, but she wouldn't have told," I assured Carl, but I knew in my heart that I wasn't telling the truth. "My friend, Toby, would call you a bad man."

"I'm not ... bad. I have a past, and it's caught up with me. I remember... you..." Carl put his fingers under my chin. "You were much younger, but those blue eyes are like pearls. Pretty and fresh."

I swiped his hand from my face, and kicked the gun from his hand. "I'm not your pearl." My legs walloped Carl in the side, and I dove to the floorboard for the gun, coming up with it in both hands, kneeling on my knees. I pointed the gun at Carl, who slapped me with the back of his hand.

Owwww!

My head slammed into the dash, and Carl snatched the pistol from me. "Girl, you're a lot like your mama, Mahlee. She's wiry and brash herself. That's why Stilley and Young had to go, too. She was talking them into siding with her, to turn me in, so I shot them. Do you hear that? Both of them. I'm not afraid to shoot a little girl, either."

Tap. Tap. Tap.

Sobbing, I wiped the blood pouring from my mouth. "Mahlee didn't shoot them?"

Chuckling, Carl replied with sharpness in his voice. "Of course not. I followed her down the trail by the river and heard her talking to Stilley. He got fresh with her and they struggled, so I took care of him." Carl rubbed his brow. "Then Young made the mistake of talking to her on the phone from my plantation. I followed them back to that abandoned house on Soda Street, in time to see her aiming her gun at him. She can't shoot, but I can. I took care of Young, too. The police will think it's her. No one will believe it's me."

I wept. "I believe it. I believe it's you. My Taddy doesn't deserve you."

Tap. Tap. Tap.

Carl shook the gun in the air. "It's your little guy. He's tapping on your window. Get rid of him. Or you'll both come up missing."

I cracked my door, and before I could speak, Tak cried, "I dropped my pearl again. I can't find it." He stopped mid-cry. "Hey, that's the man who let us come to the birthday party."

Carl tucked the gun inside his coat.

Tak licked his lips. "Thank you, Mister. That was the first time I'd had cake in, forever. Taddy told me you're the nicest man in the whole wide world."

Clearing his throat, Carl's voice rattled. "Thank you, son. You best be gone now."

Tak shouted at me. "Help me. I need my pearl."

I raised my eyebrows and glanced at Carl who removed his pocket watch from his vest, and his fingers ran over the cluster of pearls on the case. I quizzed him. "Did you happen to lose a couple of pearls?"

He wrinkled his nose. "Hmm, I did. Somehow I figure that boy has one of them."

I changed the subject. "Come on. Let us go. We won't say a word."

Carl shook his noggin. "Nope. Not until you tell me where Mahlee is."

"I can't tell you. I don't know. She's gone."

Tak tugged on my sleeve. "Help me. Please."

Carl switched to his criminal voice. "Little girl. We have to go."

Tak gave up on me and ran back to the spot on the tracks where he lost his pearl, and started digging. The *chugga-choo, chugga-choo* brought the steam engine into view, and it barreled at us. "Tak! Tak!" I screamed, but Carl held my arm, keeping me from leaving the car.

I wailed. "If that was Taddy you wouldn't let him get hit by a train. You don't have to do this. You can change, and be sorry for your bad stuff." My screams make my neck hurt, and I yanked and yanked, and I wiped blood from my face.

Carl's nose stopped twitching, and his fingers unfolded in slow motion. "Hurry, go save the boy, and save yourself."

I jumped from the car, and shot Carl one last glance, as he placed the pistol on the seat. I gave him a compliment that came from somewhere hidden inside of me. "Carl, my Taddy does deserve you, when you're like this."

He whispered, "Taddy is the son I never had."

Like lightning, I charged toward Tak, who dug in the ground. He was unaware of the train choo-chooing and whistling, of how close it was to hitting us. "Tak, we have to get off the tracks." I pulled him into my arms like a dead fish from the river, and we rolled off the tracks, down the slope like syrup jars, landing in a slushy wet creek.

The train rolled ahead, a flat-out roar toward Carl's car, and the wheels on the train sent sparks flying.

Carl put his head on the steering wheel, and I held Tak against my chest, shielding him. Pushing Tak inside the tunnel under the tracks, we held our ears. The rumbling metal sounded like thunder, and the screeching explosion of bending and crunching pierced my ears.

I peeked from the tunnel in time to see the train crimp. The boxcars tore into the woods past the spot where Carl's car once sat. Ducking back under the bridge, I hugged Tak, and he whimpered. "I just wanted my pearl."

"I know. I know."

The booming and crunching sounds lessened, and we moved to the side of the tracks. "No! Carl's not … not dead."

I ran to the car, which was now upside down, and the heat from the fire sent me back down the tracks. "No! This can't be happening!" I crumpled to the ground. "I hate it when people die."

Tak touched my shoulder. "Me, too. I miss my ma and pa."

Together Tak and me rocked in the dirt, and we huddled like bear cubs, while the crackling continued, and the train caught fire. Fire trucks rolled in and police cars, too. Sirens sounded, but no birds sang, and Tak and me cried until Mr. Marion showed up. Then we blubbered and moaned, and that's when I realized Tak's leg gushed with blood, and my … satchel …

Cheer-reek. Cheer-reek.

"No! That blasted chicken hawk took my satchel."

Pam Kumpe

Music Plays, Hearts Sing, Lives Change

Standing in the bathroom, I slipped the white dress on from my satchel. "Wrinkled! I can't wear Eleanor's dress to the dedication like this." I grabbed a washrag, wet it in the sink, and ironed the wrinkles from my dress with the damp cloth. Twirling around the cotton dress stitched by my friend from Wheelock, I floated like a cloud, a clumsy one, but light just the same.

I sat on the edge of the tub staring at the two-tone, brown and white Stride Rite shoes, the ones Susan thought I needed to have besides my red PF Flyers. I guess I'll wear them. I crammed my tennis shoes into my satchel, and hugged my bag, thankful for Crush who climbed a tree four days after the train wreck to rescue it from a branch where the chicken hawk left it. I hate that day; it's a reminder of the train slamming into the Cadillac, the awful-no-good, horrible goodbye to Mr. Carl.

Knock. Knock. Knock.

"Are you ready? We're having the ceremony. You don't want to miss it." Toby's squeal sneaked into the bathroom like a squeaky toy.

"I'm coming." I laced my shoes, slung my satchel on my shoulder, and took a glance in the mirror, rubbing the new scar on my forehead with my fingers.

I disappeared into my reflection, staring into my own eyes. I wondered why the sheriff didn't believe my version of what happened on the tracks. Mr. Sheriff figured Carl had car trouble, but I was there, I saw the whole thing. Carl let the train barrel into his door.

288

I blinked my eyes and the face of the sheriff popped into the mirror. I could see his pen tapping the desk and it made me want to kick him, even now. He didn't care about my pearl or Tak's pearl, or how we found them or where. Carl's watch must have gotten burned up, it was never found in the wreckage.

Shaking my fist at the mirror, I shouted at the sheriff. "I told you about sitting in Carl's car, about the gun pointed at me, and how he admitted to shooting his worker men. And you kept tapping that stupid pen."

Knock. Knock. Knock.

I wiped the sheriff's face from the mirror, not happy with how he handled the 'vestigation. The sheriff had his mind made up, and he's ready to arrest Mahlee, if he ever finds her. I don't expect he will. I'm glad she ran away, because no one believes she's innocent. Well, I do. Toby does, too. And Mr. Marion. Crush is doubtful, but I know my Mahlee, and she's not a killer. She's just a hobo on the run. She's lost in the pages of her own life.

Knock. Knock.

Toby bellowed. "Hurry up. The ceremony is starting."

I cracked the door open and stepped into the hall.

"Whoa! I've never seen you in a dress."

I flared my nostrils, and touched my braided hair. "Don't get used to it."

"I have a feeling I won't see you wearing a dress after today."

I glanced at my Stride Rites. "Or these." Clomping next door, to the front yard of the Soda Street house, I saw people in suits and dresses. They chatted and pointed at my grandma's house—and they were all smiling. Mr. Marion's bald spot shined in the sun, and his grin reached for blocks. He babbled with another man, whose belly was bigger than his jacket, and the two men stood perched on the freshly painted front porch with new pieces of wood.

The broken windows in the house held new panes, and the floors inside were polished to a sheen. The painters stroked clouds and rainbows in all of the bedrooms at the request of Toby.

The builders hammered day and night to connect my grandma's house with a giant hallway leading to Mr. Marion's home. He hasn't liked all the dust flying into his spotless kitchen from all the sawing, not that I have, either. I've slept on a pallet in the front room every night for the past three weeks, with Mr. Marion sleeping on the sofa with one eye open. He's making sure I don't run off before Pastor Cody picks me up tomorrow.

At first, I wouldn't tell him how to find my friends or family after the train wreck. But after I saw Tak leaving the hospital with only a small bandage, and after Mr. Marion gave the boys a forever home, I made a plan to let him send me back to Texarkana. Well, that is, until today. Now, I've got a new plan and it's taking me down the rail to a place where answers come and life is free.

"Shoelace. Come stand with us. They're going to unveil the sign. I have a feeling you're going to love it." Theodore's cheeks on his face jiggled, as he waved to me.

Theodore hasn't exactly been my friend while I've been in Jefferson, and his words caught me off guard. I stumbled in my new shoes. "I'll stand right here with Toby. Thank you."

Theodore rushed to me. "No, you have to come over here by the road, right in front, so you can see the sign. It's right above the porch, right above the blue doors."

I mouthed. "Who decided to paint the house yellow with blue trim and blue doors, anyhow?"

Tak yanked on my hand. "I like yellow. It's like the sun. When you are blue, you can walk into the sun house."

A tap on my shoulder made me twirl. "Timmons, look at you. Your face is clean. Now that is a miracle."

"Crush made us take a bath, and it's only Thursday."

I smiled, "Where is Crush?"

Toby pointed. "He's with the triplets over there. He's been lecturing them about taking care of their grades. Now that the boys are going to public school, Crush is worried they'll copy each other's work."

Tak hugged my waist. "I'm going to be in kindergarten and I'll be at Toby's school, and Timmons and me are sharing a room. We even have our own beds."

Thomas stepped between two ladies in big white hats. "Hey, do you like my new glasses?" He pushed the brown frames up his nose.

"I sure do. Where'd you get those?"

"Mr. Marion thought I should see better. And boy, can I."

The entire block became a car lot of visitors, but one person was missing from the party. My Mahlee. She hasn't been seen since I stayed in the secret room with her. Not once. But right after she left town, Mr. Marion got a letter with papers giving him the deed to my grandma's house. So I know she's alive.

I sighed, patting my satchel with my hand, and Timmons galloped to the porch to stand with Mr. Marion. I hugged my bag, proud to have the envelope from the house papers, the one delivered to Mr. Marion. I took it from the trash after he tossed it, and the return address was from Washington, Arkansas.

My daydreaming came to a halt as hands clapped in unison when this strong-shouldered man with glasses like Thomas' frames, took to the top step of the porch. "Welcome.

Welcome. We come together to dedicate this new boys' home. May the lives of every boy who lives here be changed forever."

Mr. Marion shook hands with the man, and stepped forward. "Thank you, Mayor. This is a day when love pours into my heart like syrup, fresh and gooey." He wiped his eye, and picked up Thomas. "With my adopting the Crush boys, it's my honor to open this home to other boys who need a father, who need love, who need to find music, and laughter."

From the window, a tapping on the pane revealed Theodore who waved at Mr. Marion. The mayor swung open the double doors, the majestic gate to happiness. I whispered to Toby. "The doors don't stick. Do they?"

He chuckled. "No, not anymore."

Theodore disappeared from the window and the ding-dong, singsong music floated from inside the house. I let go of Tak's hand, and sauntered through the crowd, pushing my way through backsides and long arms. I stepped up to the porch, and the mayor motioned for me to enter. Mr. Marion put his hand around my shoulders, guiding me through the foyer, turning me left where my eyes fell upon the suitcase-fireplace room.

Ding-dong. Dong. Ding. Trilly. Ding.

In the corner, near the window sat Theodore on the piano bench, and he played a song I'd never heard, but it was a song I'd never forget. I inched closer, and my fingers touched every letter on the top of the piano where Mahlee's words were etched not only in wood, but also in my heart.

I slid onto the bench with Theodore, and put my head on his shoulder, weeping my goodbye to Mahlee for real this time. Somehow I expected I'd never see her again.

The room filled up with friends and town folk, and Crush touched my arm. He smiled at me with a sincere gaze I'd not seen before. Tak cried at the other end of the piano, and Timmons wiped his nose. I looked across the room. Toby held Mr. Marion's hand, and Bingo sat on his haunches next to Thomas, and Susan clutched Lizzy Beth in her arms.

Mr. Marion moved to the other end of the piano, singing, "Shall we gather at the river where bright angels' feet have trod, with its crystal tides forever flowing by the throne of God?"

Everyone joined in with the singing. I felt like I was in church with God, like He was singing with us. At the end of the song, I hugged Theodore. "You play great. That was better than great."

"I can play some. I practice on the piano at the Kornbread Kafe, and then on my piece of wood until I master the notes. Did you know that song is Mr. Marion's favorite? It was his wife's song. She loved to play and sing."

From inside my trusty satchel, I grabbed my poem can, placing it on the top of the piano. "These are my most favorite poems, except for the one that's ripped up. Maybe you can put some music to them."

Theodore smiled. "I'd love to try. Music does something to words, and words bring music to life."

"Thanks, you're nicer than I thought."

"You are, too."

Mr. Marion interrupted the chatter. "Everyone back to the front yard. We must unveil the sign."

Outside in the grass, string waved on each end of the hidden plaque. The mayor took one piece, and the big-bellied man grabbed the other one. Mr. Marion announced, "It's my honor to thank a couple of special people for making this happen. First, I'd like to have Crush, my oldest son come forward."

Crush shuffled to the front, up the steps, and hugged Mr. Marion. Crush wiped a tear from his face. "I never dreamed my brothers, Tak and Timmons, would have it so good. Or the rest of my brothers. I love Mr. Marion like a father. He's been so good to us."

Mr. Marion stepped forward. "I had planned to send one suitcase with one invitation for the boys to become my family. When no one read the note in the first suitcase, I sent another suitcase, and another note. And a few more. I planned to tell them a few weeks back, but that's when our friend, Shoelace ran into my truck. But oh, she's changed my world forever. Thanks to her coming, and her rail-mama, Mahlee, we have this glorious house, and it sits right next to my homeplace."

Mr. Marion embraced Crush, and the people standing in the yard applauded. Then Mr. Marion motioned for me to come forward.

I shook my head.

He calmed the crowd with his hands as if swatting flies. "Come up here, Shoelace. Everyone, her given name is Annie Grace Kree, but I love her nickname. She's rescued my boys, rescued my heart, and rescued our town. She's brought us closer than we've ever been before."

My heart swelled like a river of hope, flooded with love. I'd not felt my heart ache with pangs of joy since my grandma held me that night back in '46 when I came in after midnight.

Mr. Marion called to me. "Come here. Say a word, Shoelace."

I put my hands to my ears, and stepped behind a tall man, who gave me a shove forward. I had no words for the first time in my life, but the words I'd find were tucked deeper than roots in a big oak.

A small voice next to me came with a gentle push. "I'll go with you."

I swirled around. "Lizzy Beth? My sweet little ..." I nodded, and clasped my fingers with hers and moved to the porch.

Mr. Marion hugged me, whispering, "Try and say something nice. Be gracious."

I laughed, knowing he knew me well enough to expect smart mouthing. I turned to the people. "Hi, I'm just me. Someone told me I was a messenger of hope. I'm sorry it comes with so much pain, but look, my grandma and my ... Mahlee-mama made this happen."

Crush hooted, hollering, "Shoelace. Shoelace. Shoelace."

In seconds, the townspeople, the Crush boys, Mr. Marion, Susan and even Lizzy Beth chanted my name. "Shoelace. Shoelace. Shoelace."

Clapping followed, and Mr. Marion motioned for the men to let the cover fall from the sign. I raced from the porch, spun around, and gazed up at the house. I whispered words that gave my heart its own musical notes. "The Pearl: Where Music Plays, Where Hearts Sing, and Where Lives Change."

I swallowed hard, the last month a flashback of horrible pain, and oh, but so much gain—especially since Mr. Marion's saving the piano for me until the day I can take it with me. I'll return for my love letter from my Mahlee when I'm bigger, but for now—the rail is a-calling, and I have to see if Arkansas holds the answer to the next chapter in my life.

Gone for Now

Back in my overalls and my PF Flyers, with the clock ticking into the night, I tiptoed into Mr. Marion's kitchen. "I'm just getting a drink of water."

Mr. Marion's voice rang out from somewhere in the house. "Be sure and get all your clothes together. Pastor Cody should be here early in the morning. I'm going next door to check on the boys. I've hired Ginny from Carl's plantation to be our housemother. She's always wanted a family, and now she's got one."

I grimaced. "Yes, sir. I'm all packed."

Toby walked up to me, catching me with my hand on the screen door. "Where are you going?"

I jerked my fingers from the latch. "Nowhere. I'm … getting some water."

"Sure you are." Toby embraced me with the tightest hug ever. "I knew you wouldn't stay. I had a feeling. You're on this amazing ride, and you're the bravest friend I've ever had. May the Lord be with you."

I exhaled. "Thank you. But I'm not so brave. I'm … just me."

Toby preached me a final sermon. "God has rescued you from the lion like David in the Old Testament. You are brave. You have God with you." He opened the screen. "Be careful, and let the music of your heart be a song for God. Go find your life. And every time you see a cardinal, remember to hold your head high, stand up tall, and fly like the wind in your red PF Flyers."

I stopped on the porch, looking back at Toby. "Are you ever going to talk like a regular boy?"

"No, I don't suppose I will. I've given up the idea of going to Hollywood. There's plenty of action right here in my hometown, and don't worry I'll stop screaming when I preach."

I hugged his neck. "Bye, I'll never forget you."
Choo-choo-choo. Choo-choo. Choo-choo-choo.

**

I cut through the woods, chasing the boxcars headed north from the train station. I reached with my arms, running with a force, stretching for the side ladder on one of the cars. Huffing and puffing, I vaulted, "Geronimo!!" Grabbing the rung, I landed with both feet on the ladder, and swung my body inside the boxcar. I rolled like a ball, my arms tangling with my over-packed satchel.

Scud-tle. Scoot-tug. Scud-tle. Scoot.

Dusting myself off, and propping myself against the wall, shadows bounced through the cracks in the boxcar.

Scud-tle. Scoot-tug.

"Who's there?" I made a fist with my hand. "Who's there?"

The shadow stomped forward, swinging a familiar brown suitcase. "It's me, Crush. I'm riding with you. I've got my clothes in this suitcase, and I've always dreamed of riding the rail. I figure you'll show me the ropes."

"How did you know I'd jump a train?"

"Toby was my lookout, and told me you'd left. I ran ahead of you, and jumped into this boxcar before you got out of the woods. And look, now you're riding with me."

"What if I'd decided to wait for another train?"

"It's not like I couldn't see you running back there."

I launched my satchel at Crush, slamming him upside the head, causing his body to sway like a tidal wave. "You scared me to death. This is the first rule on the rail. Don't ever sneak up on me. Ever."

Crush offered me his rule. "Don't ever hit me again." He rubbed his temple. "What do you have in that satchel?"

I clutched my bag. "Oh, I forgot. I have a jar of Marion Kane Raike Syrup."

"Great. I probably have a concussion."

"Oh, you're fine. Stop whining. Why are you even here?"

"I'm looking for adventure."

Shaking my head, I argued. "I don't believe you. Mr. Marion will be worried about you. What about Tak and Timmons? And the rest of the boys?" I slugged his arm. "Mr. Marion called you his son. His son! Is this how you thank him, by running away?"

Crush sat down on the boxcar floor, shifting his engineer cap and crossing his legs. "You wouldn't understand. This is more complicated than you would ever believe. I'm running with you, not away."

"Complicated? Everything in Jefferson is complicated. You get a family and you leave. You're not in your right mind."

Rubbing his chin, Crush nodded. "You're a fine one to talk about being in your right mind. You're the one who rides the rail. You're the one who is running away."

I sat down on the floor away from Crush, the bouncing of the boxcar told me we were picking up speed. "You can still get off. I'm looking for my life, and I don't need you."

Crush blew on his hands. "I'm looking for mine, too. You have no say in what I do."

298

"And you have no say in what I do."

I held my satchel close to my chest as the thud-thud of the train's wheels roared, sending us away from Jefferson, on our way to another place, with another chapter.

Meow. Meow.

"What's in your suitcase? You don't have a cat."

I knelt in front of Crush, and he popped the latches on the suitcase. "Here, this is for you."

"Where did you find him?"

"He's a she."

I cradled the kitten in my lap. "She's so little. She needs me." Her scratchy tongue licked my fingers between meows.

"That's what I figured. Susan has a friend whose cat had kittens, and Mr. Marion brought this one home to surprise you in the morning. He won't see you, so I brought her along. I named her Tinkle. She looks like a lion in the face, with those bushy whiskers."

Laughing, I rubbed her ears. "Tinkle?"

"Yes, after my little brother, Tink. He was small like her."

I squinted my eyes at Crush, and he grinned, giving me one of those teen boy smiles that made me want to wallop him. I wasn't sure if he was trying to get on my good side with this kitten, but my heart burst at having her.

Crush tilted his head. "You like her, don't you? Lizzy Beth got a kitten, too. Her kitten is orange like yours."

Choking, I kissed Tinkle's nose. "She has one like mine?"

"Yes, only two kittens were left. Two girls. Sisters. Now they're separated, but they're both being taken care of."

Tinkle purred in my arms. "Thank you. I do love her."

Crush moved closer, rubbing Tinkle's ear. "She's a wild thing like you. You'll need to watch out for her."

"Like I need to watch out for you?"

"Me? Not me."

"Whatever." Nodding, I mouthed, "It's going to get cold. You don't even have a coat."

"I have a quilt." Crush tapped his suitcase. "And my coat is in here. I'm prepared."

Scoffing, I cleared my throat. "Fine. You'll need it." I put Tinkle up to my face, whispering under my breath to her. "We're going to ditch him tomorrow, but you're with me."

Crush mouthed, "I can hear you."

I put my lips on kitty's ear. "Ignore him. He's a bratty boy. We're on our own." I sat back on the boxcar wall, and Tinkle curled up in my lap.

Crush unfolded his legs, and leaned backwards, sitting next to me. We goggled at the trees swishing by the opened boxcar door, as the shadows of sunset set in, and we sat in silence.

I petted my orange kitty, wondering if this train ride would be calm like a kitten purring. Or if the ride included lions lurking across the river in Arkansas.

Rescue of Undaunted Spirit

Discussion Guide

1. Crush displayed courage in rescuing Tak and Timmons, his brothers, and he also took in Thomas, Theodore, and the triplets, Thor, Tripp, and Thicke. Have you shown mercy to someone who is lost or alone? How did this change you?

2. Marion Kane Raike brought stability to Crush after the flood. He became a father image to him. Who has touched your life with kindness? Who has cared for you like a father?

3. Toby Raike had a goal to become famous in Hollywood or to become a preacher? His practicing revealed his commitment to learning the Bible. After he endures a most trying week, Toby focuses his heart on only serving God. Do your dreams line up with God? Are you willing to change them so they will?

4. Gladys Suzanne Winston (Susan) adopted Lizzy Beth and tended to be clean, organized, and committed to her family. Her husband, Boyd, lost his eyesight, but she's strong and willing to make the most of her life. How have your risen above trials you face? Where does your help come from?

5. Carl's ghosts rose up to haunt him, and the voice of his past shouted at him in Texarkana from the face of Tin Can Mahlee. Have you faced your past? How did it change you? Did you feel like the train of your choices raced at your down the track? How can you reconcile that?

6. Lizzy Beth lived every day with a bouncy, loving joy. She made friends easily, and remembered Shoelace. She had no idea Shoelace was her half-sister, but she loved her like a sister just the same. How can we learn from this toddler?

7. Shoelace tumbled down the stairs in a fight with Taddy, and lost Mahlee all in the same weekend. Feeling alone and abandoned, how did she handle this? How do you handle times when you lose your footing, or when it appears no one loves you?

8. Timmons and Tak attached themselves to Shoelace, and enjoyed being with her. They brought innocence, and an endearing, and carefree spirit to the friendship. As survivors, the boys met each day with resilience. What can we learn from these two boys? How do they find the strength to live with joy?

9. Mahlee ran away to protect Shoelace, but her tendency to run has something to do with how she handles adversity. How do you handle things when the day gets hard? What are you running from? How do you trust God through hard situations?

10. Archie carried handkerchiefs and left them for those he met. His ability to calm others and to bring peace to those along the rail is a trait we can emulate. How can we comfort others? Who can you think of right now who needs a handkerchief or a prayer, or a hug or even a smile?

The Lord who rescued me from the paw of the lion
and the paw of the bear will rescue me from the hand of this Philistine."
Saul said to David, "Go, and the Lord be with you."
I Samuel 17:37 NIV

Pam Kumpe

Jefferson, Texas

A Boasting Ghost
by
Shoelace

Crush came in with a rush
But oh, his boys gave me such joy.
Until, I bumped into a dead man.
Then I had to hush.

Not once. But twice,
I found a body
Life felt so shoddy.
I ran and ran.
I hid and hid.
But then I met the killer
And the killer met the train.
Dang!

Somehow running away
Felt like a place to stay.
In Jefferson, Texas with the ghosts
But I can only boast
That I am still alive.
Tak is, too.

But without my Tin Can Mahlee
I am ever so blue.
So it's time.
Geronimo to a boxcar
This is my cue.

The answers are somewhere in Arkansas
I'm up for the call if I don't fall
Or get caught by the law.

Pam Kumpe

Annie Grace Kree Chronicles Series

1 Untied Shoelace
2 Unknown Soul
3 Rescue of Undaunted Spirit
Book # 4 Unwanted Sidekick (Summer 2016)

Other Books by Pam Kumpe

See You in the Funny Papers

A Scoop of Inspiration

Things I Learned in Jail

In the Lick of Time

My View from the Bridge

www.pamkumpe.com